What the critics are saying about...

Ellora's Cavemen: Legendary Tails I

5.0! "This anthology is one of the best I have ever read. All the novellas are quite diverse in settings, subject matter, and hero/heroine interactions... I highly recommend this anthology for quick, exciting stories that will put a spark in your day or keep you up all night. " – *Callista Arman, Mon Boudoir*

5 Cups! "All of these stories were great for me and I couldn't pick just one. I thoroughly enjoyed the differences in them all and found all of them to be wickedly sensual and greatly appealing." – *Sheryl, Coffee Time Romance*

5 Hearts! "Ellora's Cavemen: Legendary Tails 1 is a fantastic collection of stories that I enjoyed reading from start to finish. Normally when I read collections like this there might be one or two stories that aren't as good as the rest, but this time every one of them shined..." – *Julia, The Romance Studio*

"Six stories written by six different authors all with a flavor of their own, ELLORA'S CAVEMEN: LEGENDARY TAILS 1 is sure to spark a few deeply hidden fantasies of your own." - *Terrie Figueroa & Sinclair Reid, Romance Reviews Today*

ELLORA'S CAVEMEN: LEGENDARY TAILS II

Love Spell
By Charlene Teglia

Lucy Wilson wants to get carried away. Literally. The inept witch has a history of relationship failure. Without passion, she fears she won't find lasting love. To prove that she's the object of his desire, she wants a man who will capture her body and her heart.

Mitch Davis is too conservative and controlled to be the passionate lover she yearns for. After months of platonic dating, Lucy knows what she has to do. Give up on Mitch and go after the man who will be everything she needs — with a love spell that can't go wrong. Or can it?

Club Rendezvous
By Jan Springer

Finally free of an abusive relationship, "Shy Girl" Emma McCall sheds her inhibitions and explores her sexual side at Club Rendezvous, a swinger's club specializing in the Alternate Lifestyle. Here she meets up with the dashing Logan Masters, a sexy hunk she's secretly fantasized about since college. With the help of his gorgeous twin brother, Luke, Emma will experience her ultimate fantasy…a scorching ménage a trois.

Freak of Nature
By Shiloh Walker

He had nerve. Zoe couldn't *believe* Micah had come back up her mountain, not after he had used her all those years ago. So what if she still dreams of him at night…so what if she still loves him. She didn't want to see him again…so why did she melt, just from looking at him.

But Micah's not here just to fan an old flame—he's here because her life is in danger. Again.

Vampires and Donuts
By Tielle St. Clare

There are two things Kendra craves but knows are bad for her: vampires and donuts. When a vicious vampire attack sends her to Brand—the one vampire who tempts her beyond wisdom—for healing and protection, the close proximity to this man she can't resist is just too much temptation.

And Kendra discovers the good thing about donuts…they don't bite back.

Demon's Fall
By Margaret Carter

Caught between Heaven and Hell! When fallen angel Kammael takes human form under orders to seduce Erin Collier away from her destiny, he becomes strangely attracted to this mere mortal. He can't bear to see her harmed and when the Infernal Powers attack Erin, he may have to make the ultimate sacrifice for his newfound love.

Garden of Eden
By Jaci Burton

Dr. Eden Mason has spent the past hundred years orbiting the Earth in stasis. She and a handful of scientists are the only survivors of a global meltdown.

One special passenger has joined them — Adam, an alien sent to recreate what was once a thriving, beautiful planet. But Adam needs Eden to fulfill his goal, in a way she never expected.

With Adam at her side, Eden hopes that life on new Earth will be a lush garden of sensual pleasures. But Adam's not telling her everything, and his secret may end up destroying them both.

NEED A MORE EXCITING
WAY TO PLAN YOUR DAY?

ELLORA'S
CAVEMEN
2006 CALENDAR

COMING THIS FALL

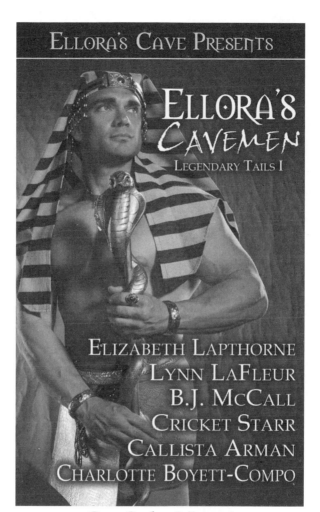

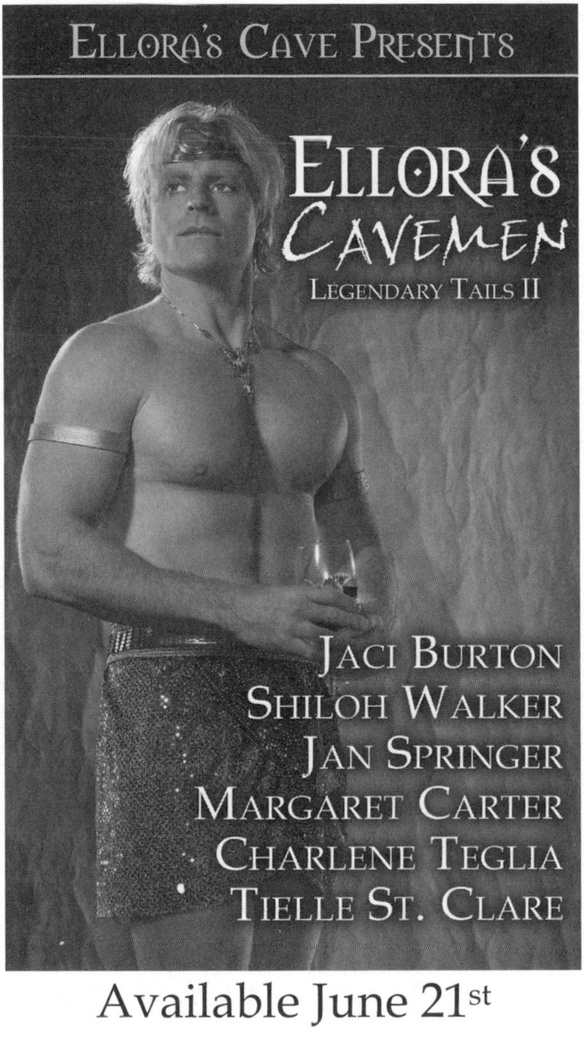

Available June 21st

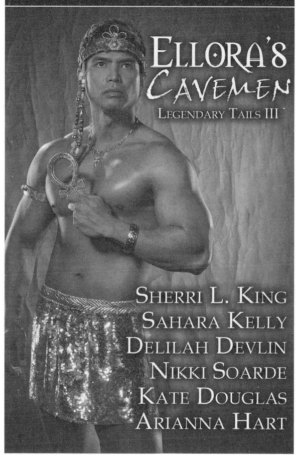

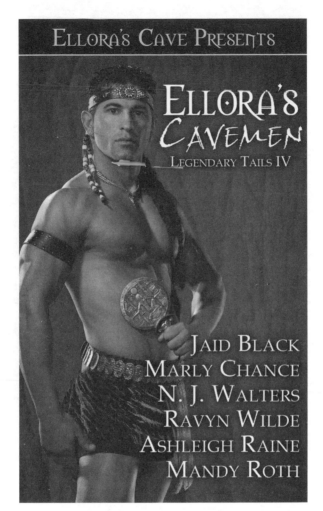

Available December 21st

ELLORA'S
CAVEMEN
LEGENDARY TAILS II

ELLORA'S CAVEMEN: LEGENDARY TAILS II
An Ellora's Cave Publication, June 2005

Ellora's Cave Publishing, Inc.
1337 Commerce Drive, #13
Stow, OH 44224

ISBN # 1-4199-5152-1

Digital ISBN # 1-4199-0154-0
Other available formats: ISBN MS Reader (LIT), Adobe (PDF),
Rocketbook (RB), Mobipocket (PRC) & HTML

Edited by *Raelene Gorlinsky*.
Cover design by *Darrell King*.
Photography by *Dennis Roliff*.

Warning:

The following material contains graphic sexual content meant for mature readers. *Ellora's Cavemen: Legendary Tails II* has been rated E-rotic by a minimum of three independent reviewers.

Ellora's Cave Publishing offers three levels of Romantica™ reading entertainment: S (S-ensuous), E (E-rotic), and X (X-treme).

S-ensuous love scenes are explicit and leave nothing to the imagination.

E-rotic love scenes are explicit, leave nothing to the imagination, and are high in volume per the overall word count. In addition, some E-rated titles might contain fantasy material that some readers find objectionable, such as bondage, submission, same sex encounters, forced seductions, and so forth. E-rated titles are the most graphic titles we carry; it is common, for instance, for an author to use words such as "fucking", "cock", "pussy", and such within their work of literature.

X-treme titles differ from E-rated titles only in plot premise and storyline execution. Unlike E-rated titles, stories designated with the letter X tend to contain controversial subject matter not for the faint of heart.

ELLORA'S CAVEMEN: LEGENDARY TAILS II

Love Spell
By Charlene Teglia

Club Rendezvous
By Jan Springer

Freak of Nature
By Shiloh Walker

Vampires and Donuts
By Tielle St. Clare

Demon's Fall
By Margaret Carter

Garden of Eden
By Jaci Burton

LOVE SPELL

Charlene Teglia

Chapter One

She had to stop seeing him.

Lucy Wilson nibbled on her lower lip while she laid tarot cards in a Celtic Cross. Not that she expected the cards to tell her anything. She wasn't good with cards. She wasn't good with candle magic, either, and she'd given up using her athame when she cut herself with it.

She wasn't much of a witch, when it came right down to it. And Mitch Davis was just one more example in a long line of things she wasn't much good with.

A person could only cope with so much failure in life. She wasn't willing to give up on magic. Which left Mitch. So she should stop seeing him.

Morning sunlight slanted through the lace curtains on her windows, warmed the golden oak floor of her kitchen, touched the cards she'd laid on her kitchen table with a soft ray of illumination. She was using her favorite deck, Whimsical Tarot, and the illustrations from familiar fairy tales made her smile.

Her spread, predictably, included the devil in the position of her present predicament and the lovers as the future. Lucy sighed.

The major arcana card depicted as a puppet and puppeteer indicated that something was bedeviling her, and that something was the reason she had to stop seeing Mitch. Because lovers they weren't, and not for lack of trying on her part. It also indicated that she was the one trapping herself. She was in this situation because she hadn't been willing to free herself from it.

She looked at the future outcome, the lovers depicted as Beauty and the Beast twirling in a dance. That was what she wanted, and she wasn't going to get it with Mitch.

"Face it, Lucy," she muttered as she gathered the cards up. "He is not interested in you in a physical way."

Unfortunate, because she was interested in him in a physical way. Very interested. Too interested for platonic dating to go on. More to the point, it was demoralizing for her to keep saying yes to Mitch when it meant saying no to getting what she wanted. What she needed. What she deserved.

Nobody knew better than Lucy that without passion, without some spark, no relationship could hope to withstand the ups and downs of long-term commitment.

She'd been there, done that, and now she had the divorce certificate to prove it. No matter how compatible a man seemed to be, without the necessary fire to keep love alive it was going to burn out and leave nothing but ashes.

Her ex-husband hadn't been interested in her. And now she was repeating the pattern of self-defeating behavior by dating another man who wasn't interested in her, because for some stupid reason her mouth kept saying "yes" every time Mitch asked her out while her brain kept shrieking "no, no, no!"

It was hard to say no to Mitch, because he was so big and solid and he made her feel so good just by being there. The way his hazel eyes took everything in told her he paid attention to details and thought things through before he acted. Lucy liked that about him. He was reliable.

But he was also cold and distant. His big hands never touched her in any way and she'd never gotten close enough to find out if his wavy chestnut hair was as soft as it looked. She wanted to get close. Emotionally and physically, and she didn't see how she could have one without the other.

Well, things were going to change. Tonight was the first Friday after the new moon. The perfect night to cast a love spell to call her true love to her. And today she was going to keep the lunch date she hadn't been able to stop herself from agreeing to with Mitch and end it for good.

She was going to override her treacherous mouth and tell him. She was going to stop seeing him, and that was final. She'd free herself from this impasse, stop being a puppet, go after what she really wanted.

Lucy finished gathering the cards and stuffed them into a purple velvet bag with gold tassel ties. Then she stood up from the table, leaving breakfast dishes scattered next to the bag of cards, and headed for the shower.

Time to get dressed, get to work, and get going on her resolution. It was October, and that meant Samhain and a new year. No better time to say goodbye to the old and welcome the new than now.

Chapter Two

He should stop seeing her.

Mitch Davis knew this the way he knew that the sun rose in the east, the moon affected the tides, and spring followed winter. It was a fact as immutable as any law of nature—if he kept seeing Lucy, sooner or later he was going to do something that would get him arrested or disbarred.

The trouble was, every time he was with her he got distracted by her pansy-brown eyes and forgot why he should end it before anything dangerous happened. And then, before he knew it, his mouth opened all by itself to ask her for another chance to play with fire.

His buffed and shining black dress shoes carried him up the wooden steps, past the wide window that displayed a colorful selection of books and tarot cards along with the glittering fanciful creature that was The Crystal Dragon's namesake.

He watched as his own square hand closed over the brass door handle and swung the door open, drawing him into the New Age shop filled with books for hippies of all ages seeking enlightenment, crystals to promote harmony, and a woman guaranteed to disrupt his orderly life.

It was just lunch, Mitch reassured himself. What could happen at lunch? Lunch was safe. Business crowds filling restaurants with sober suits and PDAs, meetings conducted informally.

Clandestine meetings, a treacherous voice in his head whispered back. Lovers sneaking away for a nooner. Maybe even doing it right in the parking garage in broad daylight while just a few feet away oblivious suits scheduled future events inside restaurants and office buildings.

Or maybe doing it in the elevator, stopped between floors. Lucy wore dresses frequently. All he'd have to do would be to stand behind her, lift her skirt in back, unzip his pants...

Mitch closed his eyes briefly. It was her. She put those kinds of thoughts into his head. It had to be her because he'd never had them before he met her and now all he could think about was Lucy. Sex with Lucy. Hot, explicit, illicit sex with Lucy in public places and in positions still forbidden by the blue laws. Carrying Lucy off and tying her up while he used sex to master her and bind her to him forever. Going down on Lucy while she went up in flames.

He was going to get arrested. He was going to get sued. Lucy would never go along with the kinds of ideas he had about her, and if he even hinted at what he wanted to do to her, she'd file for a restraining order and his career would end in scandal and embarrassment.

The only thing that had saved him so far was that he hadn't ever let himself kiss her or touch her in any way. If he did, he'd snap.

Boise was too conservative a community and in many ways too like a small town for him to get away with carrying on with Lucy the way he wanted to, and he wanted to do more forbidden things to her more urgently every day.

He had to stop seeing her. It was the only solution. Somehow, he had to find the will to end it before it ended him. He had to tell her. Today.

Then Lucy was in front of him, and her eyes were so warm and her smile was so wide and her body was so lush and inviting. He could be happy just looking at her, Mitch thought. Maybe he didn't have to end it just yet.

She wasn't smiling at him. She was talking to a customer and waving her hands in animated conversation. The customer was smiling back, because nobody could fail to respond to the warmth in Lucy's smile. Her nutty shop full of flaky ideas and flakier merchandise did a booming business because Lucy made everybody feel good. They'd buy something just to carry a piece of that good feeling home with them.

Mitch never wanted anything but Lucy to take home with him, where he could keep her and all the good feelings she generated cuffed to his bed. If he was smart, he'd buy a calming aromatherapy candle instead.

She was wearing a floral print dress with a flowing long skirt and a gauzy lace-trimmed top. So feminine. So sweet. So old-fashioned.

So why did he see her in a skintight black vinyl catsuit with one metal zipper that would go from her throat to her crotch and lay her curvy, lush body open to his gaze when he pulled it down with his teeth?

Her shoulder-length curly hair looked like taffy streaked with sunshine. Her pansy eyes and her soft, pink, smiling mouth looked far too innocent for the carnal ideas he had about her.

Lucy might be some sort of New Age witch, but she wasn't the least bit wicked.

Mitch was the wicked one, hiding his secret thoughts behind an impassive face, a conservative suit, carefully trimmed nails and shined shoes. A well-groomed, conservative, professional-looking man did not give the appearance of a sexual deviant, something his clients probably appreciated when he represented them in court.

But all he had to do was look at her and the only thing conservative about his wild imaginings was that they focused on Lucy and Lucy alone.

So he was a completely monogamous deviant. That wasn't going to earn him any points if he stuck around Lucy long enough to lose control, rip open that gauzy, lacy covering over her full breasts and fill his eyes with her before he filled his hands and mouth with her.

The fabric looked flimsy enough to tear easily with the slightest pressure. Mitch's big, square hands flexed at the thought.

That did it. He had to stop seeing her, for her sake if not for his. This was the last time. It had to end.

His voice was more abrupt than he meant it to be when he spoke. "Are you ready yet, Lucy? We have a reservation."

Her hands froze in midair and her eyes swung to his. "Mitch. Hello. I'm just finishing up, I'll be right with you."

She said something else to the customer that Mitch couldn't hear, pressed a vial of essential oil into the woman's hand and motioned towards the cash register. "If that doesn't do the trick, just bring it back," Lucy said, more audibly. "But try it."

The woman went, and smiled as she pulled out her wallet.

Lucy came to him and stopped about a foot away. Mitch wished she'd stopped a little sooner. She was close enough for him to grab her.

She came up to his shoulder, which made him want to tuck her into his side. Her streaky taffy curls would flow down his arm if he did, and she would be nestled close enough for the scent of sandalwood, sunshine and woman to go straight to his head.

He wanted to feel her body warm and snug against his. He wanted to sink into her snug warmth. Right there and then. The customers could just go around them.

Mitch took a step back to a safer distance and motioned for Lucy to follow. "We're running late, so we'd better get going."

His voice came out short to the point of rudeness again. He couldn't help that. If he didn't clamp down on his voice the way he clamped down on every other part of himself, he would just come right out and say it. *I want to fuck you, Lucy. I want your skirt up around your waist and my cock buried in your cunt. And I want to keep you tied to my bed until I'm finished fucking you, which should take about fifty years.*

And the words would be said out loud. They would hang in the air between them where he couldn't take them back and unsay them. And she would be offended. Hurt. Possibly even scared.

Those were not the kinds of words he should say to a woman like Lucy.

She deserved sweet words, soft words, romantic words.

Maybe he'd been a lawyer too long, but he didn't have any soft, romantic words left in him—if he'd ever had them to begin with. He'd seen and heard it all, the side of human nature that wasn't pretty and couldn't be prettied up no matter what words covered it.

He didn't want to hurt her. He didn't want to scare her or make her feel cheap. He just wanted her in a hot, raw, primal way, and it was getting harder to hide.

Thank God this was the last time he'd ever see her, or he would say it, and she'd probably slap him. Right before she burst into tears.

Lucy followed him to the parking lot and got into the passenger side of his Mercedes. He didn't miss the way she cuddled her backside into the leather seat. It made him hard. It made him want to see her enjoying the cushion of leather with no clothes blocking the sensation at all, just her bare ass squirming in pleasure.

Everything about her made him hard, which was exactly the problem. Even an innocent car seat could become an object of carnal imaginings if Lucy was anywhere near.

Mitch closed the door for her, harder than he meant to. He stalked around to his side, climbed in, closed that door with a solid sound too, and started the engine. He didn't say anything. He didn't trust himself to talk. Maybe Lucy wouldn't mind the silence or maybe it would annoy her enough to make ending things between them easier.

Something had to make it easier, because he hadn't been able to bring himself to do it yet and he didn't have any idea how he was going to do it now.

He drove the short distance from her Hyde Park shop to the upscale restaurant on downtown's Main Street in carefully bottled-up silence, turned off the engine, and got out of the car immediately. He didn't dare linger in the enclosed space with her. It would be too easy to put his hand between her knees under that flowery skirt and slide it up until he could touch her right between her legs.

Unreasonably, Mitch felt a flare of anger over the way she dressed.

If she knew what was good for her, she'd stop wearing those damn dresses and put some pants on. They were practically an invitation for him to come and get her. She wore nothing but sandals on her feet so there wasn't even the flimsy barrier of pantyhose to protect her virtue, not that that would stop Mitch if he got his hands under her dress even once. He'd shred anything between him and her skin and then he'd get inside her with no further preliminaries.

Mitch knew his resentment over her clothing was completely irrational. The problem was his, not hers. She made him insane, that was all. So he'd end it and stay the hell away from her forever and keep his mind on legal briefs and court filings where it belonged.

Somehow he got her door open and Lucy out and into the restaurant where she was seated safely away from him, on the other side of the table.

Lunch was ordered. Lucy toyed with her water glass, her fork, folded and unfolded her cloth napkin, and Mitch watched her hands fidget. He was making her nervous, he knew. He was acting abrupt, gruff, rude. He should say something to put her at ease, but he was at a loss as to what words might do that. The words that sprang most readily to his mind in her presence were not ones Miss

Manners would recommend for graceful social discourse. "I want your cunt for dessert" didn't strike him as the ideal opener.

"Nice weather," he said finally. "Not too cold yet." The uncharacteristically long Indian summer made the fall weather inviting, with sunny days and just a hint of coolness in the air. It felt refreshing after the drugging heat of summer.

Lucy looked up at him. Her hands went still. Her soft pink lips parted to say something to him, but the waiter appeared just then with their lunch and she closed her mouth again.

"What were you going to say?" Mitch asked when the waiter left.

She gripped her napkin again, crushing the folds of fabric in her fists. She stared down at her plate.

A feeling of foreboding gripped him. Lucy looked very serious.

The silence seemed to stretch out forever. Time slowed and the sounds of other diners receded into the distance. There were only the two of them present, Lucy staring down and not speaking words he increasingly felt certain he did not want to hear.

And then she looked directly into his eyes and said them.

"I don't want lunch. I don't want to see you, ever again. I want to leave now."

It shouldn't have come as a surprise. He'd been rude and he knew it. And this was exactly the result he'd intended, only he'd meant to be the one saying the words. Not so abruptly. He'd meant to let her down gently. Still, he couldn't stop himself from asking her, "Why?"

She sighed, stuffed the napkin under the table along with her fisted hands and answered him. "Because I want things you can't give me."

"What things?"

"Things," Lucy mumbled, evading the question.

"You're dumping me," Mitch stated. There was nothing to lose now by being blunt. To hell with Miss Manners. "I think you at least owe me an explanation. What things, Lucy?"

She looked furtively around the restaurant to see if anybody else was seated within hearing distance. Nobody was, but she leaned forward and pitched her voice low just to be safe. "I was married once, you know."

Not what Mitch expected to hear, but in fact he had known. It wasn't a secret. It wasn't unusual, either. Divorces happened.

He shrugged. "So?"

"So my ex was like you. Very conservative. He didn't approve of me, and…" Lucy's eyes were starting to swim with emotion and Mitch wanted to find her ex so he could plant a fist in the man's mouth for making her cry.

"And he didn't want me," Lucy went on. "I didn't excite him. I didn't interest him. I was just not what he wanted. Not enough for him. And I divorced him because I couldn't take living with that, and now I'm dating you and it's like I'm living it all over again."

Lucy sat up straighter, which made her full breasts move under the thin gauzy fabric in a way Mitch deeply appreciated. "I don't deserve to be with somebody who doesn't want me, Mitch. Physically. I'm talking about desire. I have needs."

Mitch could understand that she had needs of her own. He had needs he was entirely too aware of whenever she was around, but she was on a roll now. The words had apparently been building up inside her for some time and they were pouring out faster and faster.

"I don't want platonic dating," Lucy was saying. "I don't want to spend my time with a conservative suit who's too afraid of getting wrinkled to kiss me. I want a man who will get wrinkled. Or better yet, naked. I want sex. I want a man who will break into my room in the middle of the night because he's dying to have me. I want a pirate who will kidnap me and drag me off to his ship for immoral purposes and give me a choice between being eaten by sharks or eaten by him."

He was paralyzed by her words, which was a good thing because otherwise Mitch would be tempted to give her exactly what she wanted, right there, on top of the table, in the middle of the restaurant.

He could throw her down, rip off her panties, drive his tongue into her and make her scream out her release while the other diners watched in shock if that was what she wanted, because only the fear that Lucy didn't want him the same way he wanted her had kept him in check up until now. Well, that and the fear of legal reprisals. Okay, that, the fear of legal reprisals, and a strong desire not to torpedo his career.

"I want to be wanted, Mitch, can you understand that? I want to make a man insane with passion. I want him to drag me off by my hair to fuck me until I'm incapable of running away and do it so well I would never want to. And don't you dare laugh at me." Lucy stood abruptly and threw down her napkin. "I don't ever want to see you again."

And because he was still paralyzed by her words, by the image of himself as the pirate taking her captive, or maybe as the Neanderthal dragging her off, she got away. She was gone before he'd recovered himself enough to motion for the check and go after her.

Well, hell. He'd finally found out that sweet, innocent Lucy wanted all the things he wanted to do to her and he wasn't busy doing them to their mutual satisfaction right now because she'd dumped him.

His instincts had known it all along. His crazy thoughts about her hadn't been so crazy after all. They'd been right on the mark, telling him how to win her. Only he'd been too civilized to follow his instincts and he'd lost her. Now what?

Mitch retrieved his Mercedes and headed back to his office. A strategic retreat while he considered his options and planned his next move seemed in order.

For starters, how difficult would it be to rent a boat?

One thing he was certain of. Now that he knew how perfectly Lucy's needs meshed with his own there was no way he was letting her get away from him to have those needs met by some other man. She'd escaped him in the restaurant only because she'd taken him by surprise. He was going to be the only man to meet every need she had, and he would meet them so completely she would never think of dumping him again.

Of course, that might take some time. She'd seemed pretty upset and pretty definite about not wanting to give him a second chance.

Mitch made a mental note to investigate long-term boat rentals.

Chapter Three

Lucy got through the rest of the day somehow, but she kept seeing Mitch's frozen face while she all but yelled that she needed sex, including oral, in the middle of a classy restaurant full of conservative business types, many of them probably his clients.

The way he'd looked at her made her sigh with embarrassment. She'd probably sounded like a crazy woman. A sexually frustrated crazy woman, too pathetic to get a man, hence her secret hopes that one would simply appear and take what nobody apparently wanted.

Maybe if she dyed her hair a brassy blonde, she could look less wholesome. Maybe if she moved into a trailer park and burned all her granny dresses and wore jeans that rode low on her hips and went braless, maybe she could look less like a good girl and more like a good time.

Probably not. She'd probably just look dumb, like she was wearing a costume that didn't fit her very well. Exactly what it would be.

She wasn't the low-riding tight jeans type. She was the flowery dress type. Men probably looked at her and pictured her in the kitchen baking cookies. They did not picture her getting naked and spreading herself out on the kitchen counter to offer herself up as a snack. She apparently just wasn't the type to inspire anything but Betty Crocker fantasies, where the only thing getting hot was the oven.

It was probably a good thing that Mitch had never kissed her. She would have flung herself at him and embarrassed them both by begging him to take her. He probably knew that, which was why he'd never given her any encouragement.

He could be gruff and distant. He could be aloof and austere. But Lucy knew that Mitch had never wanted to hurt her feelings and that the scene in the restaurant had probably upset him. Not so much because she'd freed them both from an increasingly awkward situation, but because he wouldn't have wanted to upset her enough to cause a scene in the first place.

Honestly, she'd meant to be more dignified. Things just sort of got out of hand. She'd started to tell him how she felt and the feelings just kept finding more words to express themselves with, until fleeing the restaurant and Mitch's frozen look had been the only possible thing left to do.

Well, maybe it wasn't done gracefully, but it was definitely done. It was over. That much had been very clear, at least. "I never want to see you again" sounded considerably more dramatic than their platonic relationship warranted, but it did get the point across.

Goodbye, Mitch. Hello, new year and new man.

She already had everything she needed to cast her love spell at home. She'd studied the book of shadows carefully. It was a very simple sort of spell, almost as simple as a rock cairn. Impossible to screw up, even for her. She was going to do it. Tonight. And nothing would go wrong this time.

Her decision firm, Lucy did her best to focus on her shop and her customers until closing time.

The Crystal Dragon was a magical place, and not just because of the items she sold. Walking in the door made her feel good. It was her place, the place she'd made her own and used to make her own life with. She'd chosen everything, from the paint on the walls to the items in the window display and the artwork on the shop's sign.

She carried the usual assortment of incense and essential oils but she used good air filters and ventilation to keep the conflicting odors from becoming overwhelming. Her shop smelled inviting and exotic, not like an explosion in a patchouli factory.

Crystals hung in front of the windows and sunlight made them sparkle. A selection of CDs on a rack invited browsers to take sounds of nature or soft music home with them to create a tranquil environment there. Samples of those CDs played softly through the speakers in each corner of the shop.

Racks of books on self help, magic, tarot, and a variety of related subjects provided practical guidance for anybody interested in exploring themselves and the realm of spiritual possibilities. If a man wanted to learn how to make a drum to tap his way to enlightenment, he could find what he needed in Lucy's shop.

Lucy liked giving people a way to help themselves, in whatever way appealed to them. She'd found her own help during her dying marriage and it had saved her emotionally. It had saved her financially, too, when she'd opened up The Crystal Dragon the day she'd gotten her divorce.

And now magic was going to help her save herself from repeating the mistakes of the past, pining away for a man who didn't want her, dying inside every day because she knew she didn't measure up in his eyes.

She was going to have the right man, the one she was the right woman for. He would want her just the way she was. And he would show her just how much he wanted her, how perfect she was in his eyes.

At six o'clock, Lucy flipped the sign on her door to "Closed", said goodnight to her assistant, locked up the shop and walked the few blocks to her North End cottage.

She liked living in Boise's historic North End. Hyde Park was a great location for a business, and the neighborhood attracted a mix of artistic types, teachers, families, people who had originally bought up the old houses and renovated them when they couldn't afford to live anywhere else. Now those houses were prime real estate. The eclectic mix of architecture was as big a draw as the thriving business district.

It was also a very old-fashioned sort of neighborhood where people knew each other. A rarity in any big city.

Lucy didn't meet any of her neighbors on her way home, and that was fine. She wasn't in the mood to chat. She wanted to be quiet, to let the right mindset for the spell unfold. She wanted to look at trees and late-blooming mums and pumpkins on porches. She wanted to feel the ground under her feet giving her a sense of connection with something larger than herself.

By the time she'd reached her own front porch, a sense of tranquility wrapped around her. She collected her mail but didn't look at it, setting it aside for later. She stuck her dinner in the microwave and ate quietly, letting herself feel the moment.

Then it was time to begin.

Lucy set out a small, brightly colored fabric sachet of herbs, placed a pink candle next to a crystal holder, and lit a stick of jasmine incense. As the fragrant smoke curled around the end of the stick, she closed her eyes and visualized a protective circle around herself and the small draped table that served as her altar.

She unrolled a piece of parchment and wrote, stopping often to twine a strand of curly hair around her finger as she thought, then jotted down another phrase or scratched out a line and rewrote.

The incense was reduced to a smoldering stub when, finally satisfied that the list was complete, she set the parchment aside and took out a vial of rose oil. She coated a fingertip with the oil, traced a line down the candle and consecrated it. She opened the sachet, poured out vervain and rolled the candle in the herbs. Then she stood the candle in the holder, lit it, and softly chanted the incantation.

"Moon of love, shining bright, aid me in my spell tonight. Guide my true love to me; as I send, so mote it be."

Lucy gazed into the candle flame and envisioned the man who would embody all of the qualities written painstakingly on her parchment. The man who would be her soul mate, her knight in shining armor, her pirate, her passionate and adoring lover. She said the words that called him to her three times, completing the rite.

On the third repetition, a gust of wind from an open window made the candle flicker and the picture in her mind wavered, then changed from the fantasy pirate of her erotic dreams to the repressed Armani-suited image of her nightmares.

Instead of a lusty hero come to sweep her away into a deeply satisfied happily ever after, she saw a certain frozen-faced, suit-wearing, buttoned-down, aloof and austere, emotionally and sexually withholding lawyer.

Lucy swore, blew out the candle, and scattered the herbs on the altar with one impatient hand.

"Thanks for nothing," she muttered, instead of the traditional prayer of gratitude.

And she'd been so sure nothing could go wrong this time. She was a terrible witch. She couldn't do the simplest spell.

Was a man who wanted her too much to ask for? Why had she seen Mitch, a man she knew perfectly well found her completely resistible?

So much for love spells. Maybe she should try a dating service, instead.

Frustrated and defeated, Lucy stalked down the hall to her bedroom, yanked off her clothes and left them in a heap on the floor, climbed into bed and hauled the covers up over her head. She was more than ready for this day to be over.

Sleep came eventually.

Chapter Four

The firm masculine hand that closed over Lucy's mouth brought her abruptly out of her fitful dream and into a waking nightmare.

Her heart pounded as she stared into the eyes of a stranger, his face obscured by a dark mask that left only his mouth and chin exposed. The rest of him disappeared into the shadows and Lucy realized he must be dressed all in black.

How had he gotten in? Her eyes left his and went to the open window she'd forgotten to close. She let out a muffled groan at her own stupidity.

She forced herself to look directly at him again, to meet those eyes that glinted in the moonlight. She brought her hand up to shove his aside and free her mouth to speak. "You don't want to do this," she said. *Be cool. Be in control. Be firm.* "You won't be able to undo that much bad karma in this lifetime."

"Oh, but I do," he answered, leaning forward until the mask touched her nose. "I do want to do this."

Then his hard slash of a mouth closed over hers. Lucy lay frozen between shock and a nagging sense of something not quite right, a piece of the puzzle she was missing in her barely awake fog.

That voice. She knew it. She'd heard it earlier today.

It was Mitch's voice. Mitch Davis, Mr. Straight Arrow Attorney. A man who would rather pass her the salt than make a pass. A controlled, dignified man who wouldn't be caught dead dressing up like a cat burglar and breaking into a woman's bedroom in the middle of the night to ravish her.

But then, maybe Mitch had hidden depths. Mitch had never kissed her before, either. He was certainly kissing her now. Hungrily. Urgently. Like a dieter who'd broken under the strain of prolonged denial and gone for the forbidden double fudge brownie with single-minded fervor.

She dragged her mouth free of his long enough to gasp out, "Mitch?"

Her wrists were trapped easily by strong hands and her lips were recaptured by his devouring kiss. "Shut up," he growled against her lips as they parted in amazement. "Just shut up and kiss me."

Unable and mysteriously unwilling to do anything else, Lucy pushed aside all the reasons why he was all wrong for her and kissed him back.

After what seemed like an eternity, Mitch's mouth left hers and he yanked her upright by her captured wrists. The sheet and comforter slithered down, leaving her nearly naked in front of him. She had gone to bed in just her panties, and only the covers around her lower half hid her body from view.

Not that he seemed to be interested in looking just then. He shoved a piece of paper into one nerveless hand and a pen into the other, cursed in a low voice, found a book to shove under the paper as a support and flipped on the light by her bed so she could see the print.

"Sign this. Hurry up."

Lucy stared stupidly at his masked face, not understanding.

"It's a waiver," Mitch snapped out in explanation. "I'm taking you across state lines. That's called kidnapping, unless you give me permission. Then there's also abduction and detaining you against your will. Give me permission, Lucy. Sign the goddamn waiver."

"Mitch?" Lucy said again. Why was he doing this?

"Your tits are magnificent. I want them in my mouth. Sign the waiver, Lucy, I don't want to go to jail for what I'm going to do to you."

"What are you going to do to me?"

"Everything." Shoving the paper and pen aside for the time being, Mitch shoved her down on the mattress, dragged the covers away to bare the rest of her to his sight and climbed on top of her. He rubbed his erection between her parted legs to demonstrate very graphically just what everything included.

"I'm stealing you. I'm a pirate and you're a lady. I saw you, I wanted you, and now I'm taking you to my ship where you will surrender your body to me."

Mitch pressed harder into the cradle of her hips, thrusting the hard length of his penis along her clitoris, and that alone was almost enough to shoot her off into the night like a Roman candle even though he was fully clothed and she still had her underwear on. Lucy gasped at the sensation.

"I'm going to fuck your brains out," he grated out, continuing to ride her. "I'm going to put my mouth between your legs and suck your clit until you beg me to stop. I'm going to have you every way I want to and nobody will hear you scream because we will be all alone.

I'm going to ram my cock into you any time I feel like it, and you are going to let me, aren't you, Lucy?"

Lucy was beyond speech. Just a little more pressure, just a little harder...there, oh, right there. She gasped, moaned, and then she did scream as he made her come without even getting inside her.

Mitch rolled off her, pulled her into a sitting position and wrapped her fingers around the pen again with the supported paper shoved into place beneath it. "Sign, dammit, sign the waiver before this kills me. I can't wait, Lucy. I have to have you."

Mitch wanted her? Mitch had to have her? What was this about state lines and a ship?

Lucy didn't even look at the paper. She would never be able to focus enough to read it or make sense of the words in her current state of mind, anyway.

The important part was perfectly clear.

Mitch wanted to play pirate with her. And being a lawyer, he wanted to make sure whatever they did was legal and consensual with no room for ambiguity or misunderstandings. He probably couldn't help that.

She didn't mind, really. It wasn't exactly unromantic of him to break into her bedroom and give her an orgasm and tell her he wanted to steal her away to have his way with her. Again and again. Including orally. He had been listening to her at lunch.

Lucy shivered in the aftermath of the most powerful orgasm she'd ever experienced. It was clearly only a prelude to everything Mitch intended to do. If she wanted more, it was going to require her signature.

She wanted more.

She signed the paper.

Mitch grabbed the waiver back, folded it, and stuffed it into his pants pocket. Then he grabbed Lucy and yanked the sheet free from her bed. He rolled her up in it, leaving her dressed in nothing but a sheet and her underwear, put her over his shoulder in a fireman's carry, and made for the front door.

"Where's your key, Lucy? I'll lock up."

"Table. By the door," Lucy managed to answer.

Mitch found her key ring, got the door open and both of them through it and locked it on the other side.

She was being stolen by a pirate.

Lucy tried to wrap her mind around that fact and failed. Her fantasy was coming to life with the least likely candidate she could have imagined.

Mitch Davis was carrying her off into the night to do things to her. Things that involved oral gratification, and actual penetration, too. Lots of penetration, if she'd understood him correctly.

The night was turning out a whole lot better than she'd expected. If she'd known what it would lead to, she would have ended their relationship a lot sooner.

Which reminded her, suddenly, that it was supposed to be ended.

"Mitch," she said, hanging over him like a roll of carpet, "we broke up."

"Right," he answered. "The old relationship, which consisted of dates in safe public places where I never laid a hand on you, is over. You ended it, Lucy, and I appreciate that fact. I respect your decision to stop dating me. This is completely different. I'm not taking you on a date, and my hands are going to be all over you. They'll be inside you, too."

Mitch tipped her right-side up, set her briefly on her feet while he opened the car door, then stuffed her into the passenger seat. He went around and got into the driver's seat in record time.

"Are you a member of the mile high club?" he asked as he started the engine.

"What's that?" Lucy asked.

"You're going to find out. Right before you get your wings," Mitch answered. He yanked the mask off his head and threw it into the backseat. Then he reached into the glove compartment and pulled out a blindfold. He tied it around her head so that her eyes were covered. "Almost forgot that part."

Wrapped up in her sheet like a mummy, Lucy couldn't move her arms or legs. The blindfold enclosed her in darkness. She was blind and helpless and she'd signed a waiver she hadn't read giving him permission to do heaven only knew what.

She wouldn't have any idea where he was taking her, what was happening around her, who else might see her trussed up and practically naked.

It was incredibly exciting.

Whatever Mitch had planned, Lucy hoped they would get someplace where he could start putting his hands all over her and inside her very soon.

Being stolen by a pirate made her wet. Her panties were damp and clinging, her clitoris was throbbing, and the sheet was rubbing against her nipples in a really interesting way.

Lucy leaned back into the seat. "Drive fast," she urged.

Mitch did.

Chapter Five

The car came to a halt and Mitch plucked her out and put her over his shoulder again practically before the engine shut down all the way. It amazed her, coming from Mr. Deliberate. Maybe it had taken him a while to make up his mind, but when he finally decided to make his move, he didn't drag his feet about it.

Good. Her needs definitely called for a man of action.

If he changed his mind now, or worse, delayed implementing his plans for her, Lucy would kill him. Or sue. Maybe the waiver had some legal verbiage that gave her conjugal rights or something she could hold over him if he tried to hold out on her any longer. She made a mental note to find out. Later.

Mitch pounded over an asphalt surface and up some steps. Then she was lifted off his shoulder and seated again. Mitch buckled her into the seat.

"I want you to know," he breathed into her ear while his hands worked the buckle, "that the minute this thing is in the air, this seat belt is coming off and so is everything else."

"We're on a plane?" Lucy asked. She tried to focus on something easier to grasp than everything coming off. Although everything off meant everything accessible. But would anybody but Mitch be looking? Or doing anything else, for that matter?

"Private plane," Mitch answered, running his hands over her sheet-wrapped body. "Very private."

Lucy decided his definition of private needed more clarification. "Mitch, is this just for us, or were you planning to make me the centerpiece in an orgy?"

"Now there's a thought. You're very creative, I never thought of an orgy. You'd make a very hot centerpiece. But this orgy is just for two. If you want somebody else to watch while I make you come, that's one thing, but nobody else is getting inside you, Lucy. Nobody else is getting their hands or their mouth on you. Only me."

His big, square, strong hands closed over her breasts and squeezed. "These are mine, Lucy. Get used to it."

Then he let her go to buckle himself in beside her. A short time later, she felt the engines build up, the plane begin to roll, and the almost imperceptible sensation of liftoff as it left the ground.

And then, as promised, the buckle and everything else was coming off.

She heard Mitch's buckle unsnap, heard the rustle of clothing as he stripped. Her own buckle was unsnapped and her sheet-bound body was laid on the plushly carpeted floor of the plane. Mitch unwrapped her in two quick yanks. Then he literally tore her panties off her.

"I'm going to bury my tongue in your pussy, Lucy," he rasped out, and suited actions to words. He thrust his tongue into her wet, waiting sheath and Lucy groaned at the sensation.

Still blindfolded, every sensation seemed magnified. His mouth was so hot, so mobile, so hungry. He latched onto her clitoris and sucked. He let go as she started to buck up against him and licked his way back inside her, withdrew to tease her clit with his tongue, and then sucked hard on it again.

Lucy fisted her hands in his hair in case he planned to stop before she was ready and lifted her hips up to meet his mouth. "Mitch. Yes. Like that. Don't stop, don't stop!" she gasped out.

He devoured her, licking and sucking and moving his mouth over her, and her climax hit her almost without warning. She screamed and moaned and didn't care if the pilot could hear her.

While she was still convulsing, Mitch slid his mouth up her belly, over her breasts, and then settled himself on top of her. He entered her with one hard, fast thrust and it triggered another orgasm.

He fucked her furiously and Lucy came over and over, until he finally came too, and collapsed on top of her, still buried deeply inside her.

"You have now been initiated into the mile high club," Mitch told her. He flexed his hips against her. "That was too fast. I'm going to fuck you slower next time. I'm just getting started, Lucy. I'm going to fuck you until you can't run away, and do it so well you won't want to."

She gave a soft hum of pleasurable anticipation for an answer and ran her hands over his broad shoulders, down his back, across his butt. She loved the feel of his body under her hands, his weight on top of her, his penis inside her and the liquid sensation of his orgasm. It was unbelievably slutty of her, but she wanted him to come in her again and again, jetting hot liquid deep inside her.

He withdrew and slid down her body to put his mouth on her nipples, first one, then the other, licking and sucking at her breasts. His hands kneaded and squeezed them both while his mouth kept moving back and forth. Whichever nipple wasn't in his mouth would get rolled between his fingers, and Lucy couldn't decide which she liked better.

"I love your tits," Mitch muttered against her skin. "I could spend hours on your tits alone. But not just yet. I haven't had enough of your cunt."

His hands slid down her ribs and belly and then his fingers were plunging into her. "You're wet, Lucy, so wet. I'm going to fill you with my fingers and you're going to ride them."

She felt first two, then three fingers sliding into her, stretching her and filling her. His thumb worked her clitoris.

"Fuck my fingers while I suck your tits," he ordered her.

His mouth closed over a nipple again and sucked hard. The joint sensations of his hand inside her and his mouth on her nipple momentarily separated her muscles from her mind.

The things he was doing and saying, the eroticism of his words and the blindfold, the sheer physical pleasure of his touch when she'd felt starved for it, the knowledge that it was Mitch giving her everything she needed left her limp and incapable of any kind of deliberate action at all. Her mind was too full of Mitch to focus on even the simplest instructions.

Reflex sent her pelvis grinding up to meet the pressure of his thumb on her clitoris. The reflexive movement helped bring her back to some semblance of control over her own body. Lucy rocked her hips against his fingers, found her rhythm, and came impossibly hard, impossibly fast.

When she found her voice again, she gasped out, "Can the pilot see or hear this?"

"Do you care?" Mitch slid his hand out of her and moved over her until his erect penis was nudging against her opening again. "If I told you he could see and hear everything, would you want me to stop?"

He slid just the head of his penis inside her, then withdrew, only to give her the tip of himself again, teasing her opening and refusing to go further.

Back and forth, barely in, barely out, until Lucy wanted him all the way inside, deep inside, and she wanted him there immediately.

"Do you care, Lucy? Do you want me to stop fucking you?"

The tip of his cock thrust inside her again and she sobbed faintly as she lifted her hips in a vain attempt to gain more of him.

"Or do you want my cock in you so much you don't care who sees?" Mitch thrust into her slowly, so slowly, filling her up until he was all the way in. "Answer me, Lucy. Do you care who sees you getting fucked by me? Do you care if the pilot can see your soaking wet pussy taking my cock?"

"I don't care," Lucy gasped. "Fuck me, Mitch, I need you to fuck me."

He did, so slowly at first she thought she'd die with each stroke. "Faster," she urged.

"You don't get to say how fast or slow," he answered. "You just get to spread your legs when I want you to."

Her legs were spread wide to accommodate him now. They were also wrapped around his waist tight enough to threaten the circulation in his lower extremities.

"Please."

"That's right, beg me for it."

"Please, I want it harder, faster, now. Please!"

"You want me to give it to you hard and fast, and you don't care who watches while I do it?"

"Yes. No. Mitch!"

He gave her what she needed, came inside her with a raw yell of satisfaction, and made her scream her release along with him.

Afterwards Mitch wrapped her up in the sheet again, toga-style so her arms were free. He dressed himself, and returned to his seat with her cradled in his lap. He touched her nipples as if he couldn't get enough of them and cuddled her close while he cupped and stroked her full breasts through the thin barrier of fabric.

"Nobody could see or hear anything, in case you're still wondering," he told her. "I'd like to say I'd be willing to put on a show if it turned you on, but while the fantasy might be exciting, I couldn't live with the reality. The truth is, I can't stand the thought of anybody else seeing what's mine. And you're mine, Lucy."

His. The thought warmed Lucy from head to toe, wrapping her in a glow of emotional satisfaction to match her physical state. Her body was utterly sated. And now her pirate was giving her the affection and closeness she needed as much as she'd needed proof of his desire.

Perfect.

He was perfect for her, and she was perfect for him, and the spell had worked perfectly after all.

Oh. The spell.

All the glowing warmth drained out of Lucy instantly.

Mitch didn't love her. Even spellbound, he hadn't said so. He didn't really want her. He'd had plenty of time to give her some sign that he did, and he couldn't possibly have misread every signal she'd given him to go ahead and make a move on her, but he never had. Until she'd manipulated him with magic.

It was wrong. She should never have done it. She hadn't meant to, but she had cast a spell on Mitch. And she had to undo it, before he did anything else he was going to regret.

"Lucy?"

Mitch must have felt the change in her body and knew something was wrong. She heard the concern in his voice and wanted to cry. She didn't deserve it.

"Sweetheart." He kissed the corner of her mouth. "Don't get nervous on me now. I'm not going to chain you up in a dungeon or do anything you don't want me to do. I'm just working from the list of needs you gave me. Although I threw the exhibition fantasy in as an extra, since it seemed to be working for you. It was certainly working for me. If you want me to stop, I'll stop."

"I want you to stop," said Lucy, miserable, and wanting anything but. "I'm sorry, Mitch. This was a mistake."

"A mistake." Mitch sat frozen for a minute and then he ripped her blindfold off so he could glare directly into her eyes in the dim cabin light.

"What the hell are you talking about, Lucy? I just made you come so many times I lost count. When you had your legs wrapped around my waist, you weren't thinking it felt like a mistake. A mistake is when the sex is lousy. A mistake is when you find out the guy is married. An eligible, unattached male making you come screaming is not a mistake, Lucy."

He was furious. He had every right to be, she thought with a sinking feeling in the pit of her stomach. "I'm sorry," she said again, knowing how inadequate that was.

"You're sorry." He stared at her, his face going frozen again. "Damn good thing I made you put it in writing, then, isn't it? That would have been one hell of a mistake on my part, just trusting you to have told me the truth about what you wanted and not claim I'd abducted you against your will after I gave it to you. At least this way, all I lose is the deposit on the boat. Not my job and my reputation."

There wasn't anything she could say that would help. She stared down at her lap and twisted her hands together and tried not to think about what she'd lost.

She'd never had it, she reminded herself.

It wasn't real.

That didn't stop the tears from sliding down her cheeks in silence.

"Damn you, don't cry."

A sob escaped her.

"Lucy." He said her name on ragged sigh and wrapped his arms tightly around her. "I really want to throttle you right now, but I can't stand seeing you cry. I'm not letting you leave like this, either. The plane's about to land. I'll take you home, but before I do, I'm taking you to the damn boat and keeping you there until you explain to me why this is a mistake."

He tied the blindfold back on her, added a gag after minute of thoughtful consideration, and when the plane landed he carried her off again.

Chapter Six

The rocking motion of the boat was soothing. Lucy was grateful for that. She could use soothing.

Mitch hadn't said another word to her. Once he'd gotten her onto the boat, he'd dumped her on the bed in the cabin and left, presumably to take them out away from the dock so he could throttle her and dispose of the body without witnesses.

When he returned, she let him undo the blindfold and gag and unwrap her from the sheet without any resistance. If he wanted to kill her, she really couldn't blame him. But she clung to the thought that Mitch was far too controlled to ever lose his temper like that.

It was uncomfortable, being naked in front of him and knowing he didn't want her. She moved her hands to cover herself, although it was a little late for modesty.

"Put your hands down, Lucy. If this is the last time I get to see you naked, I'm going to look until I'm good and finished."

"You don't want to see me naked," she mumbled.

"Have you lost your mind? I'm male. You're female and you have big tits. For that alone I'd want to see you naked."

She blinked at him. "That's ridiculous. You never wanted to see me naked before."

"Of course I wanted to see you naked. I just never dared. I didn't trust myself not to lose control and commit a crime." Mitch rubbed a hand along his jaw, contemplating her. "Sit back down on the bed."

Lucy complied. He sat beside her and took her hand in his. "I want to know what this is about. And don't try to tell me you don't find me attractive, or I didn't satisfy you sexually. If you say something asinine like that, I will be forced to prove to you again that we are absolutely sexually compatible."

"You're very attractive," she assured him. "And you satisfied me sexually." So much so that she would spend the rest of her life knowing exactly what she was missing.

"Then explain to me why you're dumping me for the second time in less than twenty-four hours. The first time you said it was because I wouldn't put out. The second time you tell me it's because I just ate, banged, and fucked you while you had multiple orgasms. What do you want from me, Lucy? Just tell me. I'll give it to you."

"You can't give it to me," she whispered.

"The hell I can't." His voice vibrated with determination. "I'm the man for you. The only man for you. And you're the only woman for me."

"No," she said. "You only think so right now because I did something terrible."

Mitch sighed. "So that's what the problem is. Sex is not something terrible, Lucy. It isn't wrong to want sex. It isn't wrong to enjoy it. It isn't wrong for you to fantasize about me playing pirate with you or having an audience, either. You don't have to feel ashamed about the fact that you're a normal woman with healthy, natural needs."

"I don't."

"Well, then, what?" He stared at her in exasperation.

Lucy took a deep breath and made her confession. "I put a spell on you."

"You sure did," Mitch agreed. "I am under your spell and I would very much like to be under your naked body while you take a turn being on top. Can we get to that part soon, please?"

"No, Mitch, I mean it. I cast a spell on you. I didn't mean to, it was an accident. But that's why you're acting this way. It's all my fault. I'm sorry. I'll undo it."

"Lucy. You are making me seriously crazy. This is your objection? That I'm not here with you of my own free will?"

She nodded.

"Okay. Let's say, for the sake of argument, that I am in fact ensorcelled by something besides your fantastic tits, which, by the way, I would like to touch again. When was this alleged spell cast?"

"Tonight. After I closed the shop for the day and went home. And then you dressed up like a cat burglar and broke into my room."

"And this is your evidence that I'm under some spell?"

Lucy nodded again.

"Are you forgetting about lunch? Let me jog your memory. At lunch you dumped me because you had needs and I wasn't meeting them. You told me, in some detail, what those needs were. And then you ran off. At which point I went back to my office and spent the rest of the day arranging this weekend so that I could meet those needs."

He pushed her back on the bed and leaned over her. "I have proof, Lucy. You can check the time and date on the boat rental. I did that about two o'clock. Hours before your alleged spell-casting. Can I touch your tits again now?"

"Yes," Lucy said faintly.

Mitch had wanted her all along? The spell had nothing to do with it?

His hands closed over her breasts. His thumbs stroked her nipples in lazy circles. "Are you done dumping me, Lucy? I don't think I could take a third time."

She licked her lips nervously. "Mitch, wait, there's something else."

He swore, loudly and violently. "What?" he roared at her, still working her breasts with his hands.

She flinched at the volume, but she had to know. "Do you love me?"

"Do I love you." He gave her an incredulous look. "I really must have fucked your brains out, Lucy, because you don't seem to have any left. Do you think I'd go through all of this just to get laid?"

She shrugged, but couldn't hide the vulnerable need in her eyes. "You never said."

"My mistake." Mitch let go of her and kneeled on the floor beside the bed. "I love you, Lucy. Not just because you're every sexual fantasy I've ever had in the flesh. I love you because of who you are inside, the way you care about everybody. It makes me feel good just to look at you, just to be with you. I want you and only you forever. I want to marry you. Please say yes. But before you do, you should know that if you change your mind and decide to dump me again I can sue you for breach of contract."

Lucy felt a slow smile spread over her face. "Breach of contract?"

"I don't want to take any more chances. I don't want to lose you, Lucy. Say yes."

"Yes."

"Thank God." He stood up and started taking his clothes off again. "Now lay back and spread your legs. This agreement is about to be consummated."

He kneeled between her open legs once he was naked and ran his hands over her mons, petting her intimately. "Tell me you love me."

"I love you, Mitch."

"Tell me you want me and nobody but me."

"I want you. Just you."

"Tell me you want my cock again."

"I want your cock again."

He thrust a finger into her, pulled it back out, rubbed it over her clitoris, and thrust his finger into her again, working her while she gasped and squirmed. "You want it now, Lucy?"

"Yes." She said the word on a low groan. His cock was definitely ready for her, thick and engorged. She reached for it and stroked the hard length of his penis with both hands.

"Do you know what magic is, Lucy?" Mitch lowered himself over her and buried himself in her to the hilt, preventing her from answering beyond wordless moans. "This."

He proceeded to demonstrate his point.

When at long last he finally rested his case, Lucy recovered herself enough to ask, "Where are we, anyway?"

"Washington. Puget Sound," Mitch answered. He tucked her into his side and toyed with her hair, tugging gently at a stray curl. "I didn't know if a boat on a lake would meet your pirate fantasy requirement, and I thought maybe you'd like cruising around to some of the islands."

Lucy laughed. "Dressed in a sheet?"

"You could start a new fashion trend. But no, there are clothes for you in the closet. I know your size and I planned ahead."

His hands wandered all over her as they talked, stroking her as if he couldn't believe she was really there, his to hold and touch.

Lucy had a hard time believing it herself.

"We have this boat for the weekend?"

"We do."

"We're not going to hit a rock or anything, are we?"

"No. We're safe. Just far enough away from the marina that you can keep having screaming orgasms without disturbing the other boaters."

"Good thinking." Lucy smiled and snuggled closer. Then a thought occurred to her and she sat upright. "Mitch, I really did it right."

"I'll say." Satisfaction rang in his voice.

"No, I mean the spell. I really did something right. Real magic. You really are my true love and that's why I saw you at the end. I thought you weren't interested in me, which is why I thought I'd screwed up again."

She'd been shown the truth in the candle flame, she realized. That she already had what she'd been asking for. All she'd needed to do was recognize it.

"I have no idea what you're talking about, Lucy, but if you think you don't have my interest, I will prove you wrong." Mitch paused, then added, "In about half an hour. I'm thirty-eight, not eighteen."

"You don't have to prove anything now." She dropped back down beside him and kissed him the way she'd wanted to for months. It took a long time.

And then she said the silent thanks she'd neglected to give at her altar.

She would never be sure, but she thought she felt an answering touch, a brush of joy.

Maybe it was magic. Maybe it was simply love. Maybe they were one and the same thing.

The End

About the author

Charlene Teglia writes erotic romance with humor and speculative fiction elements. She can't imagine any better life than making up stories about hunky Alpha heroes who meet their match and live happily ever after, whether it happens right next door, in outer space, or the outer limits of imagination. When she's not writing, she can be found hiking around the Olympic Peninsula with her family or opening and closing doors for cats.

Charlene welcomes mail from readers. You can write to her c/o Ellora's Cave Publishing at 1337 Commerce Drive, #13, Stow, OH 44224.

Also by Charlene Teglia

Dangerous Games
Love and Rockets

CLUB RENDEZVOUS

Jan Springer

Chapter One

Club Rendezvous.

Splashes of pink light from the fancy neon sign flared through the car windows as Emma McCall did a last inventory check of herself in the rearview mirror.

Blonde bob cut, neatly combed. Check.

Bangs feathered just above perfectly arched dark eyebrows. Check.

Shimmering white eye shadow highlighting brown eyes. Check.

Hot red lipstick that matched her slinky red dress that she'd bought especially for tonight because it made her too-wide hips look slimmer and her small breasts look bigger. Check.

She looked pretty, maybe even sexy? Check?

Yes. Check.

Everything looked as perfect as it could. So why was she so bleeping nervous?

Probably because she couldn't believe she'd actually come to Club Rendezvous. That she'd finally gotten enough nerve to shake off her inhibitions and agree to meet her co-worker and good friend Kylie to finally see what all this swinging lifestyle stuff was about. For a whole year Emma had been dying to break out of the sexual mold her ex-husband had forced her into during their marriage. If she didn't chicken out, then tonight she'd begin to learn to trust men again and maybe, just maybe, she'd start onto the road to being the sexually liberated woman she'd always craved to be.

And if she was lucky she'd even get a glimpse of Logan Masters tonight. She'd heard he was back home in the next town working his late dad's farm with his twin brother, divorced and once again frequenting this club.

Just remembering the teasing and bold way he used to look at her during their college days made her pussy cream and her nipples tighten with excitement. Only a year ago, right before she'd finally got the guts to leave her abusive husband, she could only dream of coming to a wickedly delicious place like Club Rendezvous and wanting to have no-strings sex with a stranger or strangers.

However, tonight she wasn't married anymore, compliments of the divorce. Thank God! No more beatings. No more verbal abuse and certainly no more boring missionary sex whenever *he* wanted it.

After undergoing a bout of intensive group therapy for battered women she almost felt normal. Her confidence and self-esteem were coming back and her life was heading in a great direction with her job at the college, her cute little apartment and the freedom to do what she wanted and with whom she wanted. She hadn't told Kylie, but tonight she planned on setting herself sexually free as well. She was going to toss aside her sex toys and get herself laid. Good and hard. Love him and leave him. No strings attached.

Maybe even a ménage à trois!

Her momentary confidence fizzled the instant she grabbed her purse, stepped out of her car into the cool spring Alberta prairie night air and walked slowly toward the three-story building. By the time she reached the open door of Club Rendezvous, butterflies gnawed at her belly and she toyed with the idea of turning and running back to the safety of her car.

Damn her for being such a chickenshit!

Just inside the door, a gorgeous hunk who looked a lot like Fabio peeked out, saw her and waved her in.

"Hey pretty lady. Don't be shy."

She clutched her black purse and with both nervousness and excitement fought for confidence as she stepped inside the warm foyer.

"Fun's within your reach. Just show me your ticket, Miss."

"Actually it's…" She'd wanted to say Mrs. But she wasn't a Mrs. anymore. She had to get used to that. Another reason she was here.

"I'm a guest of Kylie Smith. She should be here already," Emma handed him the guest ticket Kylie had slipped her at work this morning.

He nodded. "I have a message for you from her. She can't make it tonight. Something about not finding a babysitter."

Shit!

"However, feel free to go in and here…" From a nearby bouquet he pulled out a beautiful strand of pink lilacs that smelled awesome. He winked at her and said, "A beautiful flower for a beautiful woman."

Emma's face flamed with embarrassment. She was hardly beautiful. Pretty maybe. But not beautiful. Oops, there was her low self-esteem peeking through again.

"Thanks," she said, feeling awfully self-conscious at his compliment. No man had complimented her in years and her trembling legs couldn't move her fast enough away from him. Leaving the foyer she found herself on a wickedly wonderful dance floor.

Music rocked through her and she looked around to see…erotic mayhem.

Oh-My-God!

The place was literally packed. Sensually dressed women gyrated to the music with half-naked men. Some were couples. Others threesomes. Even groups danced together. Bodies touched erotically. People kissed openly. Caressed each other intimately.

She couldn't dance like that. Could she?

A sharp thrill roared through her and her senses swirled to the wild beat of the music as she told herself that yes, maybe she could dance like that.

Men and women watched her curiously as she passed them, and she tried hard not to avoid eye contact with their smiling faces. How was she supposed to act in a place like this? How was she ever going to get up enough nerve to talk to someone let alone have sex with them?

Doubts crept through her and her hand tightened around the strand of sweet-smelling lilacs Fabio had given her. Maybe she should leave. Come back when Kylie could introduce her to some of her friends.

No! She had to stay. She'd promised herself an untamed evening full of hot sex. She deserved it. Hell, she wanted it and by golly she was going to get it.

"Hi, Shy Girl."

The delicate mix of an exotic cologne and fresh man sifted into her lungs, zipping wonderfully along her nerves.

Oh boy, she'd recognize his scent anywhere. She'd smelled it often enough when he'd come to her dorm room to pick up her roommate.

Turning around, her breath backed up in her lungs and her pulses pounded as sparkling blue eyes gazed at her.

Logan Masters, her college sweetheart. Not that she'd ever let him know. She'd been so unbelievably shy back then and engaged to her ex-husband, Bob. Hence, she'd limited herself to fantasies of Logan. Blistering erotic fantasies that had made her blush then and now.

"How are you doing? Do you remember me?" he asked and despite her flaming cheeks she forced herself to meet his scorching gaze.

His gorgeous, sensually shaped lips parted to show straight white teeth she wouldn't mind running her tongue across. His smile made the cutest dimples pop out in both his cheeks. Gosh, she'd forgotten how deep those dimples were. Forgotten how his feathery chestnut-colored hair curled wonderfully against the nape of his neck.

After all these years he still looked so damn good. Heck, he looked even better. He wore his trademark sexy beard stubble that made her face burn hotter and encouraged her pussy to cream in her panties as she pictured his head dipping between her legs, the stubble brushing erotically against the insides of her thighs as his tongue parted her pussy lips and plunged into her vagina.

Oh boy, hand me a vibrator. Now!

"Sure, I remember you, Logan." Who the hell wouldn't remember him? He was one of the sexiest, cutest guys in the agriculture college they'd both attended. And he'd been totally in love with her dorm mate, Dee. She'd heard they'd gotten married after graduation and moved overseas so they could both work in her grandfather's billion-dollar grape farm in Sicily.

"How are you doing, Shy Girl? It's been a long time. You look really hot."

That was a major understatement. She was more than hot. She was on fire.

"Are you alone?" he asked looking behind her, obviously expecting someone to be with her.

She nodded.

"Great! Please come and join us. My brother and…his lady friend are in the dining room."

"Sure."

She almost bolted as his large hand slid intimately against the small of her back. No man had ever touched her so gently before. Marriage had taught her that a man's touch only gave her pain. It was another reason she'd come here tonight. To fulfill yet another goal.

To learn to trust a man again.

Chapter Two

"You okay?" His affectionate, concerned look almost made her cry at what she'd been missing all these years.

"Sure," she nodded, feeling so self-conscious that she wished the floor would swallow her whole.

"Come on, let's go meet the others. Then I want to dance with you. Talk about old times."

Old times? They didn't have any old times. Had he mistaken her for someone else?

He expertly guided her past the gyrating crowds and opened a mahogany door, which led into another area. The loud music disintegrated as he closed the door, and soft, seductive music wrapped around her like a sensual blanket. She couldn't help but gasp at the beauty of the low-lit room. Crystal chandeliers splashed a buttery glow over tables draped with white linen tablecloths and fancy silverware. Sparkling wineglasses clinked as people toasted and laughed cheerfully.

For a split second she almost forgot she was in a swingers' club and that people were actually having sex up on the third floor. Nervousness came rushing back full speed as Logan led her toward a secluded table where a gorgeous redhead was openly flirting with a very bored Logan look-alike.

Logan's brother whistled as they drew to the table. "Hey big brother, what sexy creature did you find for yourself?"

"Hi guys. This here is an old college friend of mine, Emma McCall," Logan said as his hand settled intimately over the curve of her hip. He pulled out a chair for her and she sat down opposite his twin and beside the gorgeous redhead who made no effort to hide her disappointed pout at being interrupted.

Emma couldn't help but stare at Logan and then at his brother. Good grief. She could barely tell them apart. His brother possessed the same exploding dimples, sparkling blue eyes, curly hair and model-like facial features. The only thing different was his brother had no sexy midnight shadow to brush against her inner thighs.

Oh dear, she was starting to fantasize again.

"Emma, this is my twin brother Luke, and this is…Mary Ann? Did I get your name right?"

The woman seated beside Luke threw Logan a really pissed-off look. "Actually it's Ginger," she corrected and Emma immediately made the connection that this woman looked a lot like Ginger from the classic TV show, *Gilligan's Island*. She even had the same baby-doll hairstyle and black mole on the side of her mouth.

Luke stood quickly. Leaning over the intimate table he shook Emma's hand, giving her a gentle, friendly squeeze that immediately warmed her. She didn't miss the curiosity in his hot gaze and darn it, her shyness kicked in again making her look away. Gosh, was it getting hot in here or what?

Ginger smiled at Emma, but the smile didn't quite make it to her gray eyes. It was obvious the woman did not like her.

"By the lilacs in your hand I take it this is your first time here? They only give flowers to the first-timers."

"Oh," Emma's ego deflated. She'd thought that maybe the man at the door had really thought she was beautiful. Boy, was she ever naïve.

"So? Is it your first time?" Ginger prodded taking a sip of red wine, obviously trying to hide a smug smile.

Unless Emma missed her guess there was a sexual innuendo in that question and to her surprise she felt herself bristle with a tinge of anger.

"First time, but definitely not my last."

"That's great to hear," Luke chuckled.

Ginger threw him an annoyed look.

Logan, obviously sensing trouble, moved his chair closer to Emma. Heat roared through her as his knee brushed sensuously against her thigh.

"Would you like some red wine, Emma?"

"Please."

She watched his long fingers wrap around the neck of the wine bottle and couldn't stop a vision of both Logan's and Luke's hands sliding over her body, touching her breasts, pulling at her nipples, their delicious cocks sliding into both of her channels at the same time. Or maybe Logan fucking her with that wine bottle? Her face instantly heated.

Emma looked up and found Ginger staring at her, the smug smile gone from her lips, replaced by one of open hostility.

"So tell me, Emma. What kind of scene are you into tonight? Lesbian? Orgy? Passive? Sub?"

Bitch!

"Actually, I'm looking to give head, get cunnilingus, maybe some anal, and a ménage à trois with two men, among a whole lot of other things…and you?"

Shock splashed across the redhead's face. "Ménage à trois?"

"The night is young," Logan interrupted. "We can easily arrange pleasuring Emma, right, Luke?"

"Damn straight," came Luke's somewhat hoarse and exceptionally quick answer.

Oh-My-God! Luke and Logan were agreeing to have sex with her? Just like that?

"You're disgusting, Luke Masters," Ginger snapped and stood. She cast an icy glare at Logan's twin. "You said you were just into one girl."

"I am." Luke winked at Emma.

Sweet mercy! What was going on here?

"I'm outta here. Goodbye, asshole." Ginger grabbed her purse and stomped away.

"Good riddance, bitch," Luke chuckled and leaned back in his chair, his eyes bright and alert as he surveyed Emma.

"I'm sorry you had to see that, Em." He turned to his brother. "Thanks for getting rid of Ginger for me."

Logan chuckled, "No problem. I kind of thought you didn't like her. We have the same tastes and I knew she was definitely not your type."

A sense of awful unease swept over her. Logan had brought her here just to help out his brother? Oh man, was she ever stupid to even think that these two hunks would want to have sex with her.

She made a move to get up but Logan's hand curled softly around her wrist. "Please stay, sweetheart. I really want to talk to you and dance with you." His voice lowered. "And have sex with you, that is, if you were serious about what you said."

A wonderful quiver ripped through her at the intensely eager way these two men were looking at her. It made her pussy just about explode with anticipation. Why should she care that Logan had simply used her? She wasn't looking for an emotional commitment, remember? Tonight she wanted to give her aching pussy a present. Wanted to act on her goals and get some hot and heavy sex.

With no strings. Definitely no strings.

"Don't worry, we're D&D free," Logan said seriously.

"Oh, um. D&D?"

Luke grinned. "It means disease and drug-free. The strongest thing we've tried is pot and we always use extra-strength condoms."

"Oh." What else could she say? That's one thing she'd forgotten to bring tonight. Condoms. Her face flamed yet again.

"Okay, Luke, you're making her blush. Come on, Emma. Let's hit the dance floor."

Logan stood and held out his hand.

When she placed her fingers against his hot palm, her body tingled at the sultry way he was looking at her. He led her out of the dining room and onto the packed dance floor.

She'd never been much of a dancer. Bob hadn't cared for it so she had very little experience in that department.

When she began to imitate the sensual way the other women were dancing, she felt tense and silly.

Logan, bless him, was quick to realize her inexperience. He grinned and those awesome dimples exploded in his cheeks once again, taking her breath clean away.

"Just relax, Emma. Here, let me help you."

Both his hands slid against the curves of her hips, branding her beautifully.

"Just move your hips against my hands. Nice and slow."

She did as he instructed, following the erotic way his hands made her hips move and feeling the sensual heat racing through her from his intimate touch. Gosh, his hands felt so good.

"Good! That's it. Swing your hips. Just a little more. Perfect. Now put your hands on my shoulders."

She curled her fingers over his broad shoulders, immediately feeling the flex of muscles there as he moved his hands off her hips and smoothed lower to cup her ass cheeks.

Oh boy! That felt good too! Real good.

"Did I tell you that you look really hot? You turned me on the minute I saw you step into the dance room."

She swallowed at his compliment, and followed his bold gaze as it dropped to settle on the gentle swell of her breasts. Her heart began a loud pounding in her ears almost drowning out the music as she noted the way her nipples were poking proudly against the red velvety material.

"Thank you," was all she could manage.

He was pressing his hips forward and she could feel the long, thick length of his engorged cock burning against her mons. Liquid heat dripped from her slit as she envisioned how beautifully he'd stretch her when he sank into her cunt.

Good grief! Her panties were literally soaked. She couldn't stop the tiny erotic moan from escaping her lips as he pressed even harder and she felt rather mortified at the unexpected sound.

"You don't do this very often, do you." It wasn't a question but rather a statement.

His eyes twinkled with amusement and she got the feeling he was laughing at her. She shrugged her shoulders and looked away from his heated gaze, feeling embarrassed yet again.

"No, actually...no," she stumbled. "I've just gotten divorced." As if that would explain everything.

"Oh yes, from Bob."

"You still remember his name."

"I remember a lot of things about you. The fact that you blushed every time I called you Shy Girl. Your blushes always turned me on, Emma. Why do you think I teased you so much? I should have pursued you instead of Dee. But you were engaged to Bob and it was like pulling teeth trying to get you to talk to me when I came over. I guess I should have pulled harder."

Emma smiled, remembering how anxious and excited she'd felt knowing that Logan would be dropping by on a particular night to pick up Dee and whisk her off to Club Rendezvous.

"She always told me what you two did when you came here."

The briefest nervous flutter crossed his face and then it was gone, replaced by something else.

Hope.

"So you have a pretty good idea about the swinging life."

"It's why I came here. I want to explore. I've always wanted to explore my sexual cravings but I was just too shy to do it. Until now."

The dimples in Logan's cheeks disappeared as his smile flattened into a look of utter seriousness that made her shudder against his hard length. His head dipped and he brushed his lips across her left cheek. A whisper of a kiss that had her mind reeling and her pulses pounding.

"I heard you're teaching at the agriculture college we went to," he said and sucked her earlobe into his hot mouth. He bit gently. Desperate shivers gripped her and she couldn't stop herself from digging her nails into his muscles.

"W-Who told you that?"

"Your co-worker, Kylie. Her brother and I are good friends. I spoke to her here last week, actually. She mentioned you'd agreed to come to the Club tonight with her so I thought I'd pop in and say hello."

Logan had come just to meet her? A wonderful warm rush flowed through her.

"Kylie never told me she knew you personally."

"Don't worry, I've never been with her. She and her late husband had their own crowd they hung with. Besides, I'm very picky about the women I have sex with and she's really not my type, and there is the fact she is my friend's sister. He'd kill me if I ever slept with her. He's so damn protective of her since her husband died."

"Oh, I guess that's nice to know. I mean…that you're very picky, not that he'd kill you."

He chuckled, and then his eyes grew rather dusky. "But you are my type, Emma. Especially if you meant what you said earlier… I like a woman who wants to explore sex to the fullest."

Oh my! Did you ever pick the right girl!

Chapter Three

His hands were intimately smoothing over her ass cheeks now, dipping against her crack. The erotic way his hard erection ground against her belly was really turning her on. Big time. She realized her hips were gyrating as if she were having sex right here on the dance floor with him. Gosh, she didn't know she could swivel so easily.

The music turned to a slow dance and the lights grew dimmer. The dance floor thinned out, allowing couples to enjoy some intimate time.

"I don't want to push you or anything. I mean about sex. Since it is your first night here. Most women are just curious to see if they want to swing."

"I'm serious. I've...wanted to try for a long time. Ever since... I mean... I've fantasized..." Oh gosh, this was embarrassing, telling Logan Masters that she fantasized. "I mean since this place opened during our college years, I've always wanted to try it."

"You should have tried it if it interested you so much." His warm breath caressed her flaming cheeks.

"I was shy."

"You still are. And you blush so beautifully. I really like that about you. You're still so sweet and innocent."

It was as if he'd just struck a raw nerve and she couldn't stop herself from speaking truthfully. "My husband didn't think so. He was very insecure. Didn't like me to talk to men. If I so much as looked at one and he noticed then he let me know how much he loved me when he took his fists to me at home."

Logan's eyes darkened. If looks could kill…

Oh God! Why had she brought Bob into this?

"I heard about that. I ever see him, he's dead." The cold way he said it sent chills rippling up her spine.

"I'm sorry, Logan. I shouldn't have said anything. This isn't the place for this. I came here to have a good time not to air my dirty laundry. It's over now with Bob and I just want to be free of men."

He pulled away a little and cocked a puzzled eyebrow at her.

"I mean…I'm sorry, I didn't mean it the way it sounded. I mean I want to explore."

"You mean you want sex without the strings of an emotional relationship."

"Yeah, I guess that's it."

"I can handle the no strings…for now. And if you'll let me I want to handle fulfilling your sexual needs, Emma. You just let me know when you're ready and we can head upstairs."

Emma blew out a breath at his bold statement. Her pussy quivered. Her nipples felt as if they were on fire. She needed to do this. Needed to prove to herself that she could pick and choose what man she could have sex with. She really wanted to fuck Logan Masters. Had always wanted to fuck him. And now that she was a free woman she wanted to explore her sexuality via all kinds of avenues. If she wasn't ready by now, she never would be.

His hand intimately slid against her lower back. "Let's go and grab a bite. We can get to know each other a little more."

"Sure."

She loved the hot feel of his fingertips burning her flesh as he led her back to the other room where his brother Luke was just seating himself. Thankfully he didn't have that Ginger woman with him, and to her excitement he didn't have any woman with him.

"Ah, beautiful Em," Luke chuckled as she sat down. "I saw you two out on the dance floor. If you hadn't been dancing with my brother, I would have cut in. You're my type too, y'know." He winked at her and poured her some red wine, which she eagerly sipped as she tried hard to break away from that shyness again.

"I've already ordered for us. I hope it meets with your approval, Em. Lamb chops, sweet potatoes, baby peas and carrots and for dessert we're getting thick slabs of luscious chocolate cake. Chocolate always puts me into the mood for sex."

Logan almost choked on the wine he was sipping and Emma couldn't help but laugh at the relaxed way Luke had said it.

Maybe she was silly being so nervous. Having sex was natural. For her having sex with a man would be fulfilling an ultimate goal of sexual freedom.

"It sounds wonderful, Luke," Emma replied.

"The dinner…or the sex?"

"Both." She grinned at his smile and to her surprise this time her face didn't flame.

* * * * *

Logan couldn't stop himself from watching Emma's every move. From the cute way she curled her fingers around her fork to the delicious way her lips parted as she chewed her chocolate cake, to the cock-wrenching way her nipples poked against her hot dress.

How in the hell he'd never pushed himself harder in trying to get her attention during their college years was beyond him. He'd been an idiot for pursuing the wrong girl. He should have realized Emma was a hot woman beneath a shy-girl exterior.

They'd lost years because he'd been taken with flirty Dee. A beautiful woman who, once he'd placed the ring on her finger, decided the swinging life wasn't for her anymore and wanted to move to Italy.

Shit! He'd stuck by her decision. Hadn't agreed with it but he'd been faithful. That is, until he'd found her tumbling around in their villa bed with two busty female grape pickers.

"A penny for your thoughts?" Emma's soft voice cracked the disturbing image and brought him straight to the present.

"Yeah, bro. Where were you just now? Thinking up ways of pleasing our delicious Emma?"

At Luke's comment an odd sting of jealousy zipped through Logan. Before he could stop himself he said coolly, "I'll be the one to do the pleasing, Luke."

Luke's eyes widened visibly with apparent shock. They'd always shared their women. He'd even shared Dee with him. They'd both enjoyed that lifestyle. Now suddenly Logan wasn't so sure he wanted to share Emma.

He caught her frown, the zip of fear in her eyes and instantly realized his mistake. He was being pushy. She'd said no strings.

Shit! She was just starting out with exploring the alternate lifestyle. He had no right to tell her what do to or who to do it with.

"Sorry...I mean, I'd like to be the first one to please Emma. You can join us later..." Oh man, his dominating side was rearing its head. Not good. He'd scare her off. He turned to her and decided to put the decision-making where it belonged. In her hands. "I mean, if it's okay with you, Emma?"

Her bedroom brown eyes twinkled brilliantly and her lips parted slightly giving him a lusty view of her pink tongue as she licked a piece of chocolate off her bottom lip. The sight of it almost blew him away. He couldn't wait to feel her hot little mouth feasting on his cock. Couldn't wait to slide his engorged cock into her pussy.

"I would enjoy it very much if you pleasured me first," she said softly. "And I'm ready, if you are."

* * * * *

Emma couldn't help but stare at the group of nude women laughing and giggling, their bare breasts bouncing as they wandered down the hall just outside the changing room she was peeking out of. Logan had said she could go upstairs nude or wrap a towel around herself to hide her nudity and that he'd be waiting for her just outside.

So where was he? Had he changed his mind? Had he stood her up?

Oh God! Is that what had happened? Were both Luke and Logan laughing their heads off downstairs while she was up here waiting for them?

She frowned into the now-empty hallway.

It had been too easy. Too good to be true. They didn't want to have sex with her. She'd been stupid. Naïve. An idiot for trusting them. Why would the gorgeous Masters twins want to fuck her?

She clutched the towel tighter around her breasts and was about to step back into the changing room when she saw Logan strolling into view at the end of the hall. He stopped to read something on the bulletin board. And he was totally naked!

Chapter Four

Emma's pulse skittered at the sight of his firm butt and the powerful muscles in his thighs. Not to mention the cute way his fists were clenching and unclenching. It gave her the impression that maybe he was just as nervous as she was. The sight gave her a bubbly feeling along with a good shot of much-needed courage.

It was as if he sensed her standing there admiring him and he turned around.

His look was dark. Lusty. Hungry.

She swallowed and dropped her gaze, raking over his wide muscular shoulders, a well-muscled chest. Zipping past his pebbled brown nipples, she followed the thick fluff of dark curly hair that arrowed down the middle of his flat washboard stomach to meet with a puff of hair that shrouded a most exquisite set of swollen balls and the biggest, longest cock she'd ever seen on a man. Gosh! He was at least nine inches long and so thick she didn't think he'd ever fit inside her.

She felt her eyes widen with disbelief, felt her pussy cream so hard that she could actually smell her arousal.

"Are you ready for the third floor?"

Oh my God! More ready she couldn't be.

She found herself nodding or at least she thought she nodded as she watched him stroll toward her, his huge scrotum pulled up tight against his body and his thick shaft hardening right before her very eyes. By the time he reached her she had a breathtaking view of the giant, purple plum-shaped head that had slipped out of its sheath, and couldn't miss the thick blue vein that pulsed right down the middle of his reddening shaft.

He gazed down at her with such a smoldering look she swore her heart stopped a few beats and when he took her hand into his, she felt her knees melt.

"You look gorgeous, Emma."

"You do too."

Her heart hammered insanely against her chest as he, a wonderfully naked man, led her up the lush, carpeted stairs.

"I assumed you'd rather be in a private room since you're just starting out. Unless you'd rather congregate in the main room and have sex with others?"

She cleared her suddenly dry throat. "Private is fine." For now. She could experiment when she gathered more courage.

God! She just couldn't believe she was doing this. Plain, shy, wallflower Emma McCall, a virgin until she married her husband, was walking down the hallway of the exclusive Club Rendezvous with Logan Masters. And she was planning to have sex with him and his twin brother. It was beyond her wildest fantasies. She almost had to pinch herself to make sure this was actually happening.

He stopped them in front of Room 303 where a sign hanging on the fancy gold doorknob said Vacant.

"I can leave it at Vacant, which allows others to come in and view us. They have to ask permission to have sex with us but they don't have to ask permission to watch.

Or I can flip it to the Do Not Disturb side and we'll only be interrupted by Luke a little later on."

Telling him to leave it at Vacant was so tempting. After all, she was here and she wanted to experiment with everything, but maybe Logan would get the wrong idea. Maybe he'd think she was too promiscuous?

As if he were reading her thoughts he chuckled. "Don't worry. Lots of people enjoy being watched while they're having sex. That's why they're here at Club Rendezvous, to explore. Just like you. It may be an avenue you'd like to investigate at a later time but personally I don't mind either way. It's up to you."

"Leave it at Vacant," she found herself saying in an excited rush.

God! This was so much fun! Was it actually normal to be so excited? To feel so unbelievably free? To want to experiment so liberally and easily with sex?

Oh-oh! Her lack of self-confidence was trying to take over again. Logan was absolutely right. Places like Club Rendezvous wouldn't exist if there weren't people like her who wanted to explore. What she was doing was perfectly normal for her. She'd just stifled her sexual self all these years, that's why she was feeling a wee bit…doubtful about her wants and needs.

Logan pushed open the mahogany door.

Warm air brushed against her bare legs and arms and Emma couldn't help but gasp at the intoxicating sight of the bedroom and couldn't help but do a little wiggle dance.

"Oh my God! It's so beautiful."

The room was dimly lit with flickering votive candles that hung in bronze wall sconces. A delicate vanilla aroma wafted beneath her nose and in the middle of the room she spotted a king-size bed made out of white birch logs. The bed was covered with a shimmering pink comforter and silky white pillows.

To one side stood a massage table with a furry leopard-skin blanket draped over it and nearby...

"Oh my gosh, a fireplace! And it's on!"

It took up the entire wall and was made of gray boulders. Snapping sounds and orange sparks erupted from the rosy glow flickering along the logs in the hearth, hitting the clear glass enclosure.

"I think I've died and gone to heaven," she breathed, unable to believe that Logan had secured this beautiful room for them.

"Heaven is still coming, Emma."

She swallowed at the promise in Logan's husky voice and felt his large palm sweep across her toweled ass as he guided her into the room.

"I had no idea that there were these types of rooms up here. I just assumed..."

"What? That I'd make love to you on the floor?"

Her pussy spasmed wildly at those words.

But wasn't it a little early in their relationship for Logan to be saying the L word? No man had made love to her. With Bob it had just been sex. And she'd never really orgasmed with him. He'd been selfish. Just taking and hurting.

What a waste those years had been with Bob. He'd caught her eye when she'd been young and vulnerable. Thanks to her abusive parents, who'd left her with nonexistent self-esteem, she had been easy prey to his persuasive confidence and receptive to a barrage of abuse from him.

The only times she'd really been aroused by a man were when she watched the intoxicating kisses Logan had greeted Dee with when he came to pick her up. That's when she'd secretly started to wish for a man like Logan for herself. A man who would be her hero. A man who would whisk her away from her abusive fiancé. It had taken her years to realize she could be her own hero...if she chose to be. It had taken her years to build her self-esteem and to walk out on Bob. Last year she'd done it.

Emma found herself suddenly nodding with realization. That's probably why it was so easy to trust Logan tonight, because of the way she remembered him being in college. Kind, teasing and oh-so sexually confident with Dee.

Logan's hot fingers curled around her bare upper arms, snapping Emma back to reality. He turned her around to face him and she found nerve endings she never knew existed tingling to life at the shadowy stubble around his full lips and on his cheeks. His chin seemed darker than before and she noticed the tiny lines crinkling outward from the sides of his eyes as he smiled at her. It seemed as if maybe he was laughing at her again. Laughing at her naïveté because she hadn't known about these lush rooms existing.

"Women like you are rare, Emma. I should have noticed you before. Should have pursued you instead of Dee...shit. I was young. Stupid. Horny. She had me wrapped around her finger before I even knew what hit me. She was easy to talk to. Easy to have sex with. Easy to share in the Life."

"And I was quiet, refused to come out of my shell."

"I thought it was because you were engaged that you seemed so distant with me. I resorted to teasing you. Calling you Shy Girl so I could see that erotic blush on your face."

"I'm not so terribly shy anymore, Logan."

"You're brave to come here, Emma. Brave to want to explore your own sexual cravings."

He reached out and ran the back of his fingers along her jawline. His touch was so light and feathery. It sparked something wild inside her heart. Her womb fluttered erotically.

"You're different now. You're solid. You're not a piece of beautiful fluff that makes a man horny just by looking at her."

"Thanks…I think."

"I mean it, Emma. You're pretty and strong and confident and your sexy blush just about makes me come on the spot." He tenderly slid the back of his fingers along the column of her neck and arrowed downward over her collarbone, his warm palm settling over the top swell of her breasts, over the knot that held her towel in place.

Her breath backed up in her lungs as his heat zipped into her chest. She wondered if he could feel the hard, frantic way her heart was racing.

"There's a fresh inner confidence in you. It's bubbling right before my eyes. It's so sexy and yet it gives me the idea that you might not allow me to have a chance with you. Does that make any sense?"

The power of his words made mixed emotions erupt inside her. Fear at maybe losing her newfound precious freedom to Logan, a man she'd always been interested in. There was also a roaring excitement that he was actually admitting he was interested in her. That he wanted a chance with her. Instincts told her it wasn't just because he wanted sex with her tonight.

"If you're saying you'd like for us to date and get to know each other, then yes, I'd love to. But Logan, my marriage to Bob burned me. I want to go slow with another relationship. I want to explore my sexual side too. I've always wanted to. Now I have my chance and I can't go back to being dominated by a man. I won't. Are you comfortable with that?"

He grinned and his eyes twinkled with satisfaction at her answer. "You make me so hot when you get that determined look in your eye, Emma. Yes, I'm comfortable with it."

Logan dipped his head and grazed a feathery kiss across her lips. The sensations made her knees go so weak she had to curl her arms around his warm neck to keep from falling.

His hot, moist lips slid softly against hers and she smelled his exotic cologne along with the scent of sweet wine and chocolate cake they'd shared after dinner. The aromas were intoxicating. The movements of his mouth against hers made an erotic flush slide through her. The feeling was almost beyond description. Pleasure skimmed around her lips as his beard stubble brushed her flesh. The friction brought a rush of warm feelings to the surface. Instincts that told her this was how it should be between a man and a woman. Tender. Intimate. Hot.

His tongue swiped against her lips, prodding them open, slipping inside, skimming against her teeth. She opened and accepted him, his velvety tongue clashing with hers. Mating with hers.

He tasted so damn good. His lips were warm and giving. She'd never felt so free in her life. It gave her courage. Courage to kiss him harder. To explore these wickedly beautiful sensations slamming through her.

Her tongue pressed past his and she slid into his mouth, running across those perfect white teeth. He groaned. It was a wild sound. A sound that blasted scrumptious sensations through her pussy.

She could barely think when a moment later he broke the shocking kiss.

"What do you need tonight, Emma?" he whispered, his hot breath raking along her neck as he nibbled on her earlobe.

Sweet quivers slid along her neck and she found she could hardly tell him what she wanted. "I need to know what it feels like to be a woman. A real woman."

"And I want to know what pleases you, Emma. Will you let me do that?"

She found herself nodding, totally taken aback with the way his blue eyes seemed to darken with a sexual glaze. Sensual heat screamed through her as his lower body pressed against hers. She could feel the burning outline of his cock against her lower abdomen, just as it had felt on the dance floor. Only now it seemed bigger. Much bigger.

"We can start with an erotic massage. I want to introduce you to my hands. Hands that can pleasure you in ways you can't imagine."

Oh my!

"Belly down, sweetheart."

Her lower belly contracted with excitement as he let her go. On weak legs she turned to look at the cozy massage table.

Should she take off her towel now? Leave it on? Shyness raged.

She knew he was watching her. Could feel the heat of his gaze on her. If she hesitated too long, he'd give up on her. She didn't want him to leave. She wanted him to make love to her. She wanted to live out the fantasies she'd had about him when she'd been in college. Wanted to experience what he'd done with Dee all those times they'd left her alone and fantasizing in her dorm room.

Somehow her dorm mate had screwed up. She'd let Logan go.

Even though Emma had told Logan she wanted to go slow in a relationship she suddenly realized she didn't want to make the same mistake Dee had made.

She didn't want to lose Logan. She needn't be afraid that he would dominate her like Bob had done. He'd already said he wanted a woman to freely explore sex in the Lifestyle. And boy did she want to discover this Lifestyle.

Her breath caught in her throat as anticipation raged. Her heart pounded a mile a minute. Suddenly she couldn't wait to get naked. Couldn't wait to have Logan's hands caressing her, touching her, massaging her, his gorgeous cock fucking her.

So why was she suddenly feeling so damned shy? So slow in not getting her ass out of the towel?

It was now or never. Do or die. Oh God, that sounded so passé.

Taking a deep breath of courage, she untied the small knot and dropped the towel.

Chapter Five

Warm air breathed against her naked flesh and she heard Logan's sharp intake of breath. Her face flushed and she saw the lust raging in his eyes. The passionate look literally burned her from head to toe. His breathing sounded loud in her ears, ragged, aroused.

In turn her heart hammered in her ears. Her pussy moistened. Sharp sensations rippled through her as she suddenly wondered how he'd react when he found the butt plug buried in her ass.

Holy shit!

How was he going to be able to concentrate on giving Emma a massage when all he could think about was sinking his cock deep into her pussy and listening to her moans of arousal?

The instant she'd dropped her towel, he'd gone so hard, so fast, it had literally been breathtaking. Her breasts were small yet perky. Instinctively he knew they'd fill his hands perfectly. Her nipples were long, beaded and so lusciously pink. His fingers itched to pinch them, squeeze them, maybe even clamp them.

He lowered his gaze and noticed her bare pussy.

Oh man. She really was serious about wanting cunnilingus. His mouth watered at the thought of going down on her.

When she shyly turned around to get up on the massage table her shapely plump ass looked so delicious he could barely wait until he got his hands on those round velvety-looking cheeks. Oh man, not to mention the things he could do with her asshole.

And her wide curvy hips... He could barely contain a low whistle of excitement... He could ride her good and hard holding tight to those delectable-looking hips.

She was avoiding his gaze as she nestled belly down on the massage table, her face all rosy and pretty.

Fuck! The shy way she blushed turned him on quicker than a rocket. He'd hate for her to lose that innocence. But all the women eventually lost their shyness in the Lifestyle.

As she nestled onto the sturdy table, her ass nicely up in the air compliments of the fluffy pillow beneath her hips, her arms drew up and she tucked them beneath her chin using them for a pillow. Her creamy mounds were squished against the table, but soon they would be branding his chest.

She looked over at him, her long black lashes fluttering as her hungry gaze zeroed in on his swollen, aching shaft. Her beautiful brown eyes widened ever so slightly. Shock and arousal registered.

Shit! With that look she seemed so naïve about a man's rock-hard erection.

And she was so ready.

Oh yeah, she was ready. Ready to explore the pleasures of sex.

And he was just as ready to explore it with her.

* * * * *

Emma's breath locked in her throat as Logan's warm, oiled hands touched her feet. He moved slowly, erotically, kneading her arches, each toe, then up along her calves.

"Mmm, that feels wonderful," she sighed and allowed herself to be enveloped by the erratic sound of his breathing, and the soothing feel of his tender touch.

"You've come a long way from being Shy Girl, Emma," he said softly, his fingers branding her flesh as he slowly slid over the backs of her knees.

"It's been a long inner fight," she admitted. Her eyes fluttered closed on a sigh as he found a particularly sore knot on her lower thigh.

"Inner fights make you strong."

"And tired."

"But you won or you never would have found your way here, am I right?"

"Yes."

For an instant she felt like telling him about her abusive relationship with Bob. The beatings. The verbal abuse. Her decision to leave him.

Her resurrection. A rebirth, which included following her sexual instincts and coming here to Club Rendezvous. There was a need burning deep inside her, a craving to tell him why she wanted to go slow with an emotional relationship. She'd seen the understanding flicker in his eyes when she'd told him that Bob had burned her. Some day she'd share her past with him. But not now. Definitely not now.

Her eyes popped open and anticipation roared as his oiled palms smoothed wonderfully over her ass cheeks.

She could feel her anal muscles clench as he drew closer to her back hole. Could feel a slow burn gripping her lower belly as he massaged her curves slowly, erotically, his fingers kneading her flesh until the pleasing burn ignited.

She found herself tensing as he pulled her cheeks apart. His finger slid between her crack. A strong digit massaged her outer hole.

Oh God! The tender way he touched her there made desire swell deep inside her ass. She forced herself to relax her muscles. He slipped past the tight sphincter and dipped inside.

And stopped.

Emma swallowed her excitement at his soft strangled inhalation.

He'd discovered the butt plug.

"You weren't kidding when you said all those things to MaryAnn."

"Ginger," she corrected him, taking immense pleasure at the aroused sound of his voice.

"Forget her."

"Done," she whispered and grimaced as her inner muscles protested the slow removal of her plug.

"How long have you been wearing it?"

"Long enough to know I'm ready."

He swore softly. It was an aroused noise. Excited. Heated.

She shivered at the sound and found herself whispering truthfully, "I've never had the pleasure of a man up my ass. But I want it, tonight."

She could hear Logan swallow then he said, "Your hole is too tight for me. The plug is too small. I'll leave your beautiful virgin ass to my brother. Luke's cock is smaller than mine. He can break you in. Anal is his fetish. I'd only hurt you. Turn you off to it. When we leave here I'll give you a few more butt plugs of bigger sizes. They'll stretch you. Get you ready for me."

At the mention of his brother her stomach plunged as if she were on a runaway elevator.

Ménage à trois. Tonight. She'd almost forgotten.

Suddenly she realized she could barely breathe. Could barely wait for Luke to show up.

Slowly Logan slid the butt plug from her. Her ass suddenly felt unbearably empty.

From the corner of her eye she noticed movement. Noticed how fat and pulsing his erection was now. His cock looked beautiful. Absolutely huge. Unbelievably thick and she swore she could see the web of veins lacing his red shaft pulse as it lifted toward his belly.

Emma gasped at the erotic sight. He was turned on knowing she was a virgin back there. She realized just how lucky she was having Logan with her tonight. She could have ended up with a man to whom her first anal fuck would mean nothing. A stranger who would have cared less if he turned her off to anal. He might even have hurt her. Made her think it wasn't for her.

Yes, tonight she was very lucky indeed.

Logan's touch became gentler, more intimate. His lubed finger slipped inside. And then another followed. He massaged her, stretching her anal muscles until she gasped at the brilliant pressure. Pleasure mixed with pain. But it was a blissful breathtaking pleasure-pain she liked.

He pressed deeper, stroked sensuously, and then impaled her with yet another lubed finger. The new tightness of three fingers stroking in and out of her ass as if they were a cock brought a rich sensation surging into her belly.

"This is almost Luke's size."

She found herself whimpering at his words, found her ass pressing up against his fingers, liquid heat soaring through her vagina. She wanted him to surge deeper. Erotic frustration zipped through her as he withdrew his fingers.

Fuck my ass! she wanted to cry out. Her hole burned. Her anal muscles clenched around emptiness and in the pit of her womb something beautiful fluttered.

"Lift your hips for me, sweetheart." His voice was now barely a whisper as she did what he asked. He quickly removed the pillow.

"Turn over."

Again she did as he asked. A burning tremble zipped through her as she flipped over and came face to face with his lusty gaze. The shock of the heated way he watched her small breasts jiggle as she lay down on her back just about made her come on the spot.

He leaned over and she heard the slow sliding sound of a drawer opening beneath the massage table.

"I've got some sex toys in here. Would it be okay if I used them on you?"

A burning rush of excitement made it hard for her to talk. Instead she blew out a heated breath and nodded eagerly. "You said earlier while we were dancing that you had fantasies. Any of them about me?" he asked. His gaze slowly drifted to parts south, to where her pussy lay bare and open to his scorching view. Strangely enough she didn't feel embarrassed anymore. Just totally turned on.

"Maybe one or two."

"Only one or two?" Surprise etched his voice.

He cleaned then oiled his hands, and her lower belly clenched at the delicious sight of his rippling biceps. When his warm hands slid over the curves of her shoulders she couldn't stop herself from bucking at the heated electricity slamming into her flesh. He kneaded her muscles, digging in with long, hard fingers until she felt herself loosening beneath his ministrations.

"Okay, so maybe more. Maybe a whole bunch of fantasies."

"Tell me about them."

Emma bit her lower lip realizing he'd captured her with his question. Dare she admit her wildest fantasies to Logan Masters? His gaze was fixed on her. Dark and lusty as he awaited her answer.

For a moment she couldn't answer as she felt the distinct outline of each and every long finger as they slid lower, smoothing over her collarbone. When his hot palms glided onto her tightening breasts, he watched her closely, a lusty grin splashing over his shadowed face. He wasted no time in tending to her nipples. She cried out as his fingers tweaked and pulled. Her nipples grew hard. In seconds they were tender, chafed, screaming with heat.

"Come on, sweetheart. Don't be shy. Tell me what these fantasies were about?"

"Tonight's wine bottle comes to mind."

His gaze darkened, his fingers hesitated ever so slightly on her flesh.

"Oh?" His question seemed somewhat strangled. Instinctively she knew he was picturing things he could do to her with a wine bottle.

She cried out softly as his fingers flicked at her engorged reddening nipples. Pleasure-pain erupted with every swing. And then his head lowered and his warm mouth brushed a trembling tip.

Oh sweet God! He touched her nipple softly. Oh! So softly. She moaned as pleasure pierced her breast.

"Make that a champagne bottle," he whispered, his hot breath scorched her mound. His nostrils flared as he stared at her. Emma blinked back at him, suddenly unable to remember what they'd been talking about.

"Maybe we're celebrating New Year's Eve." He kissed the tip of her angry nipple then moved to the other one. She nearly bucked off the table as he took her quivering bud into his mouth, his teeth gently rasping her tender flesh. Pleasure-pain spiraled, making her inhale sharply.

Sweet Jesus! The man knew how to bite.

He nibbled at her nub. Licked and soothed her angry flesh. Bit her some more.

She shuddered.

A moment later his mouth left her nipple with a popping sound, his lips just as red as her bud. He cupped one tight breast, the heat of his palm scorching her. Masculine fingers kneaded her globes. Calloused fingertips twisted her nipples until she burned. One hand drifted away from her left breast and she heard the soft sound of something being moved in that sex toy drawer he'd mentioned earlier. Then she felt a sharp bite and an odd pressure on one nipple. When his fingers came away she noticed the clamp there. Her lower belly tightened at the erotic sight. He seduced her other breast in the same way and before long he had her other nipple clamped.

Red-hot fire shifted through her buds and then his hands abandoned her breasts, sliding along her gently swelling belly.

"In the fantasy your legs are widespread," he continued. At his words she found herself spreading her legs wider, and her pussy trembled with excitement as his oil-slick fingers moved between her labia and he explored the inner and outer pussy lips. Tenderly he pulled each lip one by one until they burned and she was gasping at the erotic sensations. Digging her fingers into the soft leopard skin beneath her, Emma cried out as a calloused thumb slipped over her clit. He dragged his finger back and forth over her inflamed clitoris, making Emma swallow at the brutally wonderful sensations embracing her.

"I'm teasing your clit with the smooth glass mouth of the champagne bottle," he said softly.

She swallowed tightly at the awesome way the muscles clenched in his bristle-shadowed cheeks. Obviously he was restraining himself from doing something she wanted him to do to her. Like fucking her.

"I've got you so hot and horny that you're about to come. Then I slide the smooth neck of the bottle into your juicy cunt, nice and slow, making sure that it stretches your vagina wide open."

She could hear him breathing harder. Could hear herself breathing faster as two fingers slipped inside her soaked pussy.

"Then I tip the bottle so the champagne gushes into you."

Her hips rose. Desperation gripped her. A third lubed finger slipped inside her cavern. Then a fourth.

Oh God!

Muscles were tightening everywhere. Clenching deep inside her lower belly. Inside her pussy. Her vagina pulsed with warm wetness. Her ass tensed.

Oh! Yes, everything felt so...perfect. She found her eyes closing as a climax began to build. Somewhere far off she heard a strange swishing noise. As if someone was opening and closing the door. She couldn't stop the erotic tremble from gripping her thighs at the thought that someone had come in to watch them have sex.

"And?" he coaxed. "What do I do next?"

Her brain spiraled at his question. "The bottle mouth...your mouth...drinking." She gasped. Couldn't keep the sentences straight. But somehow he knew what she was asking.

"Bring your knees up, Emma," he croaked.

"What?" Emma forced her eyes open and blinked. She hadn't realized Logan was near the foot of the bed, leaning over. A cranking sound split the air and the table lowered beneath her feet. Quickly she did as he asked and moved her feet up, bending her knees.

"Best kind of massage table," he chuckled. "The bottom half collapses allowing me closer access to your pussy."

Oh God!

A low hum followed and she realized the entire table was also lowering. A moment later it stopped and his hot fingers curled around her ankles, branding her. He moved her feet wider apart. Wide enough so that she could see him standing right between her widespread thighs. He was staring at her steaming pussy. Desire raged in the blue depths of his eyes.

She found herself swallowing her excitement as he lowered himself to his knees. Her cunt burned as his scorching breath blasted against her moist pussy. Wet flames of desire licked through her, whipped her closer to a sensual edge that would tip her into a world she'd always craved to explore.

Chapter Six

She could smell the musky scent of her arousal floating all around her. His hands dug into her generous hips, tipping her up. A soft pillow slid beneath her ass. His moist mouth settled onto her pussy, warm and possessive. She cried out at the scorching impact. Whimpered as his bristled cheeks erotically scraped the insides of her sensitive thighs. His long tongue slid against her inner lips, explored her outer lips, then swirled around her aching blood-engorged clitoris.

Sharp sensations gripped her and she couldn't stop herself from bucking against him.

He chuckled against her pussy, a hearty sound from somewhere deep inside his chest. His finger flicked against her sensitive clit. It was a light touch, an erotic pain followed and she couldn't stop herself from crying out.

"Do it again, Shy Girl."

Emma blinked, not knowing what he was talking about.

Another flick against her clitoris, harder this time. She cried out again.

"Yes, that's it, Emma. The sweet sound of pleasure-pain. A beautiful sound that makes me so hard I could just explode."

Emma whimpered as he did it again. And again. Not too long into the erotic torture agonizing sensations erupted from somewhere deep inside. She mewled in distress, not knowing if she liked these raw sensations or not. By the time he was finished, her aroused pussy literally dripped with cream.

She felt weak. Weak and so utterly horny that she found herself begging him to fuck her.

He readily took her. With his mouth.

His lips fused over her clit and she climaxed. Hard. So hard that she swore she was going to pass out. She tried to cry out but only a guttural wild sound flew past her open lips.

The climax tore through her like a breathtaking storm, destroying her senses, making cries of arousal break free, shattering through the room. She kept convulsing. Her hips bucking. Gyrating against Logan's mouth as he eagerly slurped, sipped and sucked at her pounding clit.

Sweet beautiful God!

Wave after carnal wave blasted her until the orgasms came one after another, seemingly flooding together into one massive climax that made her just about lose her mind.

* * * * *

As Logan's tongue continued to swipe and swirl around and over Emma's pulsing clit he could feel it growing, filling with blood, swelling to twice its size. Instinctively he knew from the frantic way she'd come apart like a firecracker beneath his mouth she hadn't been properly fucked in a long time, if ever. He found himself grinning into her hot, succulent cunt at the thought that tonight he would only get a glimpse of the arousal he could wring from her tempting body.

There would be many more nights in the Lifestyle. Nights that would leave Emma gasping and wondering with awe that her body could bring her so much pleasure. He also realized he couldn't get enough of inhaling the musky scent of her arousal, of tasting her sweet cream as it gushed into his mouth. Even his ears rang beautifully with the music of her passionate cries. And he really enjoyed the scrumptious flesh of her curvy hips beneath his fingertips as she fought his strong hold and tried to fuck his face in her wild erotic state of orgasms.

After he was finished making love to her tonight, she'd always think of him. Hell, he'd always think of her. He'd make it a point to pursue her, romance her, and he'd give her the sensual side of the sex and love she so obviously craved. Eventually she'd learn to trust a man again. He wanted to be that man.

With her every whimper, her every tortured sigh, his balls grew harder, swelling near to bursting with his sperm. With her every erotic sob his cock throbbed and pulsed until he could barely think straight.

Instinctively he knew it was only a matter of time before he lost full control. And that disturbed him. Losing power over a woman wasn't normal for him. He'd trained himself to maintain his erection without ejaculating while he orgasmed. In the beginning it had been no easy feat, but over the past couple of years he'd practiced mastering his cock while masturbating. And he'd done it. He'd also mastered his emotions so he'd never be at the mercy of another Dee.

But tonight things were changing. Sweet Emma would tear down those walls he'd build around himself.

He didn't know how he knew it, but he did. Something deep inside his heart had melted when he'd seen her enter the building, all curves, sweet blushes and innocent eyes filled with past hurt and new hopes. He'd heard the rumors about her asshole husband. Knew she would be skittish about men. He fully understood why she wanted to go slow with an emotional relationship. He'd get her to trust again. He knew that without a doubt.

When a hand curled over his shoulder he sighed with relief.

Luke was here. It was time to bring Emma the ultimate joy of a woman's fantasy.

A ménage à trois.

* * * * *

Emma's cunt was still spasming when she heard Logan's strangled voice. "Take over here, will you? I need to ease some of my pressure before we go on."

He was talking to someone. Who?

Emma forced herself to open her eyes. Her heart crashed in her chest as through an erotic haze she looked past her clamped nipples and saw Luke kneeling between her widespread thighs. He winked warmly and then his head lowered, his blistering mouth slamming over her swollen clit, his lips sucking so hard and so fiercely that another fantastic orgasm quickly roared through her. She bucked her hips as she convulsed, her fingers once again clenching the fluffy leopard blanket beneath her.

She rode the shattering waves. Her legs shook against the onslaught. Her mouth dropped open with a soundless gasp.

Without warning Logan's hard, pulsing cock drove between her lips, stuffing her mouth full of rock-hard flesh. Instinctively her lips curled around the vein-riddled shaft and she clamped down hard as Luke's tongue slipped inside her clenching vagina and he massaged her sensitive G-spot.

Jesus! She could barely concentrate on pleasuring Logan with the sensual way Luke's tongue was prodding at her.

Having a man's penis in her mouth wasn't new to her. It had been Bob's preferred way of sex, and in comparison Logan's cock tasted so damned good and was twice as big and long. His hard flesh throbbed so hotly inside her mouth that it sent erotic tingles of sexual awareness ripping through her. She blinked at the perfectly shaped engorged balls nestled tightly against his cock. Reaching up she grabbed at his broad stalk, plunging him deeper into her mouth to where she felt relatively safe in doing what needed doing. Clasping her fingers around his flaming flesh to prevent him from going down her throat when he climaxed, she then hollowed out her cheeks and sucked his rigid flesh so hard that Logan cried out. She thought he would come. He didn't, but she could tell by the sweet agony splashing across his face, he was climaxing without ejaculating. She'd heard that some men could train themselves to do that.

Lost in his arousal Logan bucked his hips against her, tried to feed his hot cock even deeper, but Emma kept a tight grip. In and out he plunged in carnal bliss until he was shuddering. Finally a gut-wrenching cry ripped out of his throat. Soon after, he slipped his still stiff cock out of her quivering mouth. She let go of his engorged balls and he backed away.

Closing her eyes she breathed into another oncoming climax compliments of Luke's ministering tongue. All she could do was lie there, her fingers plunging once again into the plush soft leopard blanket as she held on and eagerly awaited the next climax.

It didn't come. In her dreamy state she abruptly noticed something had changed. Her pussy was suddenly empty as Luke's tongue slipped away from her sensitive G-spot. Arousal of a different kind was shifting through her now. She felt intoxicated. Defenseless as the two brothers hovered around her, whispering softly to one another.

"She's ready," came Luke's voice.

"Look at her eyes," Logan whispered. "She's dazed. We'd better hurry. If we do her now it'll be awesome for her."

Suddenly someone was lifting her. Holding her warmly, protectively. Making her stand.

She could barely do it. Her legs were so weak. Trembling. Her breathing was way out of control. Everything was hazy.

She wanted to protest, to tell them to fuck her while she was lying down, but strong hands wrapped around her wrists, grabbing her, leading her arms around a warm neck that she instinctively knew belonged to Logan.

"Hold onto me tight, Shy Girl." Logan whispered softly, his warm come-scented breath splashing against her face. "You're about to be double-penetrated."

Oh my God!

Her mind swirled, reeled that the time had finally come. She could feel hard masculine chest muscles pressing against her bare back. Sweet pain sliced into her nipples as the clamps came off and someone eagerly twisted her nipples until a line of fire erupted deep inside her vagina. Flames of pressure laced her backside as a generously lubed condom-covered cock slipped inside her ass.

Luke's cock? Or Logan's? Her heavy eyelids had closed again and so she had no idea.

She mewled at the awesome way her anal muscles were being stretched.

"Just relax, Emma." Logan's soft whisper came from immediately in front of her, which meant Luke was the one burying himself in her behind.

She barely heard Logan's soft murmurs as he instructed her to relax, so intense was the searing pressure, the hard length sliding up her ass. Luke's hard cock tunneled deeper into her, stretching her a heck of a lot more than her butt plug had ever done. She could barely stand the clenching pleasure-pain. Barely stand on her legs.

Breathe, Emma.

She found herself giving Logan a silent thanks for letting Luke do her back door. Realized she'd much rather have Logan vaginally penetrate her. He'd always been in her hottest fantasies, it was only right to have him this way now.

His soft, sexy whisper burst through her thoughts and she felt his long finger at her swollen aching clit, rubbing tenderly. Slurping sounds split the air as he gathered her moisture, spread it over her puffed clitoris for easier maneuvering.

"You're so wet, sweetheart. So ready." Logan's voice flared with lust.

She nodded in agreement, or at least she thought she nodded, and found herself moaning as his huge condom-encased thick cock stretched into the tight, soaked opening of her vagina. The pressure as he slid into her slick pussy was exquisite.

She blew out a breath, forced herself to relax. Forced herself to keep the oncoming orgasm from spiraling out of control. Instinctively she could tell it was going to be a big one. Bigger than the others Logan had given her with his mouth.

She tightened her hold on Logan's warm neck as Luke's long cock slid out of her ass and Logan's thick shaft penetrated her sopping pussy. Her vagina eagerly clenched around his thick rod and she found herself gasping at her frightening arousal.

"You're so beautiful, Emma. So goddamn beautiful when you're about to climax."

Logan's moist mouth clamped over hers, capturing her gasps. His lips scorched hers, tasted her. She was drowning in mind-shattering sensations. Sinking in erotic bliss as both men penetrated her at the same time.

Without warning she came apart. Her body convulsed. Her mind splintered. Bright stars exploded behind her eyes.

Oh God! Fantastic!

Sensitive emotions ripped through her. Erotic sensations swaddled her. Tormented her.

Pleasure shocked her. She cried out at every impact. Thrust her hips forward. Crashed her ass backward. If they weren't double-penetrating her surely she would have fallen to the floor in an erotic heap of tears.

After her orgasm faded they began fucking her in a seesawing motion. One sliding his hard shaft into her eager, wet pussy, the other sliding out of her clenching anus. Sometimes they came into her at the same time. Those were the best. Their swollen cocks filled her to bursting. The pleasure-pain rocked her.

Both men were growling, groaning, bucking. And even when they were lost in their own pleasure they continued administering to her. Luke touching and massaging her breasts, pinching her nipples, Logan rubbing her engorged clit while he hammered into her.

Emma felt her body tightening again as another climax gathered.

"Oh God!" Another one! That's all she could think as the waves of pure pleasure enveloped her once again and shattered her. Wave after sweet wave slammed into her and she spiraled into an erotic world of bliss she wished she could stay in forever. From somewhere far away she heard the cries of release as both men came, their hot semen caught in their condoms.

When the spasms in her vagina gentled she realized that both men were cradling her protectively in their arms. She'd never felt so safe before. Safe and trusting.

Instincts told her she'd just been given the ultimate gift of two heroes. Men she would be able to trust as she forayed into the challenging yet satisfying world of the Swinger's Lifestyle.

Epilogue
Two years later

"Happy one month anniversary," Logan whispered as he lifted Emma off the portable massage table he'd built for them and settled her on her feet in front of him. She couldn't help but gasp at the scorching heat of his calloused palms as they slid sensually over her ass cheeks, nor could she stop the wild hammering of her heart at the sultry look in his hot gaze.

Every inch of her skin tingled from the erotic massage he'd just given her. The nipple rings she'd allowed herself as a wedding present to him when they'd become engaged several months ago glistened in the glow of the flickering candles set in the sconces around their bedroom. The sweet scent of lilacs wafted through the open window of his late parents' farmhouse and she couldn't help but inhale the delicious scent.

She'd come a long way in two years.

Logan and Luke had been instrumental in helping her explore her sexual side at Club Rendezvous. To her surprise, after their first threesome night together she hadn't wanted sex with any other men. Just Logan—and occasionally Luke had joined them.

But mostly she wanted Logan. Wanted him with her every breath, her every being.

"You sure about this?" he asked as his warm mouth teased her lips with warm sensuous nibbles.

"Very sure. I want you to keep fucking me until you put a baby in me."

His eyes darkened with lust and she couldn't help but whimper as a shaft of aroused heat zipped through her pussy at the sight. He'd been dropping hints about them having a family since their honeymoon. It was something she wanted too. To have a son or a daughter with the man she loved so passionately that she couldn't even imagine a life without him.

"Don't think I haven't been paying attention to the way you've been volunteering us to baby-sit for Kylie's kids."

She wrapped her hands around the root of his engorged cock and twisted gently.

He groaned and his fingertips sunk into her ass cheeks, pulling her closer.

"We just might end up with twins. Remember they run in my family."

"I think twins would be blessing."

He chuckled. "And they're a handful. But I'll do my best to give you as many babies as you want. We'll fill this old farmhouse full of kids and love, just like my mom and dad did."

At the mention of his deceased parents, his eyes momentarily glazed over with pain.

"We'll make them proud," Emma reassured him. She guided his swollen shaft between her drenched pussy lips and gasped at the scorching heat as she slid him into her wet vagina.

"They're already proud, Emma. I know it in my heart, they'd have loved you like their own daughter."

At his words blissful happiness seared through her and for the first time in her life she truly felt like she belonged to someone and somewhere.

It was the best feeling in the whole world.

About the author

Jan Springer is the pseudonym for an award-winning best-selling author who writes erotic romance and romantic suspense at a secluded cabin nestled in the Haliburton Highlands, Ontario, Canada.

She has enjoyed careers in hairstyling and accounting, but her first love is always writing. Hobbies include kayaking, gardening, hiking, traveling, reading and writing.

Jan welcomes mail from readers. You can write to her c/o Ellora's Cave Publishing at 1337 Commerce Drive, #13, Stow, Ohio 44224.

Also by Jan Springer

FREAK OF NATURE

Shiloh Walker

Chapter One

Micah Cochran was dead meat.

Zoë came up out of her work-induced fugue with only that thought on her brain as a fist pounded on her door again.

It was Micah.

She knew it in her gut—Zoë wanted to scream with rage, while at the same time, she wanted to throw herself into his arms.

It had been more than five years, not since—

She cut the thought off. She wasn't going there. Not now.

She didn't want him around—not after he'd left her without a word.

Tearing down the steps, her eyes wild, she jerked the door open. "GO AWAY!"

But he only stood there, as all the force of her gift battered at him. She saw a slight tightening around his eyes from the pain he was no doubt in as she mentally shoved at him.

Guilt came and went.

All the government jackasses who had come to her door lately, and she had kept to physical violence with them, even though they made it obvious they knew what she was. Even though she had been tempted to do more damage, she'd only hit two of them...and with her fist. Much less painful than what she had wanted to do.

But with Micah, she didn't hold back. She shoved with all the power of her mind. But he didn't move.

Swallowing, she focused and drew the raw power back inside her, watching as he relaxed slightly. Quieter now, she said, "Go away, Micah."

Shaking his head, he said quietly, "I can't."

"I can make you," she countered, arching a brow at him.

He nodded, a slow, thoughtful nod, as he agreed. "You could. But then they will do something you won't like. You have to help them, otherwise you're going to be hurt."

Her face fell as his words sank in.

He was here because of *them*, her unwelcome guests over the past week. She'd hoped after two days had passed without one of the government suits showing up at her door, they would just leave her alone.

As if. They'd just chosen a different messenger.

Morosely, she wished that she had just listened to the federal agents that had first come to her door. If she had, maybe Cochran wouldn't be here.

Woodenly, she asked, "Why you? Did they think you'd have a better chance? I don't owe you a damn thing."

Micah nodded slowly. "That's true. You don't owe me anything. But I know you, Zoë. I know how to get past the walls you put up. As to why they sent me, I guess they thought our history would make you more likely to listen to me."

Zoë laughed, the sound cold and hard in the silence of the cabin. "History? Did we have a history? We worked together...*briefly*...slept together a few times. And when the case was over, you walked away without a backward glance."

His soft voice had her stiffening. "I looked back. Almost every damned day for five years. That doesn't change what I did — or make it right. But I did look back."

Casting him a cold glance, she said, "You're right. It doesn't change what you did. Not that it really matters. It's been five years, after all. Long time to mourn somebody just because he was a good lover."

"That's not how it was," he said tightly.

"Isn't it?" she asked archly. "Was there more to it than sex? More than just the job? If it was, you wouldn't have just walked away, now would you? You used whatever means you could to get close to me, to get me to help you. And if it ended up with you in my bed, so what? And when it was over, you...you just left." The careless attitude she'd adopted wavered a little as a knot formed in her throat. It didn't matter what she told him — it *did* matter. Him leaving her had destroyed her. Turning away, she blinked back the tears suddenly stinging her eyes. "That's not history, Micah. It's sex. Sex and business. That's all I ever was to you, anyway."

His mind was opaque to her. But his emotions weren't. The blast of guilt and anger that flowed from him was ugly and black. "No," he finally muttered. "But I never pretended with you. You were —"

Cutting her eyes to him, she said sharply, "Save the bullshit. Say what you want and go."

"Not that easy, baby," Micah murmured as he followed her into the living room and lowering himself to sit on the edge of a chair, watching her.

"So what do you want with me? Got a circus where I'd make a good sideshow freak? The Amazing Zoë...telekinetic, telepathic freak of nature! She knows your every thought, she can bend spoons in midair without touching them, right before your very eyes!" she called out, using a theatrical, overloud voice.

"You're not a freak," he said levelly.

She slid him a narrow look and said, "I'm not normal, either."

He grinned. "But aren't you the one who says normalcy is boring?"

Zoë met his level stare with a bright, cheerful smile. "So, if it's not the circus, or the FBI equivalent of, what do you want with me?"

"Kyle Morraine."

The blood drained out of her face and terror started to pool hotly in her belly. "Morraine is dead," she rasped, tears stinging her eyes.

He shook his head. "No, baby. He's not."

"No!" she shouted at him, scrambling out of the couch, moving around it so that it stood between her and him. "Damn it, he died! They told me he was dead. I watched him fall."

"He lived through it," Micah said gently. "They caught up with him in Mexico. Something happened in the fall that apparently weakened him. He wasn't able to free himself the way he always had before. They caught him, and for the past five years, he's been living in an isolated prison, with the population of one. You were done with it, so they didn't feel the need to tell you the truth."

Her mouth trembled. "The need? Damn it, you know what he did to me?" she shouted, her hands digging into the soft padded top of the couch. "I have to live with that filth he shoved inside my mind — it damned near drove me insane!"

"Yes. Yes," he said quietly, rising off the couch. He moved toward her slowly, as she stared at him with abject terror in her eyes. "I was there, remember?"

Tears spilled over. "Hell, yes, I remember. He was the only reason you stayed as long as you did. When he was gone, you left."

"He wasn't the only reason," Micah said flatly. "He wasn't even the most important. But at the time, he was the most dangerous. But he sure as hell wasn't the only reason I stayed so close to you. Damn it, I stayed that close because I couldn't stand not being with you."

Glaring at him, she snapped, "Yeah, like I'm going to believe *that*. When it was over, you *left*. Don't you get that? If I meant a damned thing to you, you wouldn't have left."

Micah fell silent as he stared at her with turbulent eyes. She couldn't see inside his mind — that was as true now as it was five years ago. The only time his thoughts were clear to her was when he was touching her. All she could sense from him now was just turmoil, guilt...anger. "I couldn't handle what I felt for you, Zoë. You scared the hell out of me."

She turned away, wrapping around her arms around herself. She felt so damned cold. "Leave me alone, Micah."

His voice was closer and she shivered as she felt the heat from his body reaching out to warm hers. Against the nape of her neck, she could feel the soft brush of his breath on her skin as he murmured, "I can't. Not now."

"I won't do this again, Micah. I won't be used again, not by the agency, not by you."

"I didn't use you," he growled.

Spinning around to face him, she sneered. "The hell you didn't. Why in the hell else did you fuck me? It sure as hell wasn't because you really *wanted* me. If you'd wanted me—" Zoë cut her words off before she could stay the rest, before she could say, *you would have stayed.* She wasn't going to let him know, damn it, how bad it had cut at her when he left.

"Oh, grow up," he snarled. He came around the couch after her and she dodged away from him. Narrowing his eyes, he leaped over the couch, catching her arms. "I fucked you because I couldn't stop thinking about you. You were in my every thought. And I couldn't fucking handle it."

Her eyes widened. When he touched her, whatever barrier kept her mind from seeing into his cleared, just a little, and she could feel what lay inside him. Could feel that...*no*, she told herself, shaking her head. Lies. Nothing more than lies. Slamming her shields into place, she shut herself away from him, away from the warmth and the promise that she had once almost believed in.

"Let me go," she whispered, her voice thick.

"Why? Too hard to *not* believe me when I'm touching you? You told me once...that's the only time my thoughts are clear to you, when I'm touching you. Well, I'm touching you now...can you feel what I'm feeling? Do you know what's going on inside my head?" he asked gruffly, watching her intently.

She stared up at him with shuttered eyes, too damned afraid to *let* herself feel anything. "Micah, don't," she said weakly as he skimmed one hand up her arm, tracing the line of her neck before cupping the back of her head.

"Damn, you're so beautiful. How can you be even more beautiful than you were before?"

Her belly tightened as his fingers tangled in her hair. "Stop it, Micah," she whispered, even as she rose on her toes, arching into his touch. Her nipples tightened and the lace that cupped her breasts suddenly felt too rough, abrading her tender flesh tauntingly until she wanted nothing more than to tear it away.

"Why?" he murmured. "You want me touching you. I may not be the amazing Zoë who knows your every thought, but I know that look in your eyes."

Unable to breathe, she simply stood there as he lowered his mouth to hers, swallowing down her soft, strangled, "Micah," and drank from her, pushing his tongue inside her mouth with a hungry growl. The desperate shields she'd flung up to protect herself from him feel into shambles around her and she was lost in the heat and strength of him.

Missed you, Zoë. The words echoed in his mind, leaving her no choice but to hear them as he wrapped his arms around her, cuddling her against his chest, nestling his hips against hers.

She whimpered as she felt the scorching heat of his cock against her belly, burning her through the layers of their clothes. *Heat...*how had she forgotten his heat?

People were colors, shapes, and images to her, but so many seemed cold and lifeless, even as she tried to see the life inside them.

But Micah—he had been alive from the first day, alive and hot, like a flame, warming her to the core. She had been so cold since he left... With a ragged gasp, she shoved back, scrambling out his arms as reality reasserted itself.

"Don't touch me," she said weakly, moving away from him. Sucking air into her lungs, she missed seeing the odd flash in his eyes. Slowly she breathed, waiting until she was calmer, if not completely in control. Micah smashed her control, he always had.

He quirked a brow at her and asked, "For how long?"

She laughed, the sound odd and false in the room. Licking her lips, she rubbed at her arms as the cold swept back over her body. Her voice only wobbled a little bit as she said, "I've got the odd feeling that Morraine is a threat to society again."

He smiled, a tiny little smirk as he shook his head. "You always were a quick study, babe."

Rolling her eyes, she turned away, staring out the window at the sanctuary she had built for herself over the years. She had felt safe here. Lonely, but safe. Now that was gone.

"He's out," she whispered, forcing a slow breath into her tight lungs.

"Yes," Micah said.

Turning back to him, she stared at him, fighting the urge to fling herself into his arms and cuddle against him for comfort. Bask in his warmth and just let him hold her, promise that he'd take care of her.

Zoë had done that once. She'd loved him, let herself need him. Then she'd found out he'd just been using her — he'd destroyed her.

She couldn't risk it again. "So they want me to help capture Morraine again?" she asked quietly.

"Not exactly. But kind of," he said obliquely.

"That doesn't sound very decisive," she said, a tiny bit of amusement darting through her. "Since when does FBI answer questions like that?"

An odd flutter of tension quivered in the air. He reached up, flicking his raven-black hair out of his silver eyes as he quietly studied her. The tension thickened and she fought the nerves that always rose inside her when she was subject to strong emotion. "What?" she asked quietly. "What is it?"

"It's not the FBI that sent me here," he said flatly. "They turned Morraine over to another authority — I'm here because of them."

Licking her lips, she puzzled that one out. "Another authority?" she finally asked.

He nodded. "They are sort of like the FBI, but they deal with anything...out of the ordinary," he said finally.

"Like me," she guessed, her voice flat. Walking over to the couch, she lowered herself onto the plush, plum purple cushions, drawing her knees to her chest.

"Yes. I never knew about them. They tend to be very low-key, I'm told. They would have taken care of Morraine, but then they saw us recruit you, and they are familiar with you," Micah said, his voice sounding a little edgy. And she didn't need to even guess at why.

She was the why. Nothing she hated more than being watched, examined, investigated...she had spent most of her childhood in a place that was more like a lab than a home. "They know about Zeneri." Clenching her hand into a fist, she resisted the urge to jump up and bash her hand through the wall.

"Yes. I got some information out of one of them—I think Zeneri might have been one of the guys who started their unit up."

Her voice was a bare whisper as she asked, "And Hollister?"

"No. He was an unknown to them. I got the idea that the woman in charge was...ah...displeased. I said his name and her eyes turned to ice. Made the mention that you certainly had the right to kill him, but she almost regretted none of him was left for them to deal with."

"So they know I killed him," she muttered, dragging a hand through her hair and climbing from the chair. "How fucking long have they been watching me?"

Micah shrugged. "I don't know," he said quietly.

Anger sizzled through her veins, but she tamped it down as she met his eyes and nodded slowly. "With Morraine, once I came into the picture, they didn't see the need to step up and risk exposing themselves?" she hazarded.

He nodded. "Basically. Of course, once we had Morraine, they took over. My superior at the time wasn't happy. Sanders about had an apoplectic fit, I hear. Of course, I just found all this out yesterday," he said, shaking his head.

"I never knew any of this," he repeated. "I was led to believe he was dead, the same as you." And the helpless fury he felt at that threatened to spiral out of control as he stared at her, seeing the fear in her eyes. He wanted, more than anything, to take her someplace safe, someplace where she'd never know fear or pain again.

But he couldn't. Not yet. They could stop him—for good.

Permanently. In the only way that would work. He didn't trust a jail to hold Morraine. Micah had every intention of killing the sick fuck, but without Zoë, he'd never get close.

Turning, he went back to her side, close enough that the sweet scent of her skin flooded his head. Vanilla, honey, spice…it was intoxicating, drugging. He had missed this, missed seeing her, having her scent on his body as he woke in the morning, missed running his hands through the silvery blonde silk of her hair. Missed making love to her, knowing he had found his other half.

Missed that wry, caustic humor and the way her eyes crinkled when she laughed.

Everything…*everything* about her, even that skeptical look in her eyes.

Unable to help himself, he locked his arms around her waist, pulling her close against him. She still had the dull, vaguely hurt look in her eyes, but he didn't know what it was, what to do about it. And they didn't have much time. "There's more," he said quietly.

In the circle of his arms, he felt her body shift as she sighed, the puff of breath warm on his chest. "Somehow, I think I already knew that," she said, a trace of her old humor, dry and biting, in her voice.

Stroking his hand down her hair, he cupped her neck, arching it until she lifted her gaze to meet his. "He's coming after you," Micah said quietly. When her legs buckled, he caught her and swooped her into his arms, crossing to the couch and cuddling her against him as she sat there, numb with terror.

"After me...?" she repeated. Her voice was faint, and he had a feeling she wasn't really asking him, just trying to get her mind around it. Her eyes stared ahead blankly—Micah knew she wasn't seeing anything.

"It'll be okay, sugar," he whispered into her hair, rocking her back and forth. Savagely, he held her to him as she tried to push away. *No. I'm not letting go this time,* he thought heatedly, knowing the heat and intensity of his thoughts would get through where words wouldn't. "It will be okay."

"How?" she asked hollowly. "The biggest monster known to man is coming after me."

Lifting his head, he cupped her chin in his hand, forcing her to meet his eyes. "It will be okay—because you're stronger than he is. He took one bad blow and he snapped. You've taken everything he's thrown at you, all the bullshit you had to endure as a kid, and you're still whole, still you. You're strong—you're brave."

Her lower lip trembled. With five simple words, she destroyed him. "But I'm not whole anymore."

* * * * *

So exactly what did one do when you were supposed to be bait, she mused as she stared out the window.

This was surreal. How could it be happening again?

The nightmares still robbed her of sleep, all too often. Morraine would kill randomly, violently, with such pleasure...and he hadn't always used his own body. More than once he'd used his telepathic skills take over the mind of another, and had used that other body to kill.

A husband killed his own wife.

A cop killed two fellow cops.

Guilty…but not guilty.

The husband had killed himself once Morraine finally released the hold on his mind. But the cop, Morraine had killed him, squeezing an unseen fist around his brain until it killed the poor guy, blood flowing from his eyes, his nose, mouth and ears.

Zoë woke up screaming from the memories. Because Morraine had tangled their minds together as he tried to take over her thoughts, blending them with his own. Now every horrible thing he had done in life, she had the echo of the memory inside her head.

Those memories had damn near broken her. Zoë wasn't whole anymore. The only thing that surpassed her fear of Morraine was her hatred of him.

The hatred was what had given her the strength to track Morraine down. But she had done it her way, not the way the FBI agents kept telling her to do.

Once it was over, seeing Morraine plummet over the edge of the cliff, she had thought maybe the nightmares would stop. But they hadn't.

They never would, she suspected.

She would just have to deal with it.

And pray that monster didn't add to the nightmares.

Micah hadn't had to draw a picture for her to figure it out. They had to stop Morraine, and this time for good. What better mouse to use in such a trap, besides one with very deadly teeth?

With a wry twist of her lips, she had to admit she felt very much like a mouse. A cornered, trapped one. It was when she felt the most terrified that her own deadly powers spiraled out of control. That strength, born of fear, had saved her once. Would it do it again?

Kyle Morraine wasn't a psychopath, despite what Micah and all his fellow FBI buddies thought. And the nameless "authority" that Micah had mentioned. She had no doubt they had questioned, examined and tested him thoroughly, then assigned Morraine to some neat little slot that made the men in white jackets feel more secure and organized in their world.

But some things had no label. Not sociopath, not psychopath, not schizophrenic.

The only label that fit Morraine was evil.

He'd been born evil.

Zoë should know. After all, she had grown up with him. Both of them, along with ten other children, lived at Zeneri Institute. Supposedly it was a place for the emotionally troubled, neglected youth.

In reality, it was a lab. The youths were talented, gifted children whose parents had basically sold them to Craig Zeneri. Zeneri hadn't exactly been evil—he never set out to hurt any of them or cause them pain, and he provided for them very well. Some might have thought they led a rather posh life—so long as they did as they were asked.

When they didn't...well, imposed isolation to a gifted, over-imaginative youngster was pure torment. So they learned quickly, did as they were asked, paid attention in class and participated in the daily lab sessions.

But then Zeneri died. Somebody else came in. She was fifteen when she came face to face Draven Hollister. Fifteen the first time he tried to rape her.

She had been a bad target for his experimental theory. What happens to a young mind, one already a freak of nature, when put through traumatic experience?

He'd tried Becka next. But the pyrokinetic had been as dangerous as the telekinetic. He even tried drugs to suppress their gifts, but nothing cleared a drug fog like terror and panic. The only thing that might have worked would have been completely rendering them unconscious—and how could that terrify them properly?

There were no females left—Becka and Zoë thought it would be okay.

They were wrong.

Kyle was the youngest, at thirteen, and a rather pretty boy. Maybe that was why Hollister chose him. Kyle Morraine was also the weakest, more easy to frighten into submission.

It was a very short time, though, that Hollister had him.

One night, two boys slid out of their room, tripping the locks that Hollister had been led to believe held them in at night. They came to Zoë and Becka—the two most dangerous children—and asked for help. Who better to help fight a monster than a pyrokinetic, like Becka...or a telekinetic, like Zoe?

They would break out.

They would kill if they had to. In the end, that was exactly what had happened. They had fought back, Zoë had killed him, and they all ran away from the place that had become their prison.

Too bad they hadn't acted a little sooner. The night they'd broken out, when they'd gone to get the last child, they'd found Kyle with Hollister. The bastard had brutalized the young boy — raped and beaten him just to see what would happen to a gifted mind under such trauma.

"Your fault!" Kyle had screamed at her. "You could have helped me!"

If she had known, she would have. But Kyle had always been quiet, keeping to himself, staring at everybody around him with dark, distrustful eyes. And the fact was she didn't like him. There was something creepy about the boy — and he liked to kill things. She had seen it, even blacked his eye because of it.

Kyle Morraine had always been evil. As she walked down the stairs, she did have to wonder if what might have been different if she had known, if she had been able to save him from Hollister.

But a more logical part of her whispered, *He was born evil…nothing would have been different.*

"You okay?"

She jerked, startled, as she tore herself out of the past. Turning, she stared at Micah slowly, blinking away her daze. "Yeah," she said quietly.

Spinning away from the window, she moved away from the window, rubbing at her arms. "As okay as can be expected, I guess." Hearing the hollow ring in her voice, she forced a ghost of a smile and asked, "Did you finish checking in with mommy and daddy?"

He didn't respond as he studied her.

She was too quiet. Micah didn't like the solemn darkness of her eyes or the flat, firm line of her pretty mouth. There was more than fear there. He wasn't sure what it was and since he wasn't able to see inside her mind, he wouldn't know unless she decided to tell him.

Holding out his hand, he said, "Come on. I need to get a better lay of the land."

As they left the sprawling cottage-style house, he studied everything around them. Nerves on red alert, eyes so watchful he caught the white flash of a doe's tail as she bounded back into the woods just beyond the side yard of Zoë's property.

Her land was bordered on two sides by the Great Smoky Mountains National Park and the only way in and out was a long, winding snake of a road. He really wasn't looking forward to the trip out. "How in the hell do you drive this road in the winter?" he asked irritably as they followed the stone trail around the house, the muscles in his legs working as they climbed up the steep hill.

With a shrug, she said, "You get used to it. I stockpile firewood in case the power goes out and keep plenty of nonperishables on hand." Her eyes became distant. "I don't like town much."

That was understandable. Her gift was also a curse — out here, she didn't have to shield against anything. Around people, though, that was a different story. She had to maintain her shielding constantly, otherwise she was assailed by the thoughts of others. "Are others going to come out?" she asked, a frown turning the corners of her mouth down.

After a long moment, he said quietly, "No."

She stilled in midstep, her head lowering as though she had suddenly a huge interest in the ground beneath her feet. He couldn't miss the quivering in her voice as she said, "Nobody? It took a team of twenty men to corner him last time. Twenty fucking men. And what the hell good did it do? He wasn't stopped...he went over that cliff instead of being taken down. And when they caught him, he broke out of their prison."

"A lot of good, Zoë. He was off the streets, unable to hurt people for five years. That has to count for something. And it didn't take twenty men...it took one woman. You. You were able to trap his mind and keep him from striking out at the others while they surrounded him." Micah's eyes continued to roam the perimeter of her yard, from the potted mums at the fence to the nearly empty garden bordering a storage building. "If we had ten men out there in the forest, would you know?"

He turned his head in time to see her roll her eyes. "Of course," she said dryly.

Arching a brow at her, he waited. Finally, Zoë sighed and said, "If I could tell, so would he. So we just hang around here like sitting ducks?"

"Remember what you told me five years ago? You can feel others just by sensing their thought patterns. Some are louder and more vivid than others—Morraine's was one of them. And that's how he knew you were there."

"Psychics have a more powerful feel to their thoughts," she murmured softly, her lids lowering, a thoughtful frown on her face. "I'll drown your thought pattern out. He'll feel you, but probably not until he either sees you, or is very, very close. Unless he does that, all he will see and feel is me."

"Exactly. But the more people we bring onto this mountain, the more likely it is he'll know we expect him. One person is easier to hide than ten."" And if something primitive inside him was outraged by the thought, he'd just have to deal with it.

Zoë was in danger—had been since Morraine escaped a month earlier.

And until he was caught, she would be. Micah intended on catching him very soon.

A soft voice behind him asked, "Why you?"

"Why me what?" he asked, distracted, the memories of the Morraine's past victims drifting through his mind.

"Why are you the one who gets to play bodyguard?" she asked.

Shoving the morbid details of Kyle's work out of his mind, he looked back at her with serious eyes. "Because I demanded it be me. After the welcome you gave the last few people, they knew you wouldn't so much as talk to anybody you didn't know, that I had the best chance of at least getting inside the door without you breaking my face, although I'm still kind of surprised you didn't. So I told them I'd come up and talk to you, but that I'd also be the one staying with you."

Those deep brown eyes widened and her pretty little rosebud mouth pursed. "Okay…why you?" she repeated. "I mean, why insist it be you?"

Leveling a steady stare at her, he said simply, "Because I'm the only person I trust enough with your life. Besides, they have ideas that they could maybe try to chemically subdue him, recapture him. And I'm sure they learned something from their mistakes this last time. But I want him dead."

"Chemically subdue?" Dryly, she said, "Why do I get the feeling you were told not to kill him unless that was the only option."

He grinned at her. "Because I was."

She laughed but there was little amusement in the sound. "Chemically subdue. For crying out loud. They still don't understand what they are dealing with, do they?"

Micah shrugged. "It's the way we work, FBI, CIA, any government law enforcement agency—if we don't understand, then we study until we do. But in cases like this, they would be better off just to kill. How can you hope to imprison a man who can take over your mind? Who can read your mind?"

Zoë didn't answer. They both knew the answer to that. No prison would be enough to hold Morraine forever. Sooner or later, he would get free.

Chapter Two

She didn't like the thought that when Morraine came, there would be nothing between them. But she wasn't especially fond of just having more targets for him either. He could take over a person's mind and use their body like a puppet. All too deadly.

Yet she knew that this agency, whoever they were, was just like any other and they wouldn't operate on just the chance that he'd come close, risking that either Zoë or Micah would end up dead with him.

It took a while to figure out that was why the plan seemed faulty, but by nightfall, she had come to her own conclusions and she was pretty certain they were right.

Somebody wanted her to kill Morraine. That was the only reason to leave her and Micah alone on this mountain, with no backup...with nobody to keep her from doing from she had wanted to do five years ago.

Cold, she shifted a little closer to the fire, staring into the dancing flames and brooding.

This was insane.

"Why am I doing this?" she muttered, shaking her head. Swallowing, she tried to block out all the ugly possibilities that lingered in her future.

"What?"

Glancing over her shoulder, she glanced at Micah and just shook her head. "Nothing," she murmured, rising to her feet and stretching her arms high overhead. "You going to be awake for a while?"

"Yes," he murmured, his lids low, eyes glittering as he watched her.

"I think I'm going to go to bed," she murmured, turning her eyes back to the dancing flames for a minute. "You need anything before I turn in?"

Want...NEED... That was the only warning she had to brace herself before he caught her up against him, his mouth slanting over hers. Zoë's mind exploded into a kaleidoscope of color, thought and taste. His taste, wild, hot and so very male, flooded her senses, while his thoughts flowed through her mind, a chaotic river of words, pictures and colors.

Against her breast, she felt his heart slamming within his chest, beating in tandem with her own. One hand cupped over the back of her neck, while his other hand slid down her side, gripping her hip.

Heat, glorious heat, like she hadn't felt in years, burst through her. Rising up on her toes, she twined her fingers through his hair, the black silk of it falling through her fingers. A hot, empty hole settled in her belly, a hollow ache that throbbed with every breath she took.

His teeth scraped over her lip—her knees buckled as he sucked the plump flesh into his mouth and bit down just a little harder. "Sweet," he muttered, as he shifted his grip from her neck to her hair.

His thoughts battered at her, hard and powerful, overwhelming...*too long, still so soft...* His hand fisted in her hair and Zoë cried out at he arched her neck back, raking his teeth over her throat. She felt his hand, fingers spread wide, coming up her side in one slow, firm stroke, raising the sturdy cotton on her shirt as he went.

Cool air kissed the skin of her torso and she whimpered as his hand cupped her breast, stroking a thumb over the tight bud of her nipple. Each stroke from his hand resonating in her belly, in her pussy, across her clit, almost as erotic as though he were stroking his fingers through the cream-slicked flesh of her pussy.

The room spun around her in dizzying circles as he wheeled them around, and then she felt the couch at her back. As he came down on her, she brought her knees up, cradling his hips between her thighs. Damn it. She could feel him, like she hadn't felt in years, hot, thick, pumping against the notch between her thighs.

Zoë gasped for air as his hands worked beneath her, gripping the hem of her shirt. She arched up, letting him pull it over her head. A soft sob echoed through the air as he caught the diamond-hard crest of her nipple in his mouth, sucking on it, pressing it against the roof of his mouth, working her flesh through the thin silk of her bra.

His hand cupped her and she felt the heat of his flesh through the sturdy material of her jeans. Whimpering, she rubbed the mound of her pussy against him, hungry to feel him inside her again.

As he moved to torment her other breast, Zoë dipped her hands into his hair and held him against her. The heat…her head swam from the heat, the rush of pleasure that scorched her.

Then she was cold— And he was on the other side of the room, dragging a hand through his hair as he turned to stare out the window. "Damn it. I'm sorry," he muttered.

He wasn't—not really. She could feel that, even though he had tried to close himself from her. The only thing he was sorry for was that he had felt the need to stop. With a slight smile, she had to admit to herself that she agreed with him.

* * * * *

The house was silent as he paced it one final time before settling down.

He didn't like this. At all.

Even with Zoë's rather amazing talents, they were too vulnerable here. Too much could go wrong.

Micah knew that too many people here would tip Morraine off. But, damn it, two people…against a monster like Kyle Morraine.

Moving to the window, he stared outside, unable to see anything beyond the square of light that fell through the window. "God, let me keep her safe," he whispered, his head dropping forward to rest on the cool pane of glass. "Please let me keep her safe."

The short harsh cry that echoed through the air froze his heart in his chest and he turned and ran for the stairs, taking them two at a time. Drawing his gun, he rounded the corner at a dead run, throwing caution to the wind as she screamed again.

Sliding the gun back into the holster, he dropped onto the bed. Catching her shoulders, he shook her a little. *A nightmare.* Just a nightmare. She'd had them for weeks while they tracked Morraine last time.

"Wake up, Zoë," he whispered against her brow, pulling her into his arms, hugging her against him as he stroked one hand down her back. Through the thin cotton of the chemise she wore, he felt the delicate line of her spine, heard her soft, shaky breathing as she fought her way into wakefulness.

The soft, helpless sobs in her throat broke his heart. A sense of helplessness rode heavy on his shoulders as he rubbed his hand soothingly over the fragile line of her spine. "It's okay, baby," he crooned against her temple. "I'm here. You're safe."

"I can't breathe... Micah, I can't breathe," she sobbed.

Pulling back, he cupped her face in his hands, staring down into her terror-glazed eyes. "Yes, you can," he said firmly. "You can breathe, Zoë. He's not here. He can't touch you."

She whimpered and closed her fingers around his wrists, staring up at him helplessly. "He is here. He's in my head. I hear his voice all the time, feel that blood he shed all over me," she gasped. "I can't see beyond him. Micah, he's everywhere. I feel him inside me."

No. Sheer fury boiled inside him at the thought, a rage unlike anything he had felt in a very long time. "No. He's not here. He's nowhere. Nothing," he rasped as he tumbled her down on the bed, covering her mouth gently.

"He can't touch you," he muttered against her lips, determined to blot out any sign or trace of him. "He's not inside you...he can't touch you. Feel *me*. See *me*."

Gently, he caught her hands and pinned them beside her head, feeling her fingers entwine with his, her palms pressing against his. Plunging his tongue inside her mouth, he let her scent and taste flood his senses as surely as he knew his were flooding hers. As her body softened under his, he released her hands, shifting his weight so he could catch the hem of her short chemise, pulling back just long enough to tug it off.

Catching her lip between his teeth, Micah bit down gently. His hands slid up to cup her breasts and he felt the rapid beat of her heart. "Who do you see?" he whispered, moving his mouth down to bite the sensitive area of her neck, scraping his teeth along it and feeling her shudder exactly as she had five years before. "Who do you feel?"

A soft whimper escaped her and she murmured, "You. Just you."

The terror she had felt only moments before fled under the touch of Micah's hands. Nobody had ever made her feel the way he did. Just the simplest touch of his mouth to hers had her pussy aching and wet, her body clamoring for the touch of his. "Damn it, Micah, how can you do this to me?" she gasped out.

He chuckled as he moved lower, catching one nipple in his mouth. She arched up against him as he murmured, "The same way you do the same thing to me...we belong together, Zoë. I won't leave—you can't chase me away this time."

As his tongue slid around the underside of her breast, any response she might have had faded away. Against her belly, she felt the hard, pulsating throb of his cock and she sobbed out his name, reaching up and burying her fingers in his hair, holding him tight against her.

"Your taste," he muttered. "Damn it, I can't believe I went five years without it."

She shivered at the sheer hunger she heard in his voice. "Micah, please...I need to feel you inside me. Make me forget how empty I've been."

His hands stripped her panties down her legs, sliding back up to cup her ass, tilting her hips up and rocking against the slick notch between her legs. The rough material of his jeans abraded her sensitive flesh and she shivered at the near painful friction.

Zoë's breath stopped in her chest as he shifted and cupped her in his hand, pushing one long finger inside her, pumping it in and out. Heat sizzled through her veins as he sat back and slid his finger in his mouth, licking the cream away and humming under his breath. "More," he grunted, moving down and wedging his shoulders between her thighs.

Lowering his head, he nuzzled the bud of her clit with his nose before circling the narrow opening of her vagina with his tongue.

With a sharp scream, she arched up against him, sucking air into her starving lungs, hot explosions of light flashing behind her eyes. She could smell the hot scent of her arousal, the heated flesh of Micah's body. The lashing of his tongue felt like strokes of electricity sizzling against the slick folds of her pussy and once more, she couldn't breathe, but it was sheer hunger instead of terror that had her breath hitching in her chest.

Convulsions started to flutter in her sex as she gasped for air, her body erupting in a harsh, vicious climax. He groaned against her and the vibration of it teased her flesh, prolonging the breath-stealing sensations that seized her body.

A mellow, sated feeling rolled through her as the last shudders of the climax racked her body. Hands limp at her sides, she lay there staring up at Micah through her lashes. Her ribs lifted and fell as she sighed, arching her back and stretching lazily while he jerked at his shirt.

She watched it go flying across the room and then her gaze dropped to watch his hands tearing at his buttoned jeans, opening them and dragging down the zipper. Something fluttered in her belly and she licked her lips as he moved up over her, staring down at her with hooded eyes.

Zoë felt the head of his cock nudging against her entrance and she tipped her hips up eagerly, greedy lust dancing through her veins. Reaching up, she gripped her shoulders as he pushed inside. His eyes closed, teeth gritted. She whimpered under the onslaught of physical sensations, the mind-blowing emotions that rocked her as she felt the echoes of his hunger.

He pulled back and she whimpered as he nearly left her before pushing back in. Arching her back, Zoë tried to lift her hips and pull him deeper and he laughed, sliding his hands down to cup her hips and hold her still. "What do you feel? Who is inside you?" he murmured.

"You." As he started to shaft her with short, hard strokes, she moaned, "Just you." His head swooped down and she greedily opened her mouth under his, sucking his tongue into her mouth and biting down, smiling against his lips as his big body bucked over hers and he slammed into her, his fingers biting into the skin of her ass, spreading the cheeks apart so he could trail his fingers between.

Zoë jumped at the caress, her eyes flying wide. Her nipples, tight and hard as diamonds, stabbed into his chest. Wrapping her legs around his hips, she worked her hips against the thick stalk. He moved higher on her body—Zoë screamed as the slight shift of position had his body stroking against her clit with every thrust of his hips.

150

Climax lingered just out of reach and she could all but feel it humming through her body. But before she could reach it, Micah whispered, "Not so fast," and pulled out, leaving her empty, her body screaming with unfulfilled hunger. Grabbing at him, she tried to pull him back down to her but he just laughed, evading her hands and turning her over onto her belly, shoving a couple of pillows under her hips to prop her up before he covered her body with his and pushed inside with one hard, deep stroke.

Zoë shrieked—his position had him so deep inside her, she thought she could feel his thrusts clear to her throat. Stuffed full and starving for more, she tried to shove back at him but he just bore down on her with his weight, capturing her hands and pinning them down beside her head. "You're so tight, so wet," he murmured. "You feel so good around my dick."

Groaning, she clenched the muscles in her pussy around him, trying to hold him inside. "Micah, please, it's been too damn long," she whimpered.

"I know," he purred as he scraped his teeth across her neck. "That's why we have to make this last." He echoed his words with one long, slow stroke, pulling back out until just the tip of his cock was inside her, slamming back in.

Shifting his grip, he moved both wrists to one hand. Cupping his other hand around the curve of her rump, he stroked his fingers over the silky flesh, probing the tight pucker of her ass.

Shrieking out his name, Zoë bucked back against him.

The tip of his finger pushed inside—she exploded around him, thrusting her hips back to meet his. Slowly, torturously, he rotated his finger inside the snug grip of her ass, prolonging the orgasm as it blasted through her.

Burying her face in the sheets, she gasped out a harsh, burning breath. In the braceleted grip of his hands, she fisted her own, her nails biting into her palms. Swimming in a hot pool of sensations, she shuddered, feeling everything he felt, feeling every slow stroke of his cock inside her pussy, all magnified.

"Let me in," he muttered. "I want to feel what you're feeling."

Helplessly, she lowered the shields between them and his being sank into hers. His thrusts changed rhythm, became shorter and deeper. His hunger was a biting, clawing thing that stole her breath away and spiraled out of control. He slammed into her, the head of his cock butting against the mouth of her womb and he climaxed, the hot, wet jets of his semen coating her already dew-slicked depths.

As he collapsed against her, he rolled to his side, pulling her against him and cuddling her. Zoë felt the harsh rhythm of his heart slamming against her back. Wrapped in his arms, she felt all the loneliness of the past five years just drift away, felt all the terror-stricken dreams fading into the night. Her entire soul, for once, was at peace.

Micah awoke with a hard-on. His dick was nestled against her snug backside and as he lay there, debating on getting up to make her breakfast or make love to her, she shifted and rolled forward, sprawled facedown. He sat up and stared at her, watching as she shifted a little more, drawing up one knee.

The way she lay, early morning sun pouring in through the skylight painted her flesh golden, and his eyes were drawn to the shadowed cleft between the cheeks of her ass. Voracious need punched a fist in his belly and he shifted out of bed, squatting next to her nightstand. Keeping his eyes on her still form, he slowly opened the drawer. Once it was open, he looked inside, smiling as he found the blue bottle of lubricant in there, nestled next to a rabbit. She did love her bunny vibe, he mused.

Taking the vibrator and the lube, he crawled back on the bed, easing her knee just a little higher. Slicking the lubricant on the shaft of the vibrator, he pushed it against her, eyes narrowing to slits as he worked it inside her.

Her hips shifted and a soft little moan slid out of her.

He knew the minute Zoë woke up. Her body stiffened and she cried out softly, whipping her head around and staring at him with her mouth opened in a soft "o", her eyes wide. Now that he had her attention, he flicked the power button on the vibrator and shifted it around so that the ears of the vibe were nestled against her clit. The pearl embedded inside the vibrator started to rotate around the shaft, teasing her sensitized flesh.

Lowering his head, he pressed his lips to the graceful line of her spine, nuzzling the sunny golden curls out of his way so he could lick a slow, teasing path up her neck. "Remember the last time I used this on you?" he asked gruffly.

"Yesssss," she hissed as he pulled the vibrator out and then slowly worked it back in. She sobbed and threw her head back, and he watched her knuckles go white as she gripped at the sheets tangled beneath her.

He sought out the lubricant by touch with his other hand. "I remember it, too. Your body trembling as I fucked my way into your snug little ass," he murmured. "You screaming and begging me to let you come, begging me not to stop. That memory haunts me." Dropping the lubricant down by her hip, he shifted onto his knees and gripped her hips, pulling her up so that her torso bowed into the bed, her ass up in the air. Taking her hand, he guided it to the rabbit and folded her fingers around the handle of it. "Keep it there," he ordered.

Her answer was nothing more than a soft moan. That sweet ass started to rock as she rode the vibe, her pace increasing. His cock jerked at the sight, insistently. Grabbing the lubricant, he poured some into his hand to warm it before he started to probe the snug glove of her ass.

"Sweet," he praised, shuddering as she gripped his fingers tightly. "You screamed yourself hoarse that night."

"Micah…"

"You ready to scream again for me?" he teased as the grip of her anal muscles eased just slightly. Settling back on his heels, he poured more lubricant into his palm and coated the ruddy length of his sex. Rising to his knees, he took his cock in hand and aimed for the gleaming, tight pucker of her ass, slowly pushing against it until she opened for him. The sight of that pink flesh flowering open around his cock had him gritting his teeth. The need to fuck her, hard and fast, was damn near painful.

Working his cock deeper, he groaned harshly as he felt the subtle movements of the vibe she had buried deep in her pussy. The toy had tightened her passage, and she was fist-tight already. Pulling out, he slowly worked his cock in, his head falling back as she slowly took him inside the snug grip of her ass.

She wailed and pushed back against the restraining grip of his hands, her muscles flexing around him and he bellowed out her name as his control snapped and he rammed full length inside her.

Zoë screamed as he impaled her, burying his cock inside her, his balls swinging forward to slap against her hand as she pushed against the vibrations of the rabbit. The little ears that gave the vibe its name buzzed against her clit. It was too much sensation—the scalding length of his cock, the vibrations of the rabbit ears against her clit, and the rotating little pearls that wrapped around the shaft of the vibrator.

But she couldn't come. It was still too far away…he pulled out and slammed back into her and she screamed again, writhing under the grip of his hands. He pulled out again and drove back inside her. His fingers spread wide on the curve of her hips, digging into her flesh.

She was burning up inside, too hot, skin felt too tight. Each rough stroke of his cock pushed her higher, pushed her closer.

It was like molten lava had replaced her blood. The heat spiraling out of control, threatening to burn her alive. Greedy, she shoved back against him and jolted when he lightly slapped her ass. "Always so demanding," he murmured as he shafted her.

Heaven, she had never felt so alive. So hot. So needy. "Damn it, please," she begged.

"But I am pleasing you," he murmured

"You're mean," she pouted, her voice low and rough. "Stop teasing me, Micah—I can't handle it."

"No?" he asked gently, pulling out until she could only feel the thick head of his cock lodged within the tight muscles of her ass and then he shuttled back inside, quick and hard. Another slow withdrawal before thrusting in.

Zoë hissed out a breath between her teeth and whispered, "No!" Shoving back, she impaled herself on his cock as he tried to withdraw, pumping her hips forward and back in a greedy, driving rhythm.

Zoë's hungry wail had his nerves singing. He watched, slowing his hips until she was taking him, the pink pucker of her ass opening around his cock like a hungry little mouth. She was so damned tight, so hot...a shiver raced down his spine, tightening his balls and he knew he couldn't hold off much longer. Raising his hand, he slapped her ass again and listened to her scream bounce off the walls as she exploded. The muscles in her snug little ass went into tiny, caressing convulsions all along his length. With a hoarse groan, he pulled out and slammed back into her one final time, his weight crushing her into the bed as he slid his arms under hers, his hands hooking around her shoulders as he burrowed in to the hilt.

Her breath escaped her in a rough little wheeze and he cursed softly under his breath, rolling to his side and taking his weight off her slim form. His cock, still semi-erect and wet from the lubricant and his come, slid from her and he sighed at the loss of that tight embrace.

Burying his face in her hair, he held her against him as her body continued to shudder. "I was trying to decide whether to fuck you or fix you breakfast," he whispered once he could breathe again.

"I like your choice," she sighed, smiling and cuddling back against him. His cock stirred with interest as she pressed her butt against him. Micah closed his eyes and thought, *This will kill me.*

The soft brush against his mind had him stiffening slightly as she whispered into his mind, *It could...but I can't think of a better way to go.*

Chapter Three

"When do you think he's going to try anything?" Zoë asked as she nipped a piece of bacon, watching Micah as he stood at her stove expertly turning the golden brown hash browns.

"I only wish I knew," Micah said, his mouth going into a firm, flat line, eyes grim. "I feel so blind."

Zoë shrugged. "You're not blind. Not with me," she said, lifting one shoulder, her eyes moving to the window. She'd had to draw the curtains. They couldn't risk Morraine seeing Micah. Her presence would drown out any echo from Micah until Morraine was practically on top of them. And he'd be caught by surprise, hopefully surprised enough that Micah could do what needed to be done.

But in order for this entire plan to work, she had to drop her shields. Going completely unshielded was like walking naked in a rainstorm.

The emotions she picked up from Micah had her head whirling.

It was his thick head. He was so damned stubborn, his personality strong enough, that she had a hard time seeing inside his head. Of course, he was also an intensely emotional person. And his emotions, she felt. Emotions were like colors, just like thoughts came mostly in complete words.

And the color of his emotions painted her a rainbow.

Hunger, fear, want, desire, anger...*love*. She hadn't seen that emotion of love so clearly on him before. She'd felt confusion, need, lust...but love...had he always loved her?

Did he even *know* he loved her? Whether or not he had admitted it to himself, she didn't know. Whether or not he ever planned on telling her, she didn't know. But he did love her. Love was a pure golden color underlined with the deep, rose red of desire, and the colors surrounded him.

With her shields down, she felt so much.

But that could also be dangerous.

She was leaving herself wide open for Morraine. And he'd done her enough damage already. Pensively, she stared at the table, lost in thought, lost in the morass of her fears.

"Hey."

Startled, her head flew up and she stared solemnly into Micah's eyes. His hand came up, cupping her cheek and she rubbed against it, reaching up to cover his hand with hers.

"Are you okay?" he asked quietly.

With a forced smile, she said, "As okay..."

Terror, icy and black, punched her in the gut as a low, menacing voice purred into her mind. *Now...now...now...what do we have here?*

The psychic voice was powerful enough that it echoed in the room, not just within her mind. Powerful enough that Micah heard it as well and his hands closed over her upper arms, pulling her against him. Her vision was foggy for a minute as fear seized control. For a moment, she battled the fear as it tried to overtake her, but finally, she gained control, clearing her mind and mentally bracing herself for what was coming.

Zoë swallowed and raised enough of her shielding that he could only sense what she wanted him to sense. Now that he was here, she could resume some of her normal caution. "What do you want?" she said flatly. "Your masters know you got out of your cage?"

Always so brave, Zoë. Aren't you surprised to hear from me? You all thought I was dead, Kyle crooned.

Zoë laughed. "I should have known better than to expect you to die like a normal person. You're like a cockroach, always turning up in the most unexpected places." Staring up at Micah, she forced a smile and mouthed, *I'm okay.*

His eyes were flat and hard but he nodded, cocking a brow at her and waiting.

I'm coming for you, Zoë. Do you know that?

"Well, I didn't think this was a social call. What makes you think it will be so easy?" she demanded. She stepped back away from Micah and ran her hands through her hair. Zoë was pleasantly surprised to find her hands steady.

Kyle laughed, the silky sound warm and amused. Almost pleasant. *You are weak, Zoë. Weak and soft. That's why you didn't kill me when you had the chance.*

"Trust me when I say that's not a mistake I'll ever make again," she assured him sweetly. "Why don't you come on up and I can show you?"

Kyle laughed. *No...I'm not done playing with you yet.*

Ice chilled her blood as he shoved at her mind and for long minutes, her eyes blurred and she couldn't see the sunny yellow of her kitchen anymore, just the rough-hewn warm amber beams of an exposed ceiling. Narrowing her eyes, she growled, "Get out of my head. You're not welcome in here, you pathetic excuse of a man." As she shoved him out of her mind, she broke out into a sweat and the sudden break of the link left her staggering for a minute. Slamming her hands against the table, Zoë sucked air into her lungs, scrunching her eyes tightly closed.

Micah's arms came around her and he whispered into her ear, "Are you okay?"

Turning around, she stepped up against him, snuggling against him. "Well, at least I can move enough to shake. That's better than last time," she murmured.

Under her cheek, she felt the steady beat of his heart. His hand came up, fingers threading through her hair, massaging her scalp as he cradled her against him. "He doesn't know I'm here, does he?"

Zoë could feel the smooth cotton of the Henley shirt he wore against her cheek as she shook her head. The warmth of his skin underneath. "No. He's too focused. Too focused on me."

That was going to be his downfall.

* * * * *

So focused on Zoë, so focused on making her scream and whimper and beg that he stopped thinking. He let his emotions rule his thinking and after Zoë had broken the link with him, he'd left the mountain. She could even feel him...vaguely...his presence slowly grew more and more dim, like a light in the darkness.

He got stupid. Instead of thinking with his head, he thought about how to get to Zoë and he grabbed a girl. He took her off the streets, a college coed in town for some R&R over her fall break.

Zoë could feel the girl's fear as Morraine dragged her through the woods, murmuring against her skin, using the barrel of his Glock to caress the flesh left bare by the plunging neckline of her sweater.

He hadn't been gone more than a few hours and Zoë had been aware of every step he took, aware of the girl's terror, Morraine's excitement.

Keeping her face blank as she dealt with all the emotions from the girl, she accepted the steaming cup of green tea into her hand from Micah as he crouched down in front of her. Without drinking it, she set it aside and leaned forward, looping her arms around Micah's neck and drawing him against her.

The minute his lips touched hers, she did it. Focusing and dragging him under. As he went kicking and screaming into a dark slumber, she whispered, "I'm counting on you."

And then she slid out into the dusky twilight, closing the door behind her. As she moved away, she released the hold she had on Micah's mind and whispered a prayer.

Morraine kept whispering to her as she tracked him. *She's bleeding, Zoë. Aren't you going to try and save her?*

"I'm not going to *try*. I will save her. Stupid fuck."

Morraine laughed.

Zoë knew these woods like the back of her hand, even in the night. As twilight fell, the shadows lengthened but she moved through them surely and confidently, sidestepping the branches and natural debris that littered the forest floor.

With her shields locked down so tightly, he wouldn't feel her coming until it was too late. And he was shielding from her, so she couldn't track him as well, at least not like she could if she let her shields down.

But he couldn't do a damn thing about blocking the girl's thoughts from her.

Zoë was just too strong.

And she was severely pissed.

By the time she got close enough for Morraine to feel her presence, Micah was awake. Feeling Micah's fury, she dropped her shields once more, hoping the power of her psychic presence would drown out Micah, or at least camouflage him for a little while.

"Let the girl go," she said, keeping her voice normal.

Although Morraine was still probably a quarter a mile away, she knew he'd hear her.

Just like she heard his evil laughter. "Now why should I? She's such a pretty little toy, skin so white and soft...well, at least where I haven't cut her."

"Because if you don't this is the closest you'll ever get to me," she replied. "You want me? This is your chance. But you can either let her go *now*, or I disappear. You'll kill her. I know you will. You get me close enough, the first thing you'll do is kill her in front of me. So if you want me, let her go."

"You don't have the guts to come and face me," Kyle sneered. "I let her go, and you'll just run away."

Zoë laughed, the sound hard and brittle in the air. "No. Because I want you dead more than I want to run away," she responded. "Believe that."

When Micah awoke, he exploded off the floor in a flurry of motion.

He didn't even waste time searching the house. He headed for the back door, but before he even got to the kitchen, he heard Zoë murmur, *No…he's watching that way. Follow me…*

It wasn't her voice. Not really. More like an echo, or a memory she had planted within his mind.

Damn it. When she kissed him, she had known Morraine was out there and she knocked him out so she could go after him herself.

With a snarl, he jerked his phone from his belt as he slid from the house, barking into it, "He's here. Zoë's out there."

This plan was seriously flawed. One person going after Morraine.

No…*two*.

It was as he was running through the woods, stumbling on the uneven ground, that he realized why the plan seemed so fucked up to begin with. Oh, he was sure there was a team that would come in and do the clean-up.

But they were counting on somebody else doing the dirty work.

Not Micah.

He was there to make sure Zoë stayed alive and to call them if something went wrong. But Zoë was the one they were counting on to kill Morraine. It had been the suit that had insisted Morraine be brought in alive. But the woman had been the one in charge, and now Micah understood the secrets he'd seen in her dark gaze.

She wanted Morraine dead as surely as Micah did. Only she wasn't strong enough. And apparently none of her men were either. So the ball fell to Zoë.

Problem was, it put Zoë entirely too close to Morraine—Micah wasn't at all pleased with that.

The echo of her voice guided him. He listened to it intuitively as he moved through the woods. His night sight kicked in and he didn't have to run blind anymore. The darker shapes of trees and branches and rocks lining the faint trail became easier to avoid and he moved quicker.

And soon, he heard her voice, not just the echo of a memory she'd forced inside his head. They'd be having a talk about that. But right now he was too happy to see her in one piece. Although he'd known she was alive. He'd felt it.

If something ever happened to her, he would know. He'd feel it inside his heart—and his heart would die inside him.

Sliding behind a tree, he drew his gun and prayed that whatever twist of fate kept Zoë from sensing what was going on in his mind would also keep Morraine out.

"I can always go back after the girl," Morraine said as Micah braced one shoulder against the tree. In the distance, he could hear the sound of a woman's faint sobs, the sounds of somebody thrashing through the trees.

Shit. He had brought bait. A girl to threaten Zoë with. That was why she'd left the way she had. Stubborn, irritating brat of a woman. He would strangle her.

"No," Zoë said calmly. "Because you won't leave these woods alive."

There was the sound of branches and leaves crunching underfoot and Micah chanced peering around the tree as Morraine approached Zoë. The bastard laughed as he stared down at her. "Arrogant bitch, aren't you?"

"Hmm. No, confident bitch. Arrogant is what you are, thinking you are so powerful, so mighty. And you don't even realize that I wasn't alone in that house. Any more than I'm alone with you right now."

Micah cracked a smile, shaking his head. He understood what she'd done now, traded herself for whoever Morraine had grabbed, counting on Micah to come after her. Although Zoë had the skill to kill Morraine, Micah suspected she didn't fully believe it. And even if she did, it would scar her.

"There's nobody here but us, Zoë. Don't you think I'd know? I'd hear the thoughts," Morraine said, his voice still so full of arrogance.

Moving out from behind the tree, Micah lifted his gun as he cocked an eyebrow at Zoë. "Not if my head is too thick for the thoughts to leak out. Zoë can't hear me. Why should you?" he asked as he aimed the gun squarely at Morraine's forehead.

"You *fucking* cunt!" Morraine roared, lifting his arm and backhanding Zoë across the face.

Micah saw red at the same time he felt an outside force, ugly and black, punch at his mind. *Shoot the bitch*...the whisper was dark and malevolent, so full of evil that Micah was certain it would haunt him.

But it didn't control him. Curling his lips in a smile, he said, "No. I've got my target." He saw Zoë from the corner of his eye as he pulled the trigger.

And when Morraine went down, a look of shock still on his face, he felt the relief from her as surely as if he was the one with the abilities.

She hadn't wanted another stain from Morraine inside her.

Chapter Four

Two days later, finally, all the agents from the still unknown agency had left Gatlinburg. Zoë knew damned good and well there might be more questions, but for now, she had some peace.

They'd tried to recruit her.

Zoë had suspected they might—they even tried some none too subtle blackmail and then she blasted her way into the mind of the woman who'd led them. After a few moments of shell-shocked silence, the woman simply turned and walked out.

Her full abilities were something she rarely utilized—but she knew that when she blasted her way into a mind, it was akin to somebody experiencing a sonic boom within their skull. Zoë couldn't be controlled. And she wouldn't tolerate somebody trying to.

But now she was alone. Completely alone. Micah had been gone since yesterday morning. He had slid into her room and she'd awoken to find him staring down at her. For a long, poignant moment, their gazes held and then he slanted his mouth across hers and ate hungrily at her mouth.

She was left gasping for air when he abruptly pulled away and walked out.

His way of saying goodbye?

Hell, she didn't know.

She just knew she was alone again. Achingly alone. He had to go. She knew that. He had a job to do, and just because Morraine was gone didn't mean his part in it was done.

Settled at her computer, she tried to focus on editing some pictures but she couldn't work up the interest to do more than flip through the photos.

When the knock came, she stilled. Her heart started to slam against her ribs and Zoë licked her lips nervously as she lifted her head and stared out the door of her office into the hall. From upstairs, she couldn't see the door, but her gut knew who was there.

Nervously, she climbed to her feet and walked slowly into the hall, staring down the stairway at the dark shadow through the frosted glass of the door. The knock came again, demanding. Resting one hand on the banister, she walked down the steps.

Her hand closed around the handle and for a long moment, she hesitated. A hand came from outside and rested on the glass. "Open the door, Zoë."

Reaching up, she rested her palm against the glass, opposite his, leaning her forehead against the door as she took a breath and tried to prepare herself.

He'd come back…*but why?*

Why had he come back this time? Closing her eyes, she whispered, "There's only one way to find out."

Slowly she opened the door and stood there, staring at Micah in silence.

The moment her eyes met his, a smile spread across his face and he whispered, "I told you—I wasn't walking away from you again. You're mine, Zoë."

Swallowing, she said thickly, "When did you become a mind reader?"

Micah just chuckled as he pulled her against him. "I don't have to read your mind. I just need to look in your eyes," he whispered as he threaded his fingers through her hair. "I love you, Zoë. And if you plan on pushing me off the mountain, do me a favor and make sure it kills me. That's the only thing that will keep me from you."

Pressing her face against his chest, she gave a watery laugh. "I love you," she whispered. "The only way I'll try to throw you off a cliff is if you try to leave me."

About the author

They always say to tell a little about yourself! I was born in Kentucky and have been reading avidly since I was six. At twelve, I discovered how much fun it was to write when I took a book that didn't end the way it should have ended, and I rewrote it. I've been writing since then.

About me now...hmm... I've been married since I was 19 to my high school sweetheart and we live in the midwest. Recently I made the plunge and turned to writing full-time and am looking for a part-time job so I can devote more time to my family—two adorable children who are growing way too fast, and my husband who doesn't see enough of me...

Shiloh welcomes mail from readers. You can write to her c/o Ellora's Cave Publishing at 1337 Commerce Drive, #13, Stow, Ohio 44224.

Also by Shiloh Walker

Vampires and Donuts

Tielle St. Clare

Chapter One

Kendra stood to the full stretch of her five-foot seven-inch height and glared down at the gorgeous man lounging in the visitor chair on the far side of her desk.

"Brand, if you ever put your fangs on one of my friends again, I'm going to rip them out and make myself a pair of earrings."

He didn't flinch, didn't cower. Just smiled slightly. "What an intriguing threat."

"I'm serious."

He sighed and kicked his booted feet up onto her desk. "You know..." he said, crossing his arms onto his chest, "as a client, I should be treated with more respect than this. Do you threaten your other clients?"

"Most of my other clients don't drink blood." She stopped. "Wait. Most of my clients *do* drink blood and I can blame that on you as well."

He shrugged—and looked so damned yummy that Kendra thought she'd scream. It shouldn't be possible for one man to be so stunning. Tall and muscular with long black hair—typically tied back but left hanging around his shoulders tonight—a wicked smile and crystal blue eyes. Unfortunately, the smile came accompanied by fangs and the blue eyes turned blood-red when he was angry.

Brand was a fairly new vampire, only fifty years old, but he had the vampire persona down pat. He dressed in black, wore shades at night and had just the right mix of spooky and sexy.

If he hadn't been completely out of her league—and a vampire—Kendra definitely would have jumped him years ago. But she knew better.

Vampires and donuts. The two things in this world destined to tempt and ruin her.

"What can I say? You did such a fantastic job for me, I had to recommend you to my friends."

She steeled herself against the charming smile and waves of seductive energy radiating off him. She was immune. Really she was.

"Great. Some doctors strive to be 'surgeon to the stars'." She rubbed her soon-to-be-throbbing forehead with her fingertips. "I'm the investment advisor to the undead."

"Be happy. We didn't even blame you for that little dip in the market a few years ago."

She started to bare her teeth in a growl but stopped. When it came to dangerous incisors, Brand would win, hands down.

"Can we get back to the point of this conversation?" she asked.

"I didn't know there was a point to this conversation."

"Don't bite my friends."

"Kendra, honey, you know the two things I need to survive are blood and sex. Sharon was willing to provide both."

"Did she know about the blood?"

He had the grace to look a little sheepish. "Maybe not, but she won't miss it either."

"Brand!" Kendra tried to temper her voice, to keep it from turning into a whine, but wasn't sure she succeeded.

"Fine. I promise, no more biting your friends." He rose in a swift, fluid motion and leaned across her desk, meeting her halfway. "I make no promises about you though. Trust me. The sex will be hot. Will you feed me?"

Yes! her body screamed.

"No," her mind forced her lips to say. The silent wail that echoed inside her pussy at again being denied the contact it desired almost sent Kendra to her knees but she stayed strong. He was just teasing. It was something he did to torment her. No way a guy like him was interested in a woman like her. Not that she was hideous, she consoled herself. But she was common. Brown hair, green eyes, nice breasts but a little too much padding on her backside.

She looked up and saw Brand's quirky, teasing smile.

"I don't think that's appropriate," she said primly. "We're business associates, right?"

Amusement flared in those hard blue eyes. "Right."

"Why did you come by tonight?" she asked, recalling his appearance at her office door thirty minutes ago and how she'd creamed her panties at the sight of him. He'd had this effect on her from the moment they'd met seven years ago.

It had been a night much like this one. She'd been working late, trying to do a good job for the *one* client she had and Brand had walked in. He'd said he needed someone to manage his business affairs because he traveled and his schedule was erratic. She had been so stunned by the long black hair and captivating eyes that she'd agreed without thinking. He'd become her second client.

She had worked her ass off for him, doubling his considerable assets in three months. He'd recommended her to his friends and her client list grew. Four years into the relationship, she discovered Brand and all his friends were vampires. By then, she liked them all. She'd kept their secret and their business and they thanked her in many ways. Mainly by sending her more business. Two-thirds of her clients were vampires.

Through the years, she'd become friends with Brand. Beyond business, they spent hours talking and laughing.

"I want you to be extra-careful over the next few weeks."

The gray, heavy tone of Brand's words jolted her clear of her reminiscing. "What? Why?"

He hesitated and, for a moment, she thought he wasn't going to answer. It would be just like him to present a warning like that and then not explain it. But she knew how to wait him out.

"Some vampires are trying to overthrow the current leader."

"You guys have leaders? Like a president?"

"Yes, but our elections are much more bloody. The one standing at the end gets to lead."

A thought struck her and she looked at him suspiciously. "*You're* not this leader guy, are you?"

He laughed softly. "No. His name is Marcus and he's old and very powerful. I work for him."

"Ah…so what does this have to do with me?"

His deliberately casual shrug sent warnings through Kendra's mind.

"The guy who's trying to take over has decided to distract Marcus's lieutenants—by going after the people we know. Lovers, sisters, mothers."

Kendra chewed on her lower lip and tried to figure out where she fit into that list. She wasn't his sister or mother—and she sure as hell wasn't his lover, at least not in reality. In her dreams...that was a different issue.

"What does this have to do with me?" she asked again.

"He's noticed our, uh, friendship." For the first time in their seven-year history, Brand looked embarrassed. "And Marcus thinks he might come after you."

The breath locked in her throat like an invisible hand squeezing. "Me? What did I do?"

"Nothing. The guy's crazy. Just be extra-careful for a few days until we find him and leave his scrawny body writhing in the sunlight." He sounded so cold that shudders raced down her back.

"What do I do? Stay inside? Lock my doors? Wait! If I don't invite him in, I'm safe, right?"

Brand smiled again but this grim look didn't warm her tummy.

"That whole 'invitation only' thing is a myth. You don't get an invisible shield around your house when you buy it."

Said like that, it did sound rather silly and that didn't make her feel any safer. "How do I protect myself?"

"Stakes work. Silver bullets work. Don't suppose you have any of those around?"

"Uh no. I wasn't expecting werewolves to attack."

"It works for both species but since you don't have any, you just have to be careful. Stay in the company of others as much as possible. Do you have a cell phone?"

"Of course."

"Let me have it."

Kendra handed him her phone, pleased that her fingers didn't shake. Brand quickly keyed in a new number.

"What are you doing?" she asked looking over his shoulder. Dang, he smelled good. She took a deep breath—capturing it for later when she would need it.

"Programming in my number. I'm now on speed dial one." He handed the phone back to her.

"But...but...speed dial one is Donnie's Donut Palace." It was her favorite twenty-four hour donut emporium. She called ahead and they had her order ready when she drove up.

"You can do without donuts for a few days."

Her eyes tightened and Brand knew he was heading into dangerous territory. "Is that a dig?"

He looked down at her body—curvy, tight and perfect for his hands. His fangs exploded from his gums and his cock hardened at the thought of holding those round breasts and sipping at her nipples.

"No, you're perfect the way you are," he said, meaning it, though he knew Kendra would never believe him. "But until we get this settled, you have to choose between safety and donuts."

Her lips curled into a grimace. "I suppose survival is more important than the world's best donuts...for a few days."

He had to work at not smiling in return. "I'll try to work quickly." He wanted to grab her and shake her so she understood how serious this was—but he also didn't want to panic her. He would find Trevor. He had no doubt about that. And then Brand would finally make his move on Kendra. He'd waited seven years, assuming the urge to fuck her would go away. It hadn't. It had grown worse and with this latest threat, he realized he couldn't wait anymore. He had to have her—at least once. "Keep your phone with you. If anything out of the ordinary happens, call me."

"Out of the ordinary? I work for a bunch of vampires. What do you consider normal?"

He stared down at her, not letting her see the smile that threatened.

"Fine," she sighed. "I'll keep the phone on me and if anything strange happens, I'll think donuts." He raised his eyebrows. "Trust me. I'm never going to remember speed dial one as anything but Donnie's."

He took a deep breath, letting some of the tension leave his body. The long inhalation brought in a new wave of her sensual perfume—nothing added, pure woman. Pure aroused woman. He'd noticed it shortly after he'd entered. She wanted him. Her body reacted the same way every time he came near her but she'd never responded to any of his subtle hints that he wanted more.

Maybe he needed to be a little less subtle. But not until Trevor was caught.

"I've got some things to do. Lock the door and call me when you're ready to leave. I'll come back and walk you home."

She nodded.

"You'd better get going," she said, retreating behind her façade. She lifted her chin and glared at him. "And no more biting my friends."

"I promised," he said, walking to the door. "No more biting or fucking your friends." He stopped in the doorway and looked back. He couldn't have her tonight but he might as well make it known he planned to. "I have a new treat in mind."

A warm wave of need flowed out of her center, sending the delicate fragrance toward him. Brand smiled. *Good. Give her something to think about.*

At ten o'clock, Kendra pushed back from her computer and stretched her arms up. It had taken some concentration but she'd managed to get some work done. After Brand's strange seductive farewell, her mind had wanted to focus on him, not on reviewing stocks. Normally she could resist the general charm he emitted but tonight it had been different. It wasn't a generic flirtation that would have been directed at any woman — this had been focused on her.

She rolled her shoulders and sighed. It was late but her day was only halfway done. She'd shifted her work schedule to match the majority of her client list — late nights, early mornings.

In mid-yawn, she watched her office door swing open and tensed. She'd locked the front door. A tall blond man entered. Kendra immediately recognized the crystal eyes of a vampire. Not one of her clients. She stood. Brand often sent her clients but he always warned her first.

"Can I help you?"

"You're the investment guru all the vamps are using these days."

The slow, lazy drawl had the feel of slime as it oozed from his mouth. The smarmy smile didn't help the image.

"Who are you?"

"I'm a friend of Brand's."

Triggers went off in Kendra's head. None of the other vampires every claimed to be Brand's "friend". They claimed to "know" Brand or that Brand had sent them but never made the more intimate connection. She placed her hands on the desktop, covering her cell phone with her right hand. Her eyes locked on the stranger, she surreptitiously hit the first key and held it down. Brand had said out of the ordinary and she wasn't taking any chances. She might feel silly later but for now, she was taking the cautious approach.

"Brand usually tells me when he's sending someone new."

"He must have forgotten." He stepped closer.

Kendra risked a glance down. The call had connected.

"Kendra?" Brand's tinny voice reached her ears.

Her visitor's head snapped up and his eyes turned red. Before she could blink, he flew through the air, landing beside her desk. He slammed his fist down on the phone, killing the connection.

"Calling your friend?" His hand snapped out and fingers wrapped around her throat. His grip bit into her skin and cut off her air. A mangled choking sound was her only protest. "Won't make any difference. You'll be dead by the time he gets here. It's amazing how fast a human bleeds out."

The excruciating pain clouded her hearing, muffling his words. Keeping the tight grip on her neck, he grabbed her wrist. White flashed before her eyes as he opened his mouth and she saw the deadly fangs. Pain lanced her arm. She peered around his strangling hold and saw blood pouring from open slashes across her wrist. Matching pain struck on her other arm.

Her knees collapsed as he released her neck. She gulped in desperate air, trying to think beyond the spots forming in her eyes. Freed, she swung her arm out and slugged him in the chest. He slapped her hand away and grabbed the back of her hair.

"Brand must like them feisty. Me? I like a human who knows her place." He bent her head over and drove his fangs into her neck. Kendra screamed. Fire ripped through her skin and poured into her body. It was like he was inside her, filling her with his hatred. She hung in suspended animation, frozen but feeling the deadly pull of his mouth on her skin, sickened by the sensation. Blackness rose behind her eyelids, covering her mind. She was dying. She knew it. Abruptly the pain stopped and hope flickered inside her chest. *Brand? Had he come to save her?* "Your hero will never make it," the vampire sneered, as if he could hear the hope inside her head. "Perfect. You'll be dying as he arrives."

She heard the voice in the dark and felt a thump as she hit the floor.

Brand. The silent cry lingered as her mind faded to black.

Chapter Two

Kendra's hands shook as she poured coffee into her cup. Was she even able to drink coffee now? Surely Brand wouldn't have made it if she couldn't drink it.

The events of last night had crashed down on her from the moment she'd woken in Brand's bed. The stranger, the attack and...the healing. The memories were hazy but she could still feel the darkness and cold invading her body. Death had been near. Then the warmth came, filling her mouth. Brand's voice filling her head, ordering her to drink. She'd become aware long enough to realize she was sucking on Brand's...wrist. *Ugh.* Of all the things she'd ever imagined sucking on Brand, his blood had been nowhere on the list.

She turned her hands over and stared at her wrists. The bloody tears were gone and all the remained of the gouging bite at her neck was a little pink scar.

"How are you feeling?"

She looked up at Brand's soft question.

"I'm fine," she said again. He'd asked her that five times since she'd woken in his bed. She could hear the lingering guilt in his voice every time he spoke. He blamed himself for her attack. "I feel good actually. Like it never happened."

"The vampire blood gave you the ability to heal."

So it hadn't been a dream. She *had* drunk his blood. "Uh, am I a vampire?"

His lips kicked up into a sad smile and he shook his head.

"But I drank your blood. Doesn't that turn me into a vampire? That's how they do it in the movies."

"Another myth." He brushed her hair back away from her face. "It takes a blood exchange but it also takes a more concentrated effort to Turn someone. All my blood did was give you the ability to heal." He picked up her hand and stroked his fingers across her skin. The cool touch sent new delicious shivers down her spine. Her eyes tracked his fingers along her arm, leaving whispers of need behind. The heat in the center of her stomach exploded. Such a light touch but it was more than she'd ever imagined. She squirmed, her pussy turning wet, the ache billowing out of the center of her body. It was incredible. It was like she was on fire—melting from the inside, ignited by the power of his touch.

"To turn into a vampire, you have to trust the person so much that you'll give them your soul to protect while you make the change." He leaned down and placed a whisper kiss below her ear.

She concentrated on forcing her lungs to breathe—the light brush of his lips was sapping the strength in her legs. "Is your blood causing this?"

"Causing what?" Another kiss followed his question.

"This desire." It had to be something because nothing had ever felt this good. "This pleasure." All he'd done was kiss her and she was melting with need.

"No, baby, that's all you."

Air rushed out of her lungs at his whispered statement. His lips moved in a random pattern across her skin, tasting and teasing the taut line of her throat. She felt his mouth open and the gentle scrape of his teeth across her pulse. The memory of her attack barreled into her mind.

"Please, don't bite me," she said. Her voice quivered.

He paused and she knew he heard her fear.

"I won't. I promise."

She relaxed. He kept his promises. She was safe with him.

"But I have to taste you, baby. I've been dreaming about this for seven years." His lips tickled her ear as his words caressed the very depth of her sex. "Dreamed about tasting your sweet cunt, the hot spicy flavor of your pussy." He sucked lightly on her earlobe. "It's taken all my control to not throw you across your desk and fuck you senseless."

"Why didn't you?" she groaned. She knew there was a reason this was a bad idea but she couldn't think of it.

"Because I was stupid," he growled a second before he covered her lips with his own. This was no gentle, introductory kiss. He thrust his tongue deep into her mouth, capturing and captivating. Kendra groaned as his masculine flavor enveloped her. She couldn't think, couldn't worry—all she could do was feel the hot seductive lure of his lips and his tongue. A long time later—moments before she was desperate for breath—he lifted his head. "And because I didn't know you'd taste this sweet. May I taste you?"

Without waiting for an answer—which would have been a resounding "yes"—he pulled her robe open, baring her naked skin. He pressed one knee forward, slipping between her thighs. The brush of his trousers against her sensitized skin magnified all the other cravings inside her. He skimmed his fingers across the top of her knee. Kendra heard the silent request and spread her legs just a little, giving him more access, opening herself to him.

His fingers accepted the invitation, swirling across her skin to the apex of her thighs. If it had been difficult to breathe before, it was impossible now. Brand, making love to her. It was too much for her tired mind to comprehend so she shut down the voices in her head and just let herself feel.

Brand watched his hand move across her skin, fascinated by the sight of his fingers entwined with the pale brown hair that covered her sex. Damn but he wanted her. He'd never fully appreciated his vampire senses until this moment, when he could smell her arousal, smell the sweet desire that flooded her pussy.

He knew it was wrong to take advantage of her vulnerable state but since the moment he'd seen her lying in his bed, he couldn't find the noble side to his soul. He had to have her.

He smoothed his hand down the inside of her thigh, feeling the human warmth invade his skin. He knew his hands were cool but they would heat as he touched her. As they fucked, his blood would flow and his heart would pound. *This* was why vampires needed sex—to be human. To reconnect with their human roots. It was when a vampire stopped fucking that he became dangerous, or suicidal.

"Brand?" The low groan wrapped around his already hard cock and squeezed. His fangs plunged downward, demanding penetration. Her pulse rattled just beneath the surface of her skin. But he'd promised he wouldn't bite her. Holding himself back, he whispered kisses along her neck, feeling the temptation so close.

"Shall I stop?" He weighted the answer in his favor by slipping one finger up, easing it slowly, gently into her warm, wet slit. Her chest pushed up, adding a delightful shimmy to her breasts. He drove a little deeper, finding her clit, feeling the tight, already aroused bud reach for him. "I've dreamed for seven years about touching you like this, about sliding into your tight little pussy." He swept his finger around her clit, teasing the right side with extra pressure. The sweet catch at the back of her throat made him groan—she was just as hot, just as wild as he'd imagined.

His hand left the peak of her thighs and began to draw lazy swirls across her thighs, painting her skin with the hot liquid that flowed from inside her. He wanted her blood—to feel her life flowing within him. She'd declared that intimacy beyond the limits but he had to taste her.

He sank to his knees and found the banquet of her sex open for him. Under the soft urging of his hand, she lifted her leg over his shoulder. He traced the dark pink entrance of her cunt with the tip of his tongue and felt her shudder. The flavor of her arousal drifted into his mouth and seeped into the core of his body.

"Brand?"

The sensual fear beneath his name spurred him on. She wanted this but was frightened of the sensation. He would teach her to crave it, the way he did. He kept his touch deliberately light, learning her flesh, welcoming her audible cues. The delicate gasps led quickly to low-throated groans as he circled her clit, gently sucking it into his mouth. Her hips rocked in restless need. Brand reached up and held her still, keeping her in place as he tasted her sweet flesh.

His cock throbbed inside his trousers, demanding its turn at the treasure of her pussy. But there was no way he was going to give up his treat just yet. He lost himself in her—lapping at her sex, learning and loving her. Her cries filled the room, echoing through the quiet kitchen and into his head. He had to have more of her.

He thrust his tongue into her cunt, flicking the tip against the inside walls. Her hips pumped hard against his face, as if she wanted him deeper.

She was ready to be fucked.

He stood up. Her eyes snapped open.

"Wha—?" Panic fluttered at him through her gaze.

"Don't worry, baby, I won't leave you hanging." He cupped his hand around the back of her neck and pulled her to him for a long, hot kiss, sharing her flavor with her. "Don't you taste delicious?" he asked against her skin. She laved her tongue across his lips. Her eyes clouded for a moment and he'd never seen anything more sexual. "I want more of your hot pussy juice." He felt her shiver beneath his words. "I want to spend hours with my mouth between your legs, licking your sweet cunt, feeling you come against my lips." She whimpered and clung to him. "But now, I need to have you. I've dreamed of this for too many years."

She nodded with the desperation of a woman who needed to be fucked.

The vampire inside him screamed its triumph. Brand flicked his tongue across the points of his fangs, teasing the sensitive spikes. They ached with the need to plunge into her. He stared down into her trusting green eyes. He couldn't betray that trust.

He placed his hands on her shoulders and spun her around, pushing her forward until she leaned against the counter.

"Let me have you this way," he said, hoping for some level of control. She pushed her ass back, offering herself to him. The hunger flowing through her reached out to him and drew him forward.

Brand placed the thick head of his cock against her opening and began to slide in. She was wet and hot and tight. She arched into him, begging for his penetration. He pushed halfway in, stopping when she gasped.

"Too much?" Damn but she was tight. It had obviously been a long time since she'd fucked. He felt his lips bend upward. If he had his way, she'd never go without again.

She took shallow panting breaths that eased the heavy grip of her cunt. Unable to stop himself, he pushed in just a little deeper. Again she tensed.

"Kendra?" His fangs were fully extended and his body was demanding he fuck her. But if she asked him to pull back, he would. A silent howl erupted in his head.

"When you became a vampire did you grow four or five inches?" she panted.

He bit back a groan. "No, we stay exactly as we were when we were Turned."

"So you were always hung like a horse?"

"Don't make me laugh, sweet," he said, gritting his teeth. "Not when I'm finally inside you. Tell me if it's too much." She dropped her head forward and nodded, giving him the permission he was seeking.

He gripped her hips and held her still as he pushed forward. He kept his penetration slow and steady until he filled her, until every inch was buried deep in her flesh.

Heat flowed through her into his body, bringing him alive, compelling his heart to beat. Did she realize what it meant? How powerful it was to have her give herself so openly?

He held himself deep inside her, taking a breath and savoring the warmth of her pussy surrounding him.

"Oh baby, your sweet cunt holds me so tight." He thrust forward, trying to get just a little deeper.

She groaned softly and thrust against him. His body screamed at him to pound inside her, to ride her hard and deep, but he went slow, letting her adjust to his size.

Kendra kept a firm grip on the counter, holding herself steady for his thrusts. All her strength, all her energy was centered in her sex. Her body rang with pure sensation. She'd never felt anything like this. He was hard and heavy inside her. Her pussy felt stretched and filled and so alive she wanted to scream her pleasure. Her world was focused on the long, hot slide of his cock into her body.

"God, baby, you feel so good. I want to fuck you forever." His voice spiraled through her chest, sinking into the core of her body. He pulled slowly out, inch by inch slipping from her body until she felt empty without him.

"Brand!" Sensual panic flowed through her.

"I'm here, sweet. I won't leave you." He pushed back in, slower but determined as if he wanted to feel every bit of her. She rocked her hips back but he gripped them, holding her still. He wouldn't let her move. He moved inside her, rubbing pressure points deep inside her sex until she was begging for release.

He rode her slow and deep, taking her heart and giving her his flesh in return.

The deep, pulsing massage touched a place that had never been reached before. She panted, trying to capture enough breath to survive, her body screaming for the orgasm just out of reach. As if he heard the silent pleas in her whimpers, he sped up. And the scream inside her broke free. The hollow center of her sex vibrated—the contractions seemed to flow from her cunt, driving through her body, building in strength until she couldn't contain the feeling. Her knees collapsed and she dropped against the counter. Brand's hands held her as he continued to thrust inside her. He pulled out and drove back in, giving her a full ride of his cock.

"More, give me more," he said, taking her harder.

Hearing the need in his voice, she struggled to stay upright and pushed back against him, finding strength where she had none. She pumped hard, throwing her ass back in time to his forward thrusts, driving him deeper.

"Please, Brand, come inside me." She couldn't take much more.

"Soon. Let me have more. Come for me again." He reached around her and slipped his finger into her slit, sliding over her tight clit. The subtle pressure brought a new kind of release. "That's it. You feel so good coming around my cock." He kept his hand cupped on her pussy, claiming it as he continued to thrust into her.

His mouth brushed along her neck. Unable to resist, she tilted her head to the side, baring her throat. The fiery swipe of his tongue across her skin sent the warmth into her body. He opened his mouth across her neck. She tensed, preparing for his bite but it never came. His teeth scraped her skin—not biting but a gentle nip, tempting her. "I keep my promises," he whispered, pulling back and driving hard into her again.

The sweet temptation of her throat drove him to the edge. Her heart pounded a frantic rhythm that urged him to move faster, to fill her with every part of him. His fangs ached. The need to plunge them into her throat was almost more than he could take. Red heat burned from the inside of his chest, demanding her blood.

He wanted to be gentle, to love her slowly, but there was no way—not with the vampire in him screaming to be free.

And she didn't seem to want a slow, gentle fuck. She pushed her ass back, impaling herself on his shaft. The sweet pulses helped him cling to his sanity. He stared down to where their bodies were connected, his cock sunk deep into her cunt. The warm pink of her flesh penetrated by the hard line of his cock.

He dropped his head back and released the primal scream that clawed at his throat. His woman, his pussy. He was inside it where he belonged. It belonged to him now.

The urge to fuck—to possess and conquer—tore at him and he couldn't fight it. He held her steady for his strokes, giving her everything, taking every inch of her cunt and claiming it as his own. The soft cries breaking from her lips pulled him back into himself. He ground his teeth together—hoping to heaven he wasn't hurting her or frightening her.

Her body was pulled taut, stretched out and straining across the counter and the kittenish cries were for more. He needed to feel her come one more time. He slipped his fingers between the folds of her cunt, teasing her clit.

"Yes! Oh my God, Brand!"

Her scream came seconds before she did. The tiny contractions of her pussy clamped around his cock, holding him as he drove into her, needing to be just a little deeper. He continued rubbing her clit, loving the shocked sighs that followed. Finally it was too much. He sank deep inside and let the climax take him.

Kendra leaned forward on the counter, reading the newspaper spread out before her. Her eyes were moving across the words but her mind was on the man upstairs. Her body ached with delicious overuse. She'd lost track of how many times they'd come together. Even now thinking about him made her eager for more.

What was wrong with her? She enjoyed sex as much as the next woman…okay, well, maybe not *as much* as the next woman but some of the time she enjoyed sex. Most of the time it seemed more trouble than it was worth and she felt vaguely dissatisfied with the result.

She'd felt none of those things in Brand's arms. She'd been alive and hungry, loving his body inside hers. She smiled. Her pussy. Her cunt. That's what Brand called it and she found she liked the words. Just a little bit nasty, a bit on the edge.

She felt a flutter inside her pussy and groaned. She couldn't truly be craving another orgasm. *God, baby, you feel so good. I want to fuck you forever.* Liquid pooled at the base of her sex. Maybe she was. Maybe if Brand came downstairs, all fresh from his shower, she would...

"You have the most incredible ass." The hot, molten words sent her thoughts flying. Two days ago, she knew she would have spun around and tugged on the bottom of her robe, blushing at such a compliment. Now, her body immersed in the sensual world of Brand's creating, she wiggled her butt and pushed it out.

"Glad you like it," she said, glancing over her shoulder.

Brand stood in the kitchen, his eyes focused directly on her ass. He was dressed, again wearing one of the deep gray suits he seemed to favor. His hair was damp and brushed away from his face. The crystal blue eyes glittered with renewed lust.

"I've been staring at it for years." Brand came up behind her. His hands gripped her hips and he pushed forward, trapping her between his body and the counter. Kendra turned away, letting her other senses take over. "Wanting to feel you like this while I fucked you."

She shivered at his words, feeling them deep inside. It was as if her body was filled with thousands of sparklers, each igniting and exploding with his touch. She rolled her hips back, feeling his clothed erection slip between her cheeks.

"Now that I have—I need it again. You're a sweet addiction." His mouth closed on the nape of her neck. She held her breath, waiting for the scrape of his teeth, but it never came. He straightened and stepped away.

"It's almost sunrise. I have to go to ground." The regret in his voice soothed her disappointment. "Will you stay here?" he asked, kissing her cheek.

Kendra shook her head. *I can't spend the day with a dead body in the house.* She didn't say that aloud. It seemed a little insensitive since it wasn't something he could change and she *had* been willing to have sex with him all night. "I'll be fine at my place. It will be daylight."

Brand nodded but he didn't look happy. "Trevor's still around but—"

"I was attacked by a guy named Trevor? Don't you guys have to change your names when you become vampires? Take a creepy or scary name?"

That earned her a half-smile. "*I* did, but Trevor, despite his pansy name, is a vicious killer." His eyes turned dark. He carried her hand to his mouth, placing a soft kiss on the inside of her wrist. "He wants to hurt me and he'll use you to do it." His tongue flickered out and whipped across the sensitive skin. The center of her stomach fell away at the delicate caress. He turned her palm and slowly sucked her fingers into his mouth one at a time, lovingly stroking the pads with his tongue.

"I sh-should be okay, uhm, during the daylight, uh, right?" She inhaled, trying to slow the rapid pounding of her heart. "You know, it's really hard to think when you're doing that."

"Good." His smile turned into a grimace.

"What's wrong?"

"Sun's rising."

"Go. I'll be fine."

"Stay inside. Stay with people. If we have any luck, Trevor will think you're dead." He hissed through his teeth and Kendra watched the pain rack his body.

"Just go," she said, stepping away, hating to see him hurting. "I'll see myself out."

He didn't move and she realized what was missing. She moved in, pressing up on her tiptoes and placed her mouth against his. The light connection of their lips quickly deepened. Brand drove his tongue into her mouth as if he was trying to carry her flavor with him.

He groaned but she knew it wasn't passion causing the sound. She stepped away, pushing him back when he would have followed.

"I'll see you tonight," he promised. He turned and opened a door near the front entrance. Kendra had thought it was a closet but she saw the dark stairs that led down into Stygian blackness. The door snapped shut as the first rays of sunlight cut through the open window.

Chapter Three

Kendra paced the length of her kitchen, reaching the end of the counter, spinning around and walking back.

She'd been stood up by a vampire. After she'd left Brand's house, she'd gotten a gun and silver bullets—which had been harder to find than she'd expected. She'd bought stakes and garlic cloves. She didn't know if garlic actually repelled vampires but she wasn't taking any chances.

And she'd waited, sleeping during the day and staying awake all night, expecting Brand to show up at any moment. But he hadn't. That was three nights ago.

Feminist sensibilities railed against waiting at home for a man to call but she really couldn't do much more. It didn't seem wise to wander the streets looking for Brand—not when a killer vampire was after him. And her.

Maybe he's just not into you, she thought, trying to penetrate the raging desire. It was probably a one-night thing. After all, what did she have to offer a man who had spent sixty years fucking women? He probably bored easily and had moved on to the next woman.

Damn it, this was why I stayed away from him. I knew this would happen. I'm going to lose a friend and a client over sex. Phenomenal sex but still, it wasn't worth it.

There was no way she could work with him now. Not after that night together. She wasn't that kind of woman.

She had never managed to maintain a friendly relationship with a former lover. The memories were too strong. When she finally saw Brand, and she was sure she would eventually, she would be a bitch. There was little she could do about it. It was just her nature.

It was easier to cling to the anger. Anger did a wonderful job of suppressing the pain. A twinge still flickered in her chest. Damn it, they'd only spent one night together but they'd been friends for seven years. She took a deep breath, feeling the emotions well up beneath the lid of anger. She brushed away the tears.

Her heart wasn't broken, she told herself. She *would not* let herself become attached to Brand.

Too late.

She ignored the officious voice inside her head, whipped around and retraced her path.

She snagged the last donut out of the box and took a deep bite while she talked to herself. It was just a one-night stand. He'd needed the sex to survive and she wanted it as well. It was no big deal that he hadn't called.

It sounded very sophisticated inside her head but she knew none of it was true. The painful ache in her chest refuted her own words.

A knock on the door snapped her out of her thoughts and sent her spine straight. Her house was rarely tidy enough to have people just drop in, so her friends had learned to call before coming by.

Pushing her shoulders back, Kendra picked up one of the stakes and walked to the door. She put her eye up to the peephole. Micah, one of the vamp clients Brand had recommended her to, waited in the hall. She backed away from the door, fingering the sharp stick in her hand.

"Kendra, open up." Micah's voice was soft through the closed door. "I know you're there. I can hear your heart beating."

That was probably true. It was thudding in her chest.

"Brand needs you."

A band squeezed around her heart and she wavered toward the door before jerking to a stop. It could be a trick. Micah could be working with Trevor.

"Kendra, come on. They sent me because you know me. Brand's been hurt."

She leaned against the door, her mind resonating with the need to open it and vibrating with the fear of doing the same thing.

"Trevor attacked him three nights ago. Brand's barely hanging on and he needs you."

Kendra chewed her lower lip. Damn it. She didn't know what to do. But if Brand was hurt, she had to take the chance.

I'll see you tonight. He'd said it with such sincerity, with a hunger that still made her knees weak. Hell, he'd almost gotten burned by the sun because he'd wanted one more kiss.

"Kendra?"

"I'm coming," she called through the door. Not knowing what else to do, she grabbed the gun, which she'd learned to shoot in the past few days, checked that the safety was on, and put it in her pocket. That would be her secret weapon. Her blatant one was the stake she held in her right hand. She opened the door. Micah stepped back, as if trying to give her some safety room. It was something Brand would have done.

"Where is he?" she asked.

"At Marcus's."

"What's wrong with him?" Her voice was cold and demanding. She wouldn't let emotion sway her right now. She needed a clear mind.

"He was attacked, leaving his house." Micah stayed back and held up his hands as if to show he was unarmed. "Brand and I were supposed to meet three nights ago—the night after you and he finally..." He let the words fade away.

Micah knew that she and Brand had made love? What? Did vampires have some sort of sexual sixth sense?

"We all know that Brand's feelings for you go deeper than just a client relationship," he said as if reading her mind. Before she could open her mouth to ask how he knew that when *she* didn't even know that, he shrugged and explained. "Brand recommended you as an investment advisor and then threatened anyone who came near you. If anyone showed any interest in you beyond your business advice, Brand carried out his threats quite efficiently."

Kendra felt her eyes widen. That hadn't been the confession she was expecting.

"Let's go," she said, feeling slightly better toward Micah. If he were leading her to her doom, he could have grabbed her already or told her an extensive sob story. She followed him to his car and allowed herself to be seated inside, keeping her stake firmly in her grip and clearly visible.

The drive across town was silent. When they finally arrived, it was in an expensive neighborhood with large houses and security perimeters. Whoever Marcus was, he had money.

Micah waited as she climbed out of the car, then led her up the walk and opened the door.

She stepped into the house and was struck by the weak lighting. She knew about the sensitivity of vampire eyes and had redesigned the lighting in her office to accommodate them — but this was definitely on the dark side. Voices in the other room rumbled low, quiet...and male. She strained to listen. She didn't recognize Brand's voice among the others. His tones were distinctive and she felt sure she'd be able to pick him out.

The talking stopped.

Kendra tensed, hearing the shuffle of feet across a hard wood floor. She started to back away. Micah moved behind her, blocking her exit. Gripping the stake in one hand and the gun in the other, she mentally braced for an attack.

"So this is Brand's little accountant. Quite lovely."

Kendra faced the arrogant voice and gasped. It was better than laughing. *This* was so *not* what she'd expected from a Master Vampire, but from the way the three vampires — two of whom were clients of hers — flanked him, she was pretty sure he was their leader. He was short and balding. His eyes were the same piercing blue as Brand's but the rest of his features were average. No one would look at him and think "vampire" let alone "leader of the vampire world".

But his eyes held a wicked intelligence that warned Kendra not to underestimate him. He didn't fit the image but she had no doubt he'd clawed his way to the top of the vampire pile with every nail and tooth sharpened.

"How do you do, Kendra? I'm Marcus." His voice was laden with deep sensuality and Kendra could easily imagine that he didn't need stunning good looks to get women. All he needed was that voice and those captivating eyes.

Not sure she was willing to trust him—at least not until she'd seen Brand and was convinced this wasn't some sort of trap for them—she nodded and raised the stake a little higher, making sure he saw it.

"Ah, a woman and her arsenal. I admire bravery in humans…" His voice trailed away but she knew there was more. She raised her chin and dared him to finish his sentence. "…it makes them so much more entertaining to kill."

The smirk on his lips was mirrored on the faces of the other vampires. Kendra felt her eyes tighten.

"I'm sorry," Marcus said with a chuckle. "I'm teasing. You just looked so fierce standing there with your stake." He waved his arm toward the living room. "Please come in."

"Where's Brand?" she asked, not moving.

"That's exactly what I want to talk to you about."

He continued to hold out his arm, expecting her to precede him into the living room. Well, polite or not, she wasn't turning her back on him. She waited, tilting her head slightly toward the open doorway.

For a moment, she thought she could outwait him. Marcus looked beyond her and lifted his chin. Massive arms wrapped around her torso, trapping her hands at her sides. She'd forgotten Micah was behind her. He lifted her and started walking forward. She briefly considered struggling but had the distinct feeling it would do no good — and quite possibly injure her pride beyond repair. Instead she hung limply in Micah's grip. He placed her in the middle of the living room and stepped back.

She flipped her hair away from her eyes and glared up at him. "I have two words for you — blue chips."

A flicker of true fear ran across his face. She knew Micah's abhorrence of conservative investments. Ignoring him, she turned her attention to Marcus.

"I don't even want to understand how you've made one of my toughest warriors shudder in fear," the vampire leader said, looking supremely disgusted at his lieutenant. "But shall we sit? We'll give you a quick explanation and then let you go downstairs and get on with your business."

Business? Kendra had no idea what he was talking about but she sat down and tried to look serene. Serenity wasn't a façade she maintained well. Irritated, pissed, really, really annoyed — those came naturally to her but serene was a pretty foreign emotion. She curved the edges of her mouth upward in a minor, arrogant tilt the way she'd seen society ladies do and looked at Marcus.

"What business is that?" she asked calmly.

"Fucking."

"What?!" Serenity went out the window.

Marcus held up his hands in the universal symbol of "calm down and I'll explain, you idiot". She calmed down.

"Brand was attacked three nights ago. Micah found him and brought him here. We've given him blood but he's barely hanging on."

"What's wrong with him?" she asked. Worry once again spiked through her irritation.

Micah sat down and took up the story. "Vampires need two things to survive."

"Blood and sex," she said. Brand had told her as much on several occasions. She figured it was the way all men "needed" sex to survive, but maybe not.

"Right. He's taken all the blood he can but his soul is still in limbo. He needs a good, hard fuck to bring it back, rebind it to his body."

She blinked. *Wow. Sex could do all that?*

"Well, I don't mean to be rude, but if that's all it takes for him to recover, why has this taken three days?"

"We tried, but none of the women we brought in appealed to him."

"So you thought you'd dig to the bottom of the barrel and bring me?" She was more than a little offended that she was their last choice to help Brand.

Marcus laughed softly. "No, you actually were the first woman we suggested but Brand wouldn't hear of it." She choked on her own saliva. Brand didn't want her? She'd never been a sex goddess but she didn't think she was that bad of a lay. He'd rather die that fuck her again? Not a good sign. "Not because of the reasons I can see circulating through that insecure human mind," Marcus continued. "Trevor is having my house watched. Brand was afraid that if you came here, Trevor would know you were alive and you'd be in danger again. Brand thought, as we all did, that with a little time he could recover." He shook his head. "It's not working. We need you."

"I'm supposed to have sex with him."

"Yes."

"That's it?"

"Basically."

She had so many questions but Micah stood up and she realized they expected her to go with them. To see Brand.

Fuck Brand.

Wasn't a bad way to save a life.

"You'll want to leave your weapons."

Kendra lifted her chin in defiance. No way she was going in unprotected.

"There's a chance Brand could use them against you," Marcus explained in that dark, serious voice that reminded her he was the leader of a group of vampires. Micah held out his hand. Reluctantly she handed him the stake. He didn't move. He was waiting for the gun. She pulled it out of her pocket and slapped it into his palm.

"Thanks."

"Bite me," she snarled back.

"And have Brand come after me? Never."

"Enough," Marcus said. "Let's go."

Marcus led the way down the stairs. His lieutenants followed. Kendra brought up the rear—the caboose in a rather morbid train. She had no idea what they would find at the end of the track. She assumed Marcus kept a room in his basement, sealed from sunlight and protected from intruders and fire. Brand had such a room though she'd never seen it. She stepped into a broad open area. Marcus and Micah walked ahead, stopping near a door before turning to face her. The other vampires stood to the side, giving her a place in the middle of the room.

"What?" she finally asked when no one spoke.

Marcus hit a button on a small keypad on the wall. The wall panel dropped to the ground revealing a window into a room. Brand was the other side, pacing a short path in the nearly empty room. Even through the glass, fury radiated from his body.

"I thought you said he was hurt. He looks fine…just pissed."

"He's being overcome by evil."

"What?" She stepped forward. "You didn't say anything about that."

"We didn't think you'd help if you knew," Micah answered honestly.

She glared at Micah and immediately began plans to sell off any of his stocks that were making money. She moved closer to the window. Brand stabbed the fingers of one hand furiously into his hair. From his scattered appearance, it looked like he'd repeated that same action a number of times. He lifted his eyes. Red glowed from their depths instead of the blue she was used to. His eyes were cloudy, shaded. Nothing like the clarity of the other vampires.

"He doesn't appear to be in the mood for sex," she said, pointing out the obvious.

"We're hoping you will change that." Marcus looked directly at her. "Blood keeps vampires alive, but it's the sex—the contact, the pleasure—that keeps us sane. Stops us from turning into the demons that you see in the movies. For lack of a better description, Brand almost died and his soul was ripped from his body. We're hoping that the feelings he has for you—combined with the sex—will rebind it to his body. That it will make him the man he was."

Sex with a furious man who is turning into a demon.

"We'll watch from here and if you appear to be in any danger, we'll pull you out."

"Watch?" These men were going to watch her fuck Brand?

"It's the only safe way."

Strange shivers of arousal raced down her back. *Great, a perfect time for latent exhibitionist tendencies to appear.*

"Any suggestions?" she asked as Micah reached for the door.

"He might not recognize you. Try to jog his memory. If there was something special he liked, bring that up."

Kendra thought back to the night they'd spent together. He'd liked fucking her from behind, and from the front, and with her on top. Hell, he'd pretty much liked everything. But he'd especially seemed to like going down on her. Taking a deep breath, she nodded and walked inside.

Brand turned as the door opened. His eyes glowed red as he stared at her. Micah gave her a slight shove, pushing her inside. The door snapped shut behind her. Brand growled and stalked toward the door. He stopped short and Kendra saw the chain wrapped around his ankle, connecting him to the wall. His hands stretched out but he couldn't reach her. With the length given him, he could sit on the bed or pace a four-foot path.

"Brand?"

He tilted his head to the side as if he didn't understand.

She was here to have sex with him. She could do this. She had to believe Brand — her friend and her lover — was somewhere inside those hate-filled eyes. Taking a deep breath, she unbuttoned her blouse and dropped it on the floor. His eyes widened.

"See anything you like?"

Chapter Four

He stared at the woman as she stripped away her clothes until she stood naked before him. The cold inside him—impenetrable and deep—sank low into his body. She was nothing to him. The blood that ran through her body would feed him. He would drain her then toss the carcass aside.

She stepped forward, her eyes watching him. All the others had pulled away but she came closer. She stopped just out of reach, beyond his touch. Her legs moved inches apart. Slowly her hands drifted down her stomach and he found himself captivated by the movement. As he watched she pushed her hand between her thighs. Her pale fingers slipped into the dark of her slit. The warm, heady fragrance of her arousal surrounded him, filtering into his body through every pore. He breathed it in. It only increased his hunger. He licked his lips, wanted that scent on his mouth, wanted to taste the spicy liquid he knew crept from inside her.

Heat radiated out of her body, centered at the peak of her thighs—heat that he suddenly wanted, needed. He roared and stretched the limits of his chain, trying to grab her. She flinched but didn't stop her seductive strokes. She dipped her fingers into her cunt, rubbing slow circles. The liquid sounds of her self-caress rang through his ears. Brand felt his chest rise and fall in long, unneeded breaths. With the air came her fire, tiny molecules floating inside him, turning the smooth edges of the cold jagged.

She pulled her hand from between her legs. The perfume of her cunt flooded the room. Eyes wide, she stretched her hand toward him.

"Want a taste?"

The desire to grab and tear the life from her body was countered by the temptation she offered. Crushing the screams inside his head that told him to destroy the weak life before him, he held out his hand, moving as slowly as he could. She stepped forward. He wrapped his hands around her wrists and pulled her closer. Her rapid pulse vibrated through his palms, inspiring his own heart to beat. It would be simple to kill her but the lure of her cunt was too great. He pulled her fingers to his mouth and closed his lips around them.

The flavor exploded on his tongue. He licked each finger clean, consuming the delicate combination of her pussy and the subtle spice of her skin. She was delicious.

"Want more?"

He raised his head and looked into her eyes. Something about her was familiar...he'd tasted her before. Eaten her pussy.

He hooked his hand around her waist and jerked her forward. A sharp cry rang through the air but he couldn't stop. He had to taste her, needed the heat hovering just inside her. The warmth of her arousal drew him. He dropped to one knee and buried his face between her thighs, delving his tongue into the wicked heat that called him. She cried out again but this time he recognized the noise as pleasure. The sound warmed a different part of his body — settling into his chest.

Spinning around, he pushed her onto the bed, spread her legs and covered her sex with his lips. He licked inside her wet opening—the warmth, the moisture was incredible. She wanted him. Desperate hunger drove him on.

She writhed in his grip and whispered his name. "Brand, please." He closed his lips around her clit and sucked, wanting the sweet juices that flowed from her cunt. She curled her legs around his back, smashing her pussy against his mouth. Drawing her clit between his lips he rubbed his tongue around the side.

Her scream echoed in his head and heat billowed down into his groin. Memories returned with the fire— the attack, Micah's rescue and the last three days of pain. *Kendra? Here?* He wanted to push her away, afraid he would hurt her, but the desire to have more of her was too strong.

He pushed his tongue back into her cunt, lapping the heady liquid flowing from her. The cold inside him retreated, pushed back by flames and hunger and human love. She groaned in response. There was no time for long, leisurely strokes, he needed more. He tilted her hips, pushing his tongue deeper, loving her with his mouth and hands. Sweetly, she came again and again. He felt alive, warm and hungry as her cries turned to whimpers. He looked up.

"Fuck me, Brand. Damn it, fuck me."

Still fully dressed and chained the wall, he pulled her legs from around his neck and climbed over her. He jerked his fly open and his cock sprang free. There was no preliminary—she was wet and open. He plunged inside, feeling the sweet saving grip of her cunt.

"Yes," he growled, riding her hard, releasing the pain and the frustration of the past three days, giving her the hard fuck he knew she loved. He didn't stop—even when she came, he kept on. He needed one more thing—one final kiss to bind his soul forever. "Kendra?" he whispered, asking her permission.

She placed her hand on the back of his head and drew him down, turning her head and baring her neck to him. "Take from me, my love," she whispered.

The final traces of cold evaporated as he placed his mouth gently against her skin.

Kendra tensed, preparing for the dark invasion. She held her breath as his fangs pierced her flesh—but there was no pain. A brief pop and he was inside her. In all ways he filled her—cleaning out the remnants of Trevor's attack, filling her mind and body with his presence. The steady pull of his mouth was sweet and tender, heightening the intense pleasure of his cock riding inside her pussy.

Come for me, baby.

With his voice in her mind, she sighed and let the final layers of tension slip from her body. It was a sweet climax flowing in rolling waves through her body, vibrating through her chest and sparking bright lights in her heart. Brand drew his hips back and penetrated her one final time. She wrapped her arms around his back and held him as he came inside her.

Hours later, when Brand finally seemed done with her body, he pulled out of her and rolled to the side. The chain binding him to the wall clinked against the bedframe. After the first time, when he'd returned to himself, Brand had shredded his pants to remove them but hadn't had the strength to free himself completely from the chain.

"What are you doing here?" he asked.

"Uh, making love to you?"

The answer seemed obvious to her and earned her a smile. "I meant how did you get here?"

"Micah came for me. Said you'd been hurt."

"I could have hurt you."

"You'd never hurt me," she said, feeling the truth of her words as she spoke them. "You promised."

Joy flared in his eyes. He leaned forward, Kendra stretched up to meet him.

The door burst open and slammed hard against the wall. Kendra yelped and grabbed the sheet. She didn't know who was coming in but no way in hell was anyone else going to see her naked. Vampires or not, she still had that five — no, ten — extra pounds to lose.

Trevor stepped through the door, Kendra's wooden stake clutched in his right hand. Blood dripped from the tip. Kendra promptly forgot about her body issues.

"Hello, brother," he said.

"Brother?" she asked.

"We're all brothers of the blood."

"I'm not your brother in any manner," Brand said, disdain saturating his words.

Trevor shrugged but there was an evil glee in his eyes. "Then you'll be dead. Those are your choices. I gave the same choice to the others. They seemed to think death was preferable. I have no preference, of course." He pointed the stake at Brand. "You first and then I get to see why this woman is so enjoyable."

"Leave her the hell alone."

Trevor laughed and Kendra felt the sound deep inside her. It made her sick that she was connected to him in some way, that he'd actually placed his teeth on her.

Brand stood, his right leg still chained the wall, his naked body loose and limber as he prepared for Trevor's attack. He didn't have to wait long. Trevor lunged forward, stake held high. Brand caught the downswing of Trevor's arm but couldn't halt his momentum. Both men slammed into the wall. They slid to the ground and began to struggle.

A vampire fight, she discovered, wasn't much different than a human one, just more vicious. Fists and feet were aided by claws and fangs. Brand seemed to be keeping Trevor close, not giving him a chance to use the stake for its intended purpose. Streaks of red appeared on both men's throats. Brand's chest was dotted with blood. The sight jolted her from her immobility. She jumped off the bed—the sheet clutched around her body—and searched for a weapon, some way to help Brand.

She ran to the door. Micah lay flat on his back in the outer room, a gaping hole in his chest. Her stomach turned in a sick roll. She heard noises of a fight upstairs but didn't know who would be the victor and didn't dare call out for help.

She raced back into the room, determined to help Brand, even if she had to claw at Trevor herself. Even as she thought the words, Brand snarled like a wild beast and flung Trevor across the room. The other vampire hit window hard—cracking the safety glass before sinking to the floor.

Her relief lasted only a moment before he was back on his feet. He turned from Brand and grabbed her. Trevor wrapped one arm around her neck and jerked her to his side. Brand lunged forward but the chain held him back.

Trevor laughed but the sound was forced. He wasn't as confident as he wanted to appear.

"Let's have a look at your little morsel." He grabbed the sheet and stripped it down. A cold shiver that had nothing to do with room temperature ran down her back. "Nice—and is she a good fuck?" He smirked as he stroked the base of her throat. "Does it just fry you that I had her first? And that I'll have her last?"

Brand's growl shook the broken window. His eyes were blood-red. He bared his teeth and stepped forward. The chain stopped him again. Trevor laughed. Brand didn't stop. He pulled. The links of the chain stretched. The slow creak of metal breaking filled the room. With a sharp snap, he was free.

Trevor dropped Kendra and jumped clear but Brand was on him, nailing him to the floor.

The hollow clank of wood hitting cement shocked Kendra into moving. Trevor had dropped the stake. Not giving herself time to think, she grabbed the wooden pole. The two men struggled and rolled until Trevor was on top. He lifted his head, baring his fangs, and started downward toward Brand's throat. She raised her hand and buried the stake in Trevor's back.

He shuddered, his body convulsing as he screamed— the mournful sound of a soul dying. Brand pushed the flailing vampire away and dragged himself up to standing. Kendra sensed him beside her but couldn't pull her eyes away from Trevor's body as it twitched one final time. Her stomach did a slow, steady roll and she knew she was going to lose her dinner. The long wooden stake stuck out of Trevor's back. She couldn't stand to look at it.

Without thinking, she reached out, ready to pull it out.

"Don't." Brand's fingers wrapped around her wrist with enough force to make her wince. "First rule of vampire killing, leave the stake in. It's the only way to make sure they really stay dead."

She nodded. "Hopefully, I won't have to ever do that again."

"If ever there was a vampire who deserved it...it was Trevor."

"Yeah, besides, he saw me naked." She grimaced and glared at Brand. "For that alone I would have had to kill him."

"Does that mean we're all at risk?"

Kendra spun around. Marcus waited with a smile, blood smeared across his white shirt. He looked dangerous. Deadly. And she had no doubts that this man was the vampire leader. Suddenly feeling very vulnerable, she reached down and dragged the sheet up, covering her breasts.

"Is Micah dead?" she asked, remembering his body in the hall, the huge hole in his chest. Admittedly she'd planned to screw up his investments but she didn't want him hurt.

"Yes. Has been for some two hundred years."

Kendra glared at the vampire leader. He seemed to find that amusing.

"But from this most recent wound, he should recover. He just needs some blood…and a little sex to help him heal." Marcus raised his eyebrows. "Willing to offer your assistance to him as well?"

"Eww, no."

"Micah can find his own woman. This one belongs to me." Though there was laughter in Brand's voice, she heard the conviction as well and a delicate shudder ran down her spine. Belonging to Brand. What did that entail?

Marcus nodded and began to pick blood from beneath his fingernails. "Are you going to Turn her?"

"Turn? As in make me a vampire?" She whipped around, almost dropping her sheet. Brand stared back at her with a bright light in his clear eyes.

"You don't have to, baby." He put his hand on her shoulder. "We'll talk about it. Give you a chance to get used to the idea."

"Yes, but—"

Brand grabbed her close and kissed her, further scattering her mangled thoughts. She was vaguely aware of being guided backward and the soft mattress catching their weight as they fell. When Brand finally let her up for air, her head was spinning and she was flat on her back. The sheet had disappeared and Brand was kneeling between her legs, his cock pressed against her sex. She didn't quite know how she came to this position but she heartily approved of it.

"Don't worry about the future right now," he whispered as he slipped inside her.

"Marcus?" She struggled to sit up, afraid the other vampire was still watching them.

"Long gone. It's just you and me."

She looked at the floor. Trevor's body was gone as well. That eased one bit of tension. She glared at the two-way mirror. "There'd better not be anyone watching through that window," she growled.

Brand rocked his hips, shallow penetrations that rubbed the inside of her pussy with deep intensity, and her worries disappeared. It didn't matter who the hell was watching, as long as Brand kept doing that.

Their loving was slow and long. Each time she came close to orgasm, Brand would back off. The rise and fall pattern drove her insane, her body was screaming for release and exhaustion was threatening.

"Brand please, let me come." She opened her eyes and saw the sweat on his forehead. How much sex did it take to make a vampire sweat?

"Soon."

"No, now." She grabbed his face and forced him to look at her. "We might have a future together and I'm pretty sure I love you, but if you don't let me come, I'm going to stake you."

The threat added a sparkle of laughter to his eyes.

"Well, we can't have that."

As if he knew she was verging on being too sore to fuck, he reached between their bodies and tickled her clit with his finger as he slowly pumped inside her. The gentle touch triggered massive waves of tension bursting from inside her pussy. Brand's groan quickly followed as he came.

What seemed like hours later, the universe righted itself and Kendra lifted her head off Brand's chest.

"About this whole becoming a vampire thing."

"I wouldn't have brought it up but Marcus did."

Her heart dropped like stone. "You don't want me to become a vampire?"

"No, I do." The sincerity in his voice and eyes was unmistakable and her blood began to flow normally again. "But you've had a few shocks in the past few days, I didn't think you were ready for this as well."

She considered the idea. "And I'd stay exactly the way I am?"

"Yes."

"Well then, we definitely need to wait because if I'm going to stay this way, I need to lose five pounds, no, ten would be better. I don't want to go through eternity with this much extra cushion on my ass."

Brand laughed. "I happen to like the extra cushion on your ass."

"Right." Men just said that. Then Brand squeezed her butt in his big hands and she thought that maybe he wasn't kidding.

"But it's definitely something you need to think about. It's a major decision. There's no going back. Besides…" He paused and there was a wicked tone to the silence. "You'd have to give up donuts."

She pushed up, using his chest for leverage. "Give up donuts? All donuts? Even Donnie's?" He nodded. She snagged her lower lip between her teeth and stared at him.

"You're actually considering it." Brand wrapped his arms around her and rolled her under him. "If you're willing to give up donuts for me—it must be love."

Kendra smiled. "Must be."

About the author

Tielle (pronounced "teal") St. Clare has had lifelong love of romance novels. She began reading romances in the 7th grade when she discovered Victoria Holt novels and began writing romances at the age of 16 (during Trigonometry, if the truth be told). During her senior year in high school, the class dressed up as what they would be in twenty years — Tielle dressed as a romance writer. When not writing romances, Tielle has worked in public relations and video production for the past twenty years. She moved to Alaska when she was seven years old in 1972 when her father was transferred with the military. Tielle believes romances should be hot and sexy with a great story and fun characters.

Tielle welcomes mail from readers. You can write to her c/o Ellora's Cave Publishing at 1337 Commerce Drive, #13, Stow, Ohio 44224.

Also by Tielle St. Clare

Close Quarters
Dragon's Fire
Dragon's Kiss
Dragon's Rise
Enter the Dragon anthology
Irish Enchantment anthology
Just One Night
Simon's Bliss

Demon's Fall

Margaret Carter

Chapter One

Malice lurked within the scrawny man's brain. Sensing that malice from his position just inside the door that opened onto the homeless shelter's parking lot, Karl Engel visualized it as a snake. It needed only a light prod to make it inject venom into its host and spur him into action. Applying that prod wasn't Karl's job. Other forces performed that function. His job was to spring to the rescue of the host's intended victim at the strategic moment.

In the shabby reception room of the House of Bread, he held the door for Erin Collier, the potential lady in distress. The other four-to-midnight volunteers had already gone home, leaving Karl to escort Erin, one of two paid staff members on that shift, to her car. At twelve o'clock on a summer night, the lot was empty of people, although music and laughter from a bar in the next block drifted on the humid breeze. Erin brushed a lock of her short, honey-blonde hair back from her forehead and smiled up at Karl. Her jasmine perfume teased his nose.

He welcomed that fragrance, mingled with her moist female scent, as one of the compensations of occupying a human body. By the Dark Powers, there were plenty of negatives to offset the few positives! This shell of flesh required nutrition, water and sleep, and it performed distasteful functions such as digestion. Not that he didn't enjoy some kinds of food, such as the steamed blue crabs Erin had taught him to crack for their meat or the homemade fudge she sometimes brought for dessert at the shelter. If only his body didn't have to handle those treats in such a crude way. On the other hand, it responded with a pleasant stirring of the blood to Erin's lushly curved shape. He edged closer to her, letting her aroma and the glow of her aura override one of the negatives, the odor of garbage from the dumpster at the side of the building. He wasn't sure he'd have been able to endure wearing a human body and senses if he hadn't had the power to escape from them by turning ethereal now and then.

His night-adapted eyes caught sight of another figure trudging toward them on the sidewalk, a woman. No, more like a girl, he decided, in her late teens at most. He watched her with mild annoyance, hoping she wouldn't throw off the timing of the planned confrontation. Thin except for her rounded abdomen, she wore jeans, sandals, a ragged sweatshirt voluminously too big for her, and a backpack. Uncombed brown hair straggled to her shoulders.

She planted herself in front of Karl and Erin. "Do you work here? I need a place to stay."

Erin gave the girl's shoulder a brief pat. "I'm sorry, the shelter's been closed for hours. You come back tomorrow, hon—what's your name?" Her strong alto resonated through Karl's bones like organ music. One of the few pleasures of volunteering at this refuge for outcasts was listening to her lead the "clients", as she called them, in song after dinner each evening.

"Lisa," the girl mumbled. "I'm going to have a baby."

A smile flitted across Erin's lips. "Yes, I see." She dug into the purse slung over her left shoulder and pulled out a handful of twenty-dollar bills. "This should cover a room at the Thrift-Inn. It's just half a mile that way, and the street's well lit." With a wave, she indicated a northward direction past the closed restaurants, strip malls, and car dealers. "Come back tomorrow when I start my shift at four, and we'll see about getting you some help." She pressed her business card into Lisa's hand.

"Uh, sure, thanks." Looking a bit stunned, the girl stuffed the card and money into a pocket and turned to walk up the road.

As soon as Lisa reached the next intersection, Erin said in a low voice, "Maybe I should have offered her a ride. But we're not supposed to get personally involved with the clients."

Slipping his arm around her waist, Karl said, "You don't consider giving her money getting involved? Do you really expect to see her again?" The brush of her hip against his made his loins tighten, a pleasant but unnecessary distraction at the moment.

She raised her chin defiantly and glowered up at him from the foot of difference between their heights. "Yes. I don't share your low opinion of the human race."

With another appreciative sniff of her perfume, he began, "As you've told me many times in—"

Another smell intruded, beer and stale sweat. The thin, unshaven man who'd been lingering in the parking lot sidled up to Karl and Erin as they started toward Erin's car. Karl congratulated himself on timing their exit well. It wouldn't have done for the attack to occur inside the shelter, where someone on the midnight-to-eight shift might have interfered with his heroics.

Erin paused at the sight of the scrawny man, who tried to claim a bed at least four nights a week and had to be turned away an average of half the time. His weathered skin and bird's nest of gray-streaked hair made him look older than his probable fifty years. "Mr. Weiss, you know the rules." Karl read a suppressed sigh of exasperation in her mind. She folded her arms and continued in a sympathetic but firm tone. "You know the shelter closes for the night at nine, and you know you're not allowed if you've been drinking, anyway."

"Aw, come on, Ms. Collier, can't you give me a break for once?"

"You have to give yourself one first. Come back tomorrow afternoon, and we can talk about getting you into rehab again." She kept walking.

Not for the first time, Karl wondered how she could maintain such a good-humored tone. It wasn't faked, either. Underneath the layer of impatience and fatigue, she felt sincere compassion for this worthless specimen. Given permission, Karl would have stopped the man's heartbeat without a second thought. But killing human beings outright was one thing his side wasn't allowed to do, a restriction that baffled him. Didn't millions of them die every year through disease and natural disasters? Who'd miss a few more?

Weiss shuffled in front of them to block the way to the car. "Then gimme money for a motel, like you did that pregnant kid." His tone shifted from whiny to surly.

"Sorry, I can't do that. It's warm out tonight. You won't freeze. We'll talk tomorrow afternoon."

Karl marveled at the lack of fear in her voice. No wonder he hadn't yet been able to fulfill his mission of persuading her to quit her job on the shelter's staff. She was insane, more so than the rest of these hairless bipeds.

At least she had sense enough to realize Weiss, unlike the girl, would squander any cash she gave him on a bottle rather than a room.

When Erin stepped sideways to walk around him, the drunk made a grab for her arm. "Don't blow me off, lady."

Karl's hand lashed out and slammed down on Weiss's forearm in a sharp chopping motion. With a wordless snarl, Weiss stumbled backward. Karl smelled the miasma of demon-spawned anger clouding whatever rational thought processes the man had left. Not true possession, but unnatural influence, as Karl had expected. Weiss pulled out a pocket knife and unfolded it with tremulous fingers.

Erin emitted a spike of fear, quickly suppressed. When Weiss jabbed the blade in the air and snatched at her purse, though, she didn't retreat. Recognizing his chance, Karl leaped between Erin and the attacker. Instead of letting Karl shelter her behind him, to his astonishment, she shoved him out of the way.

"No, he won't hurt me. Mr. Weiss, give me that knife." She held out her hand.

The ploy might have worked if the man's brain hadn't been clogged with more than alcohol. After a shocked pause, he lunged at her again.

This time Karl didn't give her a chance to interfere. He slapped the knife out of Weiss's hand to clatter onto the pavement, knocked him facedown, and knelt on the middle of his back. "Erin, call the police."

"No, Karl." Now her voice trembled, and he scented fear on her skin. "Another arrest on his record won't do him any good. Take the knife and let him go."

"Have you lost your mind? He'll just come after you again." Karl leaned his weight harder on Weiss, who thrashed under him and alternately groaned and cursed.

"He won't do that when he sobers up. Please, I've got more experience with this kind of thing than you have."

"That's why you jumped in front of a weapon? Your psychology degree makes you invulnerable?" Although the encounter had ended just the way Karl had planned, he couldn't help feeling outraged at the way Erin had thrown herself into danger and still exhibited sympathy for this halfwit who might have sliced up both of them. With a baffled shake of his head, he stood up to let Weiss scramble to his feet. "You heard Ms. Collier. Get moving."

The demonic influence seeped away from Weiss's brain, leaving him muddled and frightened. He flung a confused glance at each of them in turn, then shambled into the darkness. Karl picked up the weapon and folded the blade. He could still hardly believe Erin had tried to shield him as if he were the one in danger.

When she took a step toward him, though, he noticed her legs quivering with the aftershock of the encounter. He dropped the knife into a side pocket, closed the distance between them in a couple of strides, and drew her into his arms. Her head rested on his chest, her cheek pressed to the front of his shirt. The strategic moment had arrived. Surely this time she'd listen to his rationale for resigning from the shelter job, even if he had to seduce her over to his viewpoint, a prospect he anticipated with pleasure as well as curiosity.

* * * * *

Shaking, Erin wrapped her arms around Karl's waist. His firmly muscled body provided a welcome pillar to lean on. Now that the crisis had ended, belated fear washed over her. Mr. Weiss had never before done anything to hint he was remotely dangerous. She could still hardly believe he'd threatened her. The steady thump of Karl's heart under her ear calmed her own breathing and pulse. One of his hands stroked her hair, while the other traced circles in the middle of her back. She felt his lips brush the top of her head. "Are you all right?" His faintly accented voice rumbled in his chest, creating vibrations that resonated through her bones.

She nodded. His fingers inched under her hair to massage the nape of her neck. Tilting her head back, she searched his face in the light from the streetlamp. His eyes, ice-blue in daylight but heavily shadowed now, scanned her with concern and possibly more. He dropped a light kiss on her forehead. Her breath caught in her throat. His fingers glided around her neck and along her jawline to cup her chin.

When he dipped his head lower to kiss her, she was ready. For over a month he'd shown up to volunteer every night that she was on duty at the shelter. Few people who donated the lavish sums of money Karl contributed would bother to put in so many hours of personal service, too. She'd wondered whether his hovering around her meant anything more than the casual interest of a man new in town, wanting companionship. His mouth exploring hers answered that question. She parted her lips to welcome the dart of his tongue. Warmth radiated from every point where the two of them touched, spreading over her like a silken cloak. Delicious tingles danced from her lips to her nipples and the pit of her stomach. Heat pooled between her legs. She caught herself shifting position to mold her body to Karl's.

His growing erection pressed against her. With a gasp, she opened her mouth wider to thrust her tongue boldly into his. When he copied the gesture, a low growl sounded in his throat. She clutched the back of his shirt and rubbed her breasts against his chest. One of her hands strayed upward to explore his thick, black hair the way she'd secretly wanted to for weeks. It felt like the winter pelt of a furbearing predator. Soft mewling noises escaped from her. She imagined his shaft plunging into her sheath the way his tongue lashed in and out of her mouth.

His hand slid down her back to clutch her bottom. When one finger slipped into the cleft between her buttocks, caressing through her skirt and panties, the zap of lightning to her core jolted her awake from the sensual trance. *Good grief, what am I doing?* She tore her mouth away from his, shifted her grip to his shoulders, and pushed a few inches back to create a gap between their bodies.

"Erin, please—" Need roughened his voice. His hands roamed up and down her back as if he couldn't get enough of touching her.

It had been so long since any man had hungered for her that she almost weakened again. But she'd known Karl only six weeks. When his fingers spanned her rib cage on each side and his thumbs wandered to the lower curves of her breasts, she grasped his wrists to stop him. Never mind that her nipples peaked in anticipation. "Sorry. I shouldn't have let that happen." She could hardly catch her breath enough to gasp out the words.

Though his eyes still smoldered, he let go of her and took a step backward. "No, I should apologize for taking advantage of the situation. Let me drive you home. Your car will be safe here for one night. I don't think you should be alone."

"Really, I'm okay now." She brushed a lock of hair off her damp forehead. Her hand still trembled, she noted with annoyance.

"Please. I'd lie awake worrying otherwise." He added with a wry smile, "I promise not to force myself on you."

She hoped he couldn't see the blush that heated her face. "Okay, I accept the offer." She had to admit to herself that driving home alone didn't appeal to her. Not only that, she didn't want to separate from him so abruptly.

His fingers rested lightly on her elbow to guide her to his car. He drove a Mercedes two-seater, not a surprise considering what little she knew about him. Buckling herself into the passenger seat, she inhaled the aroma of leather and sighed with pleasure when the air conditioner blasted coolness onto her sweat-dampened arms.

She knew Karl had come originally from somewhere in central Europe, had moved to the United States and made a fortune in some kind of dot-com business, and now lived in affluent leisure with occasional consulting to keep him busy. Whenever she'd probed for more specifics, he'd changed the subject. Not much background information to base a relationship on. For all she knew, he might have made his money in organized crime instead of software. She laughed to herself at that notion. Contrary to the Hollywood image of the mob boss with a heart of gold, she doubted the typical man in that subculture gave five-figure donations to homeless shelters.

As the car pulled onto the nearly deserted street, she gave him directions to her place. "What in hell's name possessed you to jump in front of that knife?" His obvious frustration added an edge to the demand.

"I didn't want him to hurt you."

"Well, we have something in common. I didn't want him to hurt you, either." He shook his head in apparent despair over her recklessness.

"I don't think he would have. I probably could've talked him down. But he doesn't know you. He might have tried to cut your throat." She swallowed a lump of unexpected fear. "I can't believe I just said that. It's not like him. I wonder what came over him."

Karl shrugged. "Drugs, perhaps?"

"As far as I've seen, his drug of choice has always been booze, nothing illegal."

"Whatever the cause, now you understand why I walk you to your car whenever I can. I hate to see you putting your safety at risk. I care about you."

Erin cast a quick glance at him, then turned to the dark side window. Self-consciousness battled with a tinge of wistful pleasure at his claim of caring. He couldn't mean much by that, not on such short acquaintance. "You're exaggerating about the safety thing. I've been doing this for five years."

"Why?"

The vehemence of the single-word question startled her. "What do you mean?"

"I've wondered ever since we met." The car turned off the commercial strip into the tree-shadowed neighborhood where she lived. "You have a doctorate in psychology. You gave up private practice to work at a soup kitchen, with a drastic cut in income."

"Not soup kitchen, interdenominational ministry to the homeless." A tiny smile quirked her lips. She'd corrected him on the "soup kitchen" terminology many times. "I also gave up the hassle of an hour's drive into Washington every day, not to mention the stress of dealing with clients one on one. And I gained the satisfaction of making a real difference."

Karl stopped the car at the curb in front of her house, a two-story fixer-upper in an aging neighborhood ten minutes from the shelter's location. After four years, she still spent part of every weekend on the "fixing" projects that had come with the low mortgage. "I suspect you didn't live here when you worked in the Washington group practice."

"No, and I like this place just fine compared to the overpriced condo I sold when I took the salary cut." She unbuckled her seat belt and reached for the door latch.

"Allow me." He got out and walked around to open the door for her.

Wow, I can't remember the last time that happened. She thanked him and stepped out. When he took her hand to escort her up the sidewalk, a shiver trickled up her arm.

"Seriously," he said, "why did you take on the task of saving the world one derelict at a time? And why didn't you have Weiss hauled off to jail? It can't be just abstract idealism."

She waited until they stepped onto the porch before she answered. "You're right, it isn't just that. My younger brother died five and a half years ago. Killed himself in a one-car crash while he was drunk." She closed her eyes to blot out the momentary flashback to the night she'd received the phone call about the accident. "With both our parents dead, I tried to take care of him. I failed."

Karl put his arm around her shoulders and kissed her on the forehead with butterfly-wing gentleness. "I'm sorry. But I'm sure you didn't fail him."

She blinked moisture out of her eyes. "You're right, of course. That's what I would tell a client who felt the same way. But it was such a waste. He was a brilliant artist. He had gallery shows, made sales, got some good reviews. He was also an alcoholic, and every time he started getting his life together, he'd go back to drinking and wreck it again. Other people just looked at the multiple DUIs and wrote him off as a loser. They were wrong." Her own vehemence surprised her. She modulated her voice to a calmer tone. "That's why I'm a little more tolerant of people like Mr. Weiss than you are."

"I see your motivation, but I suppose I'll never understand it, not on an emotional level." He drew her closer to him in a side-by-side hug rather than a full frontal embrace. "Surely after five years you've done enough, though? Think of all the good work you could accomplish if you reentered private practice. And you wouldn't have to worry about getting attacked with sharp objects on the street at midnight."

With a humorless laugh, Erin said, "You don't have firsthand experience with the life of a therapist, do you? Dangerous clients pop up in pinstriped suits and high-rise condos, too, not just on the streets."

"But you'd be working in a building with full-time security, no doubt." He cupped her chin to make her look up at his face. His fingers felt hot on her throat, yet the touch made her shiver. "Won't you consider resigning?

I'll donate enough to pay a year's salary for two staff positions in place of your one."

Her eyes widened in shock. He couldn't possibly mean that. "Why on earth would you make that offer?"

Karl's thumb stretched to trace the outline of her mouth. She fought the impulse to dart her tongue out and lick the trespassing digit. "I told you, Erin, I care what happens to you. I want you safe and happy. It's not as if I'd miss the money. I have more than I know what to do with."

"I am happy." Only half-aware of what she did, she swayed toward him. Her breasts grazed his chest. The friction on her nipples through the layers of cloth made them harden and tingle.

"Are you? Completely?" His low voice made her nerves quiver.

She nodded. The question echoed in her head, though. She was happy with her work, despite the low pay, long hours, and constant scrounging for funds and supplies. It satisfied her more than her therapist career ever had. Yet maybe her happiness needed some other element to make it complete. Maybe she needed someone in her life besides friends, co-workers, and clients. It wouldn't hurt to experiment, would it? She turned in his arms to face him directly and press her body to his. Standing on tiptoe, she planted a kiss on the side of his neck. He smelled like spices, cinnamon and nutmeg with a slightly burnt tinge, like no cologne or aftershave she'd ever encountered.

He responded with a startled intake of breath. He leaned over her, his hands splayed across her back to hold her tight against him, and captured her parted lips. With a sigh, she melted into him. His tongue flickered in and out of her mouth, teasing the corners and skimming over her teeth, and she retaliated. She wanted to rub all over him like a kitten, wrap herself around him and draw him inside. She hadn't wanted anything of the kind in so long that she felt dizzy with delight. Her fiancé had broken up with her in the anguish and upheaval after her brother's death. He'd taken a dim view of her "obsession" with helping "losers", too. Since then, she hadn't risked anything more than friendship with males who crossed her path. *I'm alive after all!*

That didn't mean she intended to jump into bed with Karl on the first kiss, no matter how yummy he smelled and tasted. For one thing, she knew in the back of her mind that adrenaline fueled the heat sizzling in the pit of her stomach. People often reacted to the aftermath of danger with arousal. The tickle in her nipples and clit and the molten liquid between her thighs didn't justify leaping into a casual fling. Not even if his rigid shaft nudging her lower abdomen assured her that he would join her between the sheets in a heartbeat.

With a sigh, she broke off the kiss, turned her face aside, and wiggled out of his embrace. "Time to say goodnight."

He clenched his fists at his sides and took a couple of deep, shuddering breaths. "Yes. I know. Listen, Erin, won't you consider what I said? Resigning from the shelter? In fact, I'd rather you didn't even go back tomorrow afternoon. Who knows what Weiss might do next? You said yourself that he acted out of character. Suppose he's becoming unstable?"

Shaking her head, she fumbled in her purse for the house key. "No way, Karl. I'm touched and even sort of flattered that you're so worried about me, really I am. But this is my work. It's my life now. Don't bother trying to talk me out of it. We'd only get into a useless fight." She squeezed his hand and brushed a light kiss on his chin, too swiftly for him to take advantage of the opening or for her to succumb to the temptation of starting all over. She hurried inside and bolted the door, her head still buzzing with the excitement and strangeness of the past half hour.

She headed straight for the bedroom and peeled off her clothes. The friction of the cloth made her skin itch, her nipples and clit ache. Five years of celibacy could explain the invisible ants using her nerves for a freeway interchange, but physical frustration couldn't account for the temptation to invite Karl into the house, maybe into her bed.

Again she reminded herself how little she knew about him. Rich men seeking charity tax write-offs weren't unusual, but rich men who also stood behind a counter serving dinner to street people were. Boredom? Guilt for some past transgression? Turning on the shower and waiting for the water to heat up, she giggled aloud at that thought. Karl looked less guilt-ridden than any man she'd ever met. "Arrogant" targeted his description much more accurately. Not to mention slightly weird. Despite his excellent English, he treated ordinary elements of local culture as mysterious novelties. When she'd once invited him to an early dinner at a casual seafood restaurant, for example, he'd acted as if he'd never seen a crab before in his life. Well, granted, lots of newcomers to Maryland had problems with dismembering crabs. But she'd seen him face an Italian sub and a mocha latte with almost the same degree of mixed bewilderment and delight.

Maybe he'd turned the homeless shelter into a full-time avocation to stay near her? That crazy offer to pay for two positions in place of hers certainly hinted at personal interest. With another man, she would have suspected a joke, but Karl had less visible sense of humor than anyone she'd ever met.

Erin stepped into the shower, her skin tingling with more than the spray of hot water. What woman wouldn't feel excited by the idea that a man would go to so much expense and trouble to get acquainted with her? She coated her palms with liquid soap and swirled it over her breasts and stomach, imagining his hands tracing the same path. *Crazy woman, building a fantasy out of a couple of kisses. Pathetic.* She massaged her mound and inner thighs, while her clit twitched with impatience. Lust was clouding her judgment, she decided. Two mature people didn't find soul-mates in each other so quickly. Well, lust she could fix.

She angled the shower hose at her chest and sprayed each breast in turn. Her nipples pebbled up, welcoming the fine needles of hot water. Her clit pulsed to the frantic strokes of her soap-slicked fingers. She leaned against the tiled wall, head thrown back, panting, while her sheath rippled with the contractions of her climax. After her heartbeat slowed and she caught her breath, she rinsed off, then stepped out to towel herself dry. Her eyes drooped with exhaustion. *There, lust all gone. For now.* She tried not to hear the voice that whispered another word, *loneliness.*

Chapter Two

Karl stalked to his car, threw himself into the driver's seat, and clenched his fingers on the steering wheel. Damn the blasted woman to the deepest abyss! Why wouldn't she pay attention to him?

He took a few long breaths to steady himself before he started the motor and pulled onto the street. He didn't mean that curse, of course. He didn't want to harm Erin in any way. In fact, what he advised was for her own good. He wanted her happy. He wanted more than that, in fact.

Dark Powers, I want her for myself! His pulse pounded in his temples. His own desire appalled him. He'd planned to use passion and physical need to weaken her resistance to his argument, not cloud his own mind. Yet his muscles ached with tension and his penis, engorged with blood, wouldn't let him focus on anything but plunging inside Erin's soft, moist body to relieve the pressure.

Damned inconvenient fleshly impulses. He wasn't an incubus. That role belonged to lower spirits, scarcely sentient, not a tempter of refined intellect like himself. So why did he suddenly feel such urgent need for sexual relief? Since taking on human form, he hadn't experienced sexual intercourse, though he'd anticipated trying the act with Erin if his mission required. His only release had occurred in sleep, with the humiliating involuntary discharge of excess fluids that his reproductive organs occasionally required. How would it feel to share that experience, fully conscious, with Erin?

He shouldn't be thinking of that scenario. He should be planning the next stage in his strategy, considering how to persuade her to quit the shelter before the critical hour arrived. While he didn't know exactly when that crisis would occur, he knew it would happen soon.

In all honesty, though, he realized he had little hope of undermining her resolution. He'd read her mind while they argued. She had no intention of leaving her current position. Incredibly, she actually enjoyed the work and liked most of the shabby people she interviewed, found beds for, and served meals to.

Not only that, she had risked her life in a harebrained attempt to protect him from Weiss. Karl laughed aloud at the absurdity of it. That fragile human female had tried to protect him, when in fact Weiss's blade couldn't have done him any permanent harm even if it had sliced his jugular. Karl would have needed only to turn ethereal for a minute, and upon reverting to solid form he would have been completely healed.

He sobered instantly when he remembered the alarm he'd read in her mind, the concern for him. She cared about him, enough to forget her own safety.

He shook his head, trying to banish these weakening thoughts. Didn't she care about all those waifs and strays at the shelter, too? The action meant nothing more than her serving soup and bread to the homeless did. Except that her passionate kisses hinted otherwise. She didn't make a habit of flinging herself into men's arms. He'd read that in her mind, too.

A sphere of violet light descended on the car. With a muffled curse and a squeal of tires, he braked and pulled into the parking lot of a closed office building. Why didn't the messenger take the trouble to understand the limitations of flesh and matter?

"Kammael." His true name echoed around the inside of the car and resonated through his bones. He bowed his head in acknowledgment.

"You performed your role and pretended to rescue the woman."

Karl/Kammael nodded. The infernal Powers, of course, watched him constantly. They didn't need to be told the outward result of Weiss's attack. What they wanted was Karl's perception of Erin's reaction. "What of the woman?" the voice asked.

He didn't have to consider the question for long. "I read her mind closely while I tried to persuade her to leave her current position. Her refusal was heartfelt and unambiguous. I conclude there is no reasonable chance of tempting her into that course of action."

A rumble of anger underlay the next words. "Did the attack not frighten her sufficiently?"

"Her devotion overrides any fear she might have."

Tendrils like ebony smoke undulated within the glowing sphere that enveloped him. "Then we must take more direct action. All signs indicate that the critical encounter we must prevent approaches within a few hours. She must be disabled for the duration of the crisis. Soon she will be attacked and injured. Do not protect her this time."

Again he bowed his head, while keeping a tight leash on his thoughts. The Powers must not suspect how he detested this latest decree. "I understand." He kept his eyes down until the violet glow contracted to a point and vanished, leaving bright spots to dazzle his vision.

Only then did he give his thoughts free rein. That conversation had forced the truth on him. He hadn't just "pretended" to rescue Erin. He couldn't stand the thought of her getting hurt, much less maimed or mutilated. The Powers couldn't kill her, but what they might do short of death sent an icicle stabbing into his heart. Regardless of what punishment he might receive, he couldn't let that happen. He rubbed his eyes as if trying to scrub away the rebellious thoughts. They wouldn't vanish.

He would fail his first mission. Deliberately.

As a young spirit, part of the generation most recently created, he hadn't dwelt long in the celestial realm before a messenger from the infernal lords had lured him into conversation. If "long" meant anything in a dimension where time ran so differently from the hours and days of earthly cycles. He'd been warned about such temptations, of course. The Dark Powers constantly tried to recruit new subjects. Yet their message had made sense to him. Why should the human race—hairless, bipedal mammals with short, violent lives and ridiculous pretensions to intelligence—have a chance to win their way into Paradise? It seemed only rational to join the side that rejected this ludicrous project.

Of course, Karl sometimes missed the realms of light. The infernal dimensions, though, had their own somber beauty. And freedom made up for being exiled, didn't it?

Thinking of Erin's fleshly but quite real beauty and her intelligence and reckless courage shook his certainty. Almost since his first meeting with her, he'd had doubts about the dogma of humanity's utter worthlessness. Now she'd thrown herself in front of a sharp implement for him and had returned his kiss with such enthusiasm that his mouth went dry at the memory, his palms itched to caress her again, and his penis tightened against his abdomen.

Enough! He should be thinking of Erin's safety, not his body's inconvenient appetites. Dark Powers, the attack could happen any time! What if the next threat caught her at home, unprotected?

He spun the car around and turned back the way he'd come. Irrational panic made his heart race. At this hour little traffic blocked his way, so he had no trouble driving to Erin's house twice as fast as legal speed would have allowed. A wry smile twisted his lips at the image of a traffic cop trying to ticket him. He'd have zapped unconscious any policeman who'd dared to pull him over.

He found her place quiet and dark, except for the light over the porch. No sign of danger. Or had she already suffered some injury that required an ambulance to transport her to a hospital? He dashed up to the front door and mentally probed inside. He sagged against the porch rail in relief when he sensed her sleeping mind. He wasn't too late.

After three rings of the doorbell, he heard her footsteps approaching. On the other side of the door, she said in a sleep-slurred voice, "Who's there?"

Glad she had enough caution not to open the door in the middle of the night, he said, "It's I, Karl. Are you all right?"

"What are you talking about? Aside from being dragged out of bed for nothing, I'm fine."

"You're in danger. Please let me in." Just watching the front of the house wouldn't satisfy his need to protect her. He'd feel safe only if he kept her within sight constantly, or at least within earshot.

Inside, the bolt snicked back. The door opened. Erin faced him with her hands on her hips. "Karl, what on earth is wrong with you? What danger?"

His breath caught in his throat. She wore a sheer, sky-blue nightgown that highlighted the color of her eyes. Though it covered her from neck to ankles, it hid very little. In the dim light of the entryway, every curve of her body showed through the translucent cloth. He could see the dark peaks of her nipples and the circles of the areolas, and his gaze involuntarily wandered to the dark triangle visible at the base of her abdomen. Her female scent sharpened, and he heard her pulse accelerate. She folded her arms across her breasts.

"Well? What kind of danger, and how do you know?"

He realized in his panic he'd forgotten to contrive a plausible answer to that question. "Mr. Weiss," he said. "When I left here, he was lurking across the street. I didn't consciously realize I'd seen him until a few minutes ago." His fingers grazed her shoulder, evoking a visible shiver. "Let me in."

"I don't know — oh!" When he took a step closer, she placed her open palm on his chest to stop him. Yet her eyes widened and softened, and her lips remained parted. He leaned close enough to inhale her mint-scented breath.

It must have been the lure of her suppressed excitement that distracted him from the man running up the sidewalk to the porch. By the time he whirled around to face the intruder, Weiss was charging straight at them. Karl pushed Erin backward, stepped over the threshold, and turned to slam the door. Weiss barreled into it, caught Karl off balance, and shoved it open.

More than natural anger clouded the homeless man's brain this time, and more than the subtle influence that had fueled his rage for the first attack. Now true possession completely submerged his human thoughts. A low-level demon, which his resentment toward Erin had unconsciously invited, rode him. To Karl's supernatural vision, the man looked shrouded in oily smoke. He held a gun.

"Bitch," he growled. "Can't blow me off like that." The guttural tone made the words almost unintelligible.

Karl pushed Erin behind him. "Get out of here!" He heard her stumble a few steps backward, but she didn't retreat any farther. With a muttered curse, he lunged at Weiss. The gun fired.

Karl's ears rang with the blast. The next instant, he felt a hard punch to his midsection, followed by a fiery pain. *He shot me!* Instinct took over. He faded to ethereal form, floating bodilessly between Weiss and Erin. But he couldn't block the attacker from her this way. Within a few seconds, Karl forced his human body to resume its solid shape. The bullet that had hit him clattered to the floor, and the pain vanished. A scream of alarm from Erin pierced his ears. He couldn't stop to calm her now, though.

He pointed at the gun, which instantly glowed red-hot. Weiss dropped it with a shriek of agony. Next, Karl pointed at the man's chest. A miniature bolt of lightning struck him in the heart. He crumpled to the floor.

Karl's own undisciplined human heart was racing. *Unholy Powers, did I kill him?* He had no idea what would happen to an apprentice tempter who broke the law so gravely. *Of course, I suppose I'm not a tempter anymore. I just deliberately sabotaged my own mission. I don't care. Erin is more important than any of that.*

Kneeling, he touched the unconscious man's neck and listened for sounds of life. He felt a pulse, heard a heartbeat and breath.

Sometime in those few minutes, Erin had left the room and returned. Now she stood beside him, staring down at Weiss. "I've just called 911. Is he dead?"

"No."

"What did you do to him?" Her voice sounded strained, as if she could barely keep from screaming.

"Hit him lightly, that's all. He must have suffered a heart attack." He suspected medical examination would diagnose just that.

"I'm sure I saw something—like a flash of flame."

"The gun going off again, perhaps."

"It only fired once." Her stubbornness was quickly overriding her fear.

Karl sighed to himself. "Things happened very fast. You could be wrong."

"Maybe." She rubbed her eyes. "I also thought I saw you vanish."

He said with a soft chuckle, hoping she wouldn't notice how forced it was, "The eyes play tricks at moments of stress." He didn't want to have to meddle with her mind to wipe out that impression.

She gave him a hard stare. "Yeah, I guess that's what it was. After all, what else could it be?"

Placing a hand lightly on her shoulder, he said, "You need to sit down. Let's go in the living room and wait for the police."

She glanced down at herself and blushed. "After I put something on."

* * * * *

After the paramedics carried Mr. Weiss to the ambulance, and the police finished taking notes and left, too, Erin collapsed onto the couch next to Karl. Before the cops had arrived, she'd had just enough time to don panties under the nightgown and throw on a terrycloth robe over it. Even in all the turmoil, she couldn't help blushing again at the thought of what the police must have imagined. Karl's explanation of what he'd been doing here at three a.m. had sounded pretty lame.

"Are you all right?" He reached for her hand.

When his fingers curled around hers, her heart started racing all over again. She nodded. "What about you? I could have sworn he shot you right in the chest." Already the memory of those hectic moments was muddled. She knew she couldn't have witnessed what she thought she had.

Karl said with a wry smile, "Do you see any blood?" He picked up her hand and pressed it to the front of his shirt, right above the beltline.

Her cheeks burned. Sensing his gaze on the V of her robe, she felt the heat rush down her neck and over her breasts like a forest fire roaring out of control. Sudden awareness of how narrowly she'd escaped death seized her. She couldn't suppress the reckless impulse that followed. "Karl, don't leave yet. I don't want to be alone." She insinuated her fingertips between the bottom buttons of his shirt. Underneath, she touched bare skin that scorched even hotter than her own.

His smile widened to a feral baring of teeth. "Your wish is my command."

"I never heard that line from a man before." She fumbled with his buttons, inching her way up his chest. He hissed between his teeth when her fingernails grazed his skin.

"What kind of men do you listen to, then?" He untied the sash of her robe and eased one sleeve off, then the other, in slow movements that skimmed her shoulders and upper arms. In contrast to the chill of the air-conditioning on suddenly naked flesh, his touch burned. "They should beg to fulfill your desires."

"Not that I've noticed lately." With one finger, he was tracing the neckline of her nightgown. The skin of her throat and chest prickled with chills, even though it flushed hot at the same instant. "My desires—" Before she could give her brain time to catch up and rein in her body's eagerness, she leaned toward him and pressed her parted lips to his.

He opened his mouth to feed on hers. The nibbles of his teeth and flickers of his tongue ignited sparks of electricity that spiraled outward along her nerves. His hands crept up her arms to her shoulders, his thumbs caressing the outline of her collarbone on either side of the throat.

Her vocal cords vibrated with an involuntary hum. She wanted his lips farther down, on her neck. At once, he nuzzled his way down and dipped his tongue into the sensitive spot at the hollow of her throat. With trembling hands, she folded his shirt open to scrape her nails over his chest. When she pinched his firm nipples, he gasped and bit into her neck.

Not sharp enough to hurt, the pressure of his teeth made her cry out, twine her arms around him, and dig her nails into his shoulders. Her nipples tightened to aching tautness. She squirmed around to press them against his chest. *Touch them, please!* Before she could draw breath to speak her wish aloud, his hands migrated to her breasts and cupped them in his palms. His thumbs circled her nipples. His mouth traveled from her throat to her lips to catch the moan that escaped her when he lightly touched her nipples and instantly returned to tracing the outlines of the areolas.

She didn't think she could stand the unrelieved tingle another minute. *Rub the tips, now!* He instantly flicked the tight peaks. *How did he know?* She didn't care. Her brain was too fogged with delight at the strumming that made her nerves quiver. *Faster!* He stroked faster. She swung one leg over his thighs and straddled his lap. He kept kissing her, while his hands never left her breasts. *I want it bare —*

Stealing tastes of her lips all the time, he slipped her gown over her head and shrugged out of his shirt. The fine hair on his chest teased her nipples. *Lick them!* He cupped her breasts again and bent to lap one nipple, while his fingers played with the other one. Her head reeled, as if she floated in a steaming whirlpool, anchored only by his mouth and hands and the growing ache between her legs.

She rubbed her pussy on his lap. Through his slacks, she felt the hard ridge of his cock. A gush of liquid dampened her panties. She rocked, growing hotter with every glide of the wet satin over her swollen clit. The pressure built, but she couldn't find the right angle to relieve it. She moaned and dug her nails harder into Karl's shoulders.

His hand and mouth reversed position, so that his tongue lapped the right nipple while his fingers serviced the now-wet tip of the left. Meanwhile, his hips pumped in rhythm with her rocking.

"I need—" She leaned back slightly so that her slit pressed against his cock, but her clit was exposed. It felt so ready, tight enough to burst. Unable to make herself speak her need aloud, she clutched his wrist. *Do my clit, quick!*

He fingered the taut bud. It tingled so fiercely she could scarcely hold still enough to let him to caress it. *There, yes, right there, faster, don't stop!*

Somehow, his mouth continued stimulating her breast, and his other hand serviced the exposed nipple. Through his clothes, his shaft pressed into the hollow of her slit, while her clit pulsed with waves of delicious release, and his tongue and fingers flickered in perfect harmony. While the aftershocks convulsed her, he slowed his caresses to a soothing pace and moved up from her breast to kiss her until her breathing slowed enough that she could talk.

The best she could manage, though, was a dazed, "Wow."

He guided her head to his shoulder and stroked her hair. "What is your next command?"

She giggled and nipped the side of his neck. "What about your wishes?" She rubbed her pelvis against his erection.

"You know what I want." Need roughened his voice. "But only if you desire it."

"Oh, yes," she breathed. "We're just getting started. And I'm still not ready to be alone."

In a single, sudden motion, he lifted her off his lap, swung her into his arms, and stood up. Finding herself abruptly suspended several feet above the floor, she gasped and wrapped her arms around his neck. He carried her to the bedroom without asking for directions.

When he placed her in the middle of the rumpled bed, she pulled him on top of her before second thoughts could intrude. "Are you ready?" She unbuckled his belt, popped open the button on his slacks, and unzipped the fly. He hissed aloud as her fingers brushed the hard ridge inside his briefs.

"Oh, yes, I'm ready." He stroked up her inner thigh, skimmed the outer folds of her pussy, and trailed down the inside of her other leg.

She felt hollow, desperate to be filled. With both hands, she shoved his pants down his hips. She bared his cock, captured it, and somehow kept a firm grip on it through most of his hurried undressing.

A growl rumbled in his throat. He thrust into her closed hand, while he kissed her, devouring her moans. She flung her legs wide, her hips involuntarily flexing. *What are you waiting for? Come in!*

She guided him to her center. The head of his cock slowly parted her slit. It felt so slick, so hot—she'd forgotten how wonderful a man's penis felt inside her. She kneaded his buttocks while he slid into her, inch by inch, driving her to a frenzy with his teasing slowness.

She arched her back to draw him in. *Deeper, faster!* He plunged to the hilt in her tight, eager sheath. Still darting his tongue into her mouth in sync with the rhythm of his cock, he thrust into her with rising urgency, answering her silent demands with all the force and speed she craved. The hair at the root of his shaft rubbed her clit, and her nipples brushed his chest with each movement. The vibrations radiated through every nerve in her body.

Her clit started to pulse again, and seconds later her canal contracted with breath-stopping ripples. *Come on, right now!* She locked her legs around his hips. He thrust into her depths, threw his head back, and let out a wordless cry. His whole body quivered with his release. A second wave of ecstasy rushed over her.

At last the waves died away, and he relaxed on top of her, his face buried in her neck. "I've never felt anything like that," he murmured. "Never. Thank you." His voice sounded hoarse, almost as if he were suppressing tears. She stroked his hair in silence until both of them resumed breathing normally.

He lifted his head to gaze into her eyes. "I have to ask again. Will you give up this hazardous work before some other homicidal idiot attacks you?"

Indignation soured the lingering remnants of pleasure. She planted a hand in the middle of his chest and shoved. He rolled off her, onto his side. How could he make that same tired request, after what they'd shared? Didn't he understand her at all? "So that's what the last few minutes were about? Softening me up to let you run my life?"

"No, nothing like that. I'm only worried for your safety. Can't you listen to reasonable advice without hearing it as manipulation?"

"Drop it, why don't you? You already know my answer."

"Because I care about you, damn it! Can't you see that?"

Against her will, the outburst thawed her anger. "You're sweet to worry about me, but it's my life, and I have to make my own decisions."

He shook his head as if her stubbornness baffled him. "Will you at least allow me to watch over you?"

Her fingers strayed to the thick, dark hair she couldn't resist stroking. "Sure, if you can do it without driving me crazy. To start with, I'll allow you to drive me to work tomorrow afternoon, since you left my car stranded there. But right now, you should go home so I can sleep."

"So soon?"

She laughed. "I'm worn out, and I have a feeling sleep would be in short supply with you here. Besides, I haven't had a bedmate in—well, you don't need to know. I want time to get used to the idea, to think it over." He might have flooded her senses with pleasure like no other man, but the innermost door she'd locked after her fiancé's rejection stayed shut. She would have to think longer before she could consider unlocking it.

The disappointment in his eyes almost changed her mind. He didn't press the issue, though. "Very well. Until tomorrow." He raised her hand to his lips and placed a lingering kiss in the palm.

Another first, she thought while she snuggled into the covers after he walked out. She'd never experienced hand kissing before. Who'd have guessed such a simple contact could ignite sparks in her exhausted body?

Chapter Three

The sky was paling to predawn gray when Karl emerged from the house. *Sweet?* He didn't know whether to laugh or snarl. Of all the adjectives he might have applied to himself, that was the least likely.

With car keys in hand, he paused to glance at the streak of pink visible through the trees to the east. He smiled at the image of Erin lying in sated sleep, pleasured to exhaustion by his touch. He could hardly wait to repeat the experience. Her welcoming warmth had infused him with joy as incandescent as his memories of the heavenly fields.

A peal of thunder burst on his ears. The shockwave that followed slammed him to the ground. At once he recognized the blow as no natural effect. The globe of sickly violet light that enveloped him a second later confirmed that impression.

"Kammael!" The voice pierced through him like a spear of ice.

He levered himself onto hands and knees. "Yes. I disobeyed." He forced out the response in a strangled whisper.

"You betrayed your lords for a short-lived female animal."

"I'd do it again. You are no longer my lords." For the first time, he clearly realized his defense of Erin entailed just that decision. "Go ahead and destroy me."

The voice carried a hint of a sneer. "You should know we cannot destroy an immortal spirit. Worse punishment awaits you. You have cast your lot with the human race. Share it completely."

Agony seared through his blood. Doubled over with cramps, with iron bands squeezing his ribs, he couldn't even draw breath to scream. He lay curled on the sidewalk, convulsing, blinded by pain. His brain shut down.

When consciousness returned, the pain had faded to a pervasive ache of weariness. The unnatural light had vanished. The gray sky and the nearly empty street indicated that only a few minutes had passed. Karl dragged himself to his feet and looked at the space where his car had been parked. It was gone.

He staggered to the nearest street light and leaned against it. Had the infernal messenger's decree meant what it sounded like? Karl closed his eyes and visualized his flesh melting, vaporizing, healing the bruises and fatigue while he floated in incorporeal bliss.

Nothing happened. *I'm human. Permanently.* He bowed his aching head on the lamppost.

All right. Billions of people lived out human lives in reasonable contentment. With a healthy body, he was better off than most of them. Except that the disappearance of the car probably meant he'd been stripped of his condo and bank accounts, too. He'd have to become one of Erin's charity cases.

Erin. Could he face her again? Becoming fully human left him free to love her like an ordinary man, but only if he could endure lying to her for the rest of their lives. *Love? Where did that come from?* And even if he could experience human love, what kind of life could he offer her? He'd lost all the trappings of his fabricated identity. Or almost all, he realized when he fumbled in his pockets. He still had a wallet containing a driver's license and cash, but no credit cards. He laughed bitterly. Maybe he had enough money to rent a room at the Thrift-Inn while planning his future, if he wanted a future at all.

A rush of wind drove the self-pity out of his mind. With it, golden light flooded his vision. A different voice rang in his ears like a crystal chime.

"Greetings, Kammael. It has been too long, cousin."

To his surprise, he recognized that voice. The Celestial Powers had sent a friend to deliver his doom. "Israfel? What do you mean by 'too long'? In the realm of Light, all times are one."

"Nevertheless, I have missed your company since you joined the resistance."

"Kind of you to say so. Go on, strike me dead and get it over with. At least I know you'll make it quick."

The glow rippled with amusement. "I have not been sent to destroy you. I bring an invitation. You have an opportunity to win your way back to the Light."

"They would let me return? After what I've done?" The memory of the celestial fields sent a pang of longing through him. *Home!*

"If you prove your repentance by completing the rescue of Erin Collier."

"You mean she isn't safe yet?" Fear clutched his heart. If another maniac with a blade or gun attacked her, how could Karl defend her now that he'd been reduced to feeble human abilities?

"She must meet that young woman at the shelter this very afternoon, or it will be too late. That meeting was the event the infernal Powers intended you to block."

"The pregnant girl? Why?"

"She carries a child destined to be a great warrior for the Light. Without Erin Collier's guidance, she will get no proper care, and both she and the infant will die in childbirth."

Anger simmered in Karl's chest. "All this, trying to terrify Erin or possibly maim her, was just to keep her away from the shelter today?"

A chime of affirmation emanated from the light. "The infernal Powers have become desperate. They are prepared to bend the rules and launch unnatural forces against her."

"I'll do anything to keep her safe. But how can I?" He spread his fingers and stared down at his now-mortal flesh-and-bone hands.

"That, you must discover for yourself," said Israfel. "For my part, I have permission to make an exception to the rules and transport you to her side. The time is now."

The golden glow expanded to a sphere of blinding whiteness. When Karl's vision cleared, he no longer stood on the sidewalk. The walls of Erin's bedroom surrounded him.

He rose from a crouch to fully upright and turned to face her. She sat up, letting the sheet slide down to reveal her naked breasts, and rubbed her eyes. In the predawn shadows, he could make out her puzzled frown. "Karl? What are you doing back already? And how did you get in here?"

"There's another danger. I have to protect you."

"Again? That's getting habit-forming, isn't it?" she said with a lazy smile. Abruptly, her face blanked to a wide-eyed stare. She pointed, mouth open in a stunned "oh".

He wheeled around. Between him and the door, a cloud of oily smoke materialized. It coalesced into an outline the size of a man and the shape of a hunchbacked wolf with jaws like a crocodile's and eyes like red-hot coals. Karl watched it round out to three dimensions, growing more solid by the second. He could strike no blow against it until it became corporeal, but it couldn't inflict any harm before then, either. He stepped closer, determined to block it from reaching Erin, though he expected to get torn to shreds in the process.

Behind him, she found her voice. "What is that?" she spoke quietly, as if she thought she might be dreaming.

He surveyed its maw bristling with fangs and the six-inch talons on its paws. "It's a damned hellhound," he said with perfect accuracy. His heart pounded and his breath labored as if he'd run a mile.

The thing lunged. Karl threw himself at it. Slammed to the floor, he grabbed the hellhound's pointed ears and struggled to hold its jaws away from his face. Its weight crushed the air from his lungs. The blow to his head from the impact, even with a carpet cushioning the hardwood, made his ears ring and his vision go gray. The creature raked him with one of its paws. The claws ripped his shirt and scored a deep gash over his ribs. He let out an involuntary scream at the pain and felt blood flow down his side.

"Erin!" he cried. "Run! Around me—or out the window if you have to." The hellhound's strength made his arms quake with the strain of holding it off. His only advantage was that these creatures normally couldn't stay physical for long, but could he immobilize it until it reached that limit?

He pretended to relax for a second, meanwhile listening for Erin. He heard the rustle of the covers as she stood up, but she didn't move otherwise. Why didn't she escape while she had some remote chance? Throwing his weight sideways, he rolled the hellhound off him and pinned it under his body. It writhed and bayed, a keening wail that hurt Karl's ears. Despite his best effort, it squirmed onto its back and clawed him again, this time in the center of his chest. Fresh blood gushed. The burn of the laceration, though, hardly registered next to the vise that seemed to squeeze his lungs. And his grip on the thing's head was growing weaker. His arms and fingers cramped.

He caught a glimpse of Erin circling as if she planned to join the fight. "What are you doing? Go!" The wheeze in his voice alarmed him.

Still naked, she reached behind her to pull open a nightstand drawer. She plucked out a piece of jewelry, a necklace glinting silver. Karl glanced at it swinging from her right hand. A cross.

Useless against an intelligent spirit such as he'd been, as if they were vampires in a horror movie, but this low brute was another matter. She didn't dare get close enough to wield the symbol, though.

She didn't know that. Out of the corner of his eye, he saw her bend within reach of the hellhound's talons. "No, Erin, get away!"

One hind leg lashed out to claw her ankle. With a shriek, she crumpled to her knees. Karl tightened his clutch on the thing's ears and dragged its head, just turning in her direction, back toward him. Its canines sank into his throat.

Again he screamed. For an instant the pain blotted out everything else. He fought to hang onto consciousness. Then he saw Erin stab the cross into one of the beast's eyes. It emitted a howl of agony and the eye burst into flame. Karl dug his fingers into the coarse hair on either side of the thing's head, gathered all the strength he had left, and twisted its neck. Its limbs spasmed and went limp. Not trusting this sign of helplessness, he wrenched its head halfway around. It stopped moving altogether.

"Give me that," he gasped. When he held out his hand, Erin dropped the cross into it. He shoved the necklace between the creature's gaping jaws and down its throat. An odor of burning hair and flesh tainted the air.

Karl rolled off the slowly charring corpse of the hellhound. Erin knelt beside him, her leg bleeding. She didn't seem to notice the wound. With harsh sobs, she pulled his head onto her knees.

The room lit up with the same golden glow he had seen outside only a few minutes earlier. Israfel's voice reverberated like organ music. "Well done, cousin. You have completed your penance."

Karl felt healing warmth spread over his chest. "No, take care of her first."

He heard Erin draw an astonished breath when the claw mark on her leg vanished. Again the glow enveloped him. The pain evaporated and his wounds closed. A tendril of illumination touched the hellhound, which disappeared in a crimson flash.

Stunned, Erin stared into his eyes. "I'm not dreaming. That thing was real. And you're not human."

"I am now." He sat up, and they gazed at each other, not touching, within the sphere of golden light.

Israfel said, "No longer, Kammael. The infernal Powers have overstepped their bounds. They will not be allowed to interfere further. This woman will complete her task, thanks to you. You have earned your welcome into the celestial realm. Say your farewell."

He summoned up a mental image of the fields of eternal light, a memory growing dimmer the longer he wore flesh. He had it on good authority that human beings, too, could eventually enter that realm. Meanwhile, earthly life, despite all its flaws, offered joys. "I want to stay this way," he said. "Human."

The golden sphere contracted thoughtfully. "You know, you will suffer pain and disease. You will grow old and pass through death. And she might refuse you. You might live out your human span alone."

Erin's enraptured gaze gave no clue to her thoughts, and he couldn't read her mind any longer. "I'll risk it."

"Very well. You have your wish." He thought he heard amused affection in Israfel's tone. "Shall I erase her memory of these events?"

"No, if it's allowed, let her remember. Please."

"Let it be so." The light extinguished itself.

Erin stared at him blankly for another minute. Then she leaned forward into his embrace. He wrapped his arms around her, and they knelt there, with his lips brushing the top of her head and her breath warm on his neck. He felt her tears trickle onto his skin.

"What are you? Were, I mean." she said. "A demon?"

"We preferred to call ourselves the resistance."

"Then everything that happened was a setup. You were trying to tempt me away from my job. My destiny, I guess."

"Only the first time." His chest ached. He wished he could read the mood behind her words. "After that, I wanted to protect you. I refused to complete my assignment."

"And when we made love? That was part of the temptation?"

"No, it was real. I won't blame you if you can't believe that, but everything I said about caring for you was real. I just didn't know it at first."

"I believe you. Come on, hold me." She stood up, clasped his hand and led him to the bed.

* * * * *

Erin's head spun as they moved from the floor to the bed, with Karl's hand gripping hers so tightly her fingers went numb. Had she dreamed the last few minutes? No, the pain of that beast's fangs had felt too real, and so had the healing light that had bathed her. So Karl's inhuman origin must also be true, along with his choice of humanity. The apprehension in his eyes confirmed the sincerity of that choice.

She helped him out of his ruined shirt. They sat side by side, her legs tucked under her, her head on his shoulder. "You can never go back, can you?" she whispered.

"I don't want to. I have to stay near you, even if it's only to watch from a distance." His breath stirred her hair.

With a shiver, she snuggled closer to his side. "It won't be from a distance, not if I can help it." She wanted to climb all over him, wrap around him, draw him in. Strange as it seemed to feel aroused after such terror and wonder, she sensed heat spreading from his flesh to hers and uncoiling through her veins and muscles like a living creature. The locked door at her center opened. She lay back on the pillow, tugging him with her.

"Stay," she breathed into the hollow of his throat.

He hid his face against her breast. "I don't have money anymore. My background was faked. The Dark Powers obliterated it."

"They didn't obliterate your mind, did they? If you still have the knowledge they put into your brain when you took human form, you can manage. I'll help."

He looked up at her, his eyes bleak. "I won't let myself be a burden on you—"

She cut him off. "Don't think that way. We'll work it out together. Later." She ran her hand down to his waistband.

"I don't expect anything from you," he began, leaning on one elbow to gaze into her eyes.

She silenced him with a hand over his mouth. "I want you. Unless you're not up for it." Her eyes strayed to his crotch, where she glimpsed a bulge.

His tongue flicked her palm. "I'm definitely up," he said in a tone of mild surprise. "But Erin, I may not be able to satisfy you anymore."

"What do you mean?"

"Before, I was watching your emotions and sensations, reading your thoughts."

"You what?" She started to sit up.

His hand on her shoulder restrained her. "I knew exactly what kind of touching you needed. Now I won't be able to sense your desires."

A laugh bubbled up. She tamed it before it could escalate to hysterics. "How do you think ordinary men and women figure it out?" With his help, she unfastened his slacks. While he finished undressing, she stripped off her gown. A minute later, they lay side by side, naked.

She fingered his throat and the bearded roughness of his jawline. "That thing almost killed you. We almost lost our chance at love."

He drew a harsh breath. "Love?"

"That's what it's usually called when people risk their lives for each other."

A visible tremor racked him. "I do love you. And I want you." He glanced down at his erection. "My body wants yours."

A contraction rippled through her sheath. The yearning in his eyes and the tension she saw in the muscles of his arms and legs made her long to relieve him. "That's mutual." She squeezed his shoulder and skimmed down his side to the hipbone.

Draping an arm over her, he inched closer. "It feels so strange to be encased in flesh. Yet wonderful, too." His hand traced a spiral on her back and came to rest just below her waist.

Impatient, she clasped his buttocks to mold her lower body to his. His penis and testicles teased her mound. She flexed her hips to rub up and down his hardness. A moan escaped him, a sound she echoed.

"What shall I do now?" he murmured hoarsely.

"Touch my nipples like before."

With one hand, he fingered each nipple in turn, quickly coaxing them to peaks. His other hand clutched her bottom to hold her against him. She felt dizzy with need and so wet she couldn't stop squirming.

"Are you ready?" he asked, still strumming her nipples in turn with frantic speed.

"Oh, yes!"

"Good," he growled. "I can't wait much longer. My—cock needs to enter your pussy."

"Do it!" She rolled onto her back, still clasping him.

"Last time," he said hoarsely, "you wanted your clitoris caressed."

"Not now! Just come in!"

She spread her legs, and he plunged inside.

"I want to please you—" He pulled almost out, then slid in, inch by inch.

"You are." She wrapped her legs around him and forced him deeper. They found the rhythm together, each stroke heating her clit and vagina closer to the explosive point. She felt his cock growing harder, larger, filling her and pulsing with imminent release. She screamed when the convulsions seized her, and his climax instantly followed.

Long minutes later, he stirred and brushed a light kiss on her cheek.

"You see," she murmured, "being human and ordinary isn't so bad."

"I can live with it," he said, guiding her head onto his chest where she could hear his heartbeat, "if I have you to show me the way."

"Always."

The End

About the author

Marked for life by reading DRACULA at the age of twelve, Margaret L. Carter specializes in the literature of fantasy and the supernatural, particularly vampires. She received degrees in English from the College of William and Mary, the University of Hawaii, and the University of California. She is a 2000 Eppie Award winner in horror, and with her husband, retired Navy Captain Leslie Roy Carter, she coauthored a fantasy novel, WILD SORCERESS.

Margaret welcomes mail from readers. You can write to her c/o Ellora's Cave Publishing at 1337 Commerce Drive, #13, Stow, OH 44224.

Also by Margaret Carter

Dragon's Tribute
New Flame
Night Flight
Things That Go Bump In the Night II
Virgin Blood

GARDEN OF EDEN

Jaci Burton

Dedication

To Charlie—life with you is my own version of
Paradise in the Garden of Eden. I love you.

Chapter One

Eden shut down the landing system, blinking away a century of sleep. She checked each of the remaining five pods. All were in working order. They were still in stasis, their biological functions registering normal.

Over a hundred years and everything she'd known of Earth was gone, obliterated by the global meltdown from a nuclear war no one thought would ever occur.

Thankfully NASA and the United Nations had a plan. Twenty-six spaceships, each containing six people in life-sustaining pods, had been launched into orbit before the war began. Biostasis kept their bodies alive until Earth became habitable again.

Location readings indicated the other ships hadn't landed yet. She had time. Her father had left specific instructions, loaded into the ship's computer. She fought back tears, mourning his death as if it had just occurred. For her, it had.

But now there was work to do. And that work started with Adam.

Sucking in a breath of courage, she stepped to Adam's pod and stared down at his sleeping form. Only a space blanket covered his lower body, giving her a close-up view of his broad chest and shoulders and a face that was hauntingly beautiful. Strong, rugged features. Long nose, square jaw, a hint of stubble and a mouth that made her pussy wet just imagining what he could do with those full lips. Black hair that was a little too long for her taste, but it curled at the ends and she found that oh-so…sexy.

He was perfect. She'd never seen a more beautiful man before. And she hadn't expected to find him on board her ship. Her father's revelation had shocked her.

Savior? How could one man be their savior?

As a scientist she was trained to be skeptical. Her father's notes didn't make sense, yet she trusted him implicitly. What she would be required to do with Adam made her body flush with heat. Besides, Adam might not find her appealing. What was attractive about dull blonde hair, nondescript hazel eyes and a body that spent too much time in the lab and not enough in exercise? Why hadn't Father confided in her before he put her in that pod? Why hadn't he told her about Adam, about his discoveries, about their future?

She missed her father so much. Not only was he the most brilliant scientist in NASA, he was her whole life and she had gladly followed him into space research. They'd been inseparable since he'd raised her alone after her mother died. How was she going to make it without him? Why had he insisted on remaining behind, giving Adam his spot in the pod?

None of that mattered now. What was done was done and she'd put her emotions aside as her father had taught her. Emotion had no place in science. Swiping the tears from her cheeks, she zipped up her cloth jumpsuit and pressed the buttons on Adam's pod, scanning the readings as the system slowly brought him to alert status.

His biological scan was bizarre. From the readings, he should be having a stroke right now. Instead, his chest rose slowly, his respirations typical for an adult human male.

Weird. Must be a system glitch.

The pod's vacuum seal broke with a loud hiss. She grabbed the jumpsuit that had been prepared for Adam and stood beside the pod, watching for any signs of space sickness.

His breathing seemed normal, but he wasn't awake. She reached into his pod and searched for the pulse at his neck, her fingers pressing down on very hot skin.

Fever? Couldn't be. The bio-signs didn't indicate any illness. She gasped when a hand encircled her wrist. Her gaze flew to his face and she was greeted by deep pools of turquoise. His lips curled upward in a smile.

"Eden."

Her heart slammed against her ribs. "Adam. We've landed on Earth."

Still holding her wrist, he climbed out of the pod. She fought the urge to gape at his naked body, but couldn't resist as he unfolded his massive frame.

At five-foot-seven she wasn't small. But Adam was huge! At least six-four, maybe six-five, with long legs, muscular thighs and a cock so long and thick her throat went dry. She was supposed to...with *that*?! It was erect and pulsing, the mushroomed head an angry purple.

"Do I pass inspection, Dr. Mason?"

Embarrassed at being caught staring, she glanced up, her cheeks burning. "I...needed to assess you for any signs of space sickness."

"Traveling in space doesn't affect me in the least. I've done it thousands of times."

Thousands? It was hard to believe she stood in front of an alien, someone from another planet. Adam had been under her nose for two years and her father hadn't told her. Why not?

"My father left...notes."

Adam looked around the tiny space capsule and then back at her, nodding. "This place is too constricting. Let's go outside."

She handed him the jumpsuit. He took it and laid it in the pod.

"Aren't you going to get dressed?"

He rubbed her wrist with his thumb and she was certain he could feel her racing pulse. "I don't need clothes yet. No one can see me but you."

Oh, God. What had her father done to her? The way Adam looked at her was more than a little disconcerting. She'd spent all her time in labs conducting experiments and barely possessed rudimentary social skills. Like her father, she was a hermit, preferring computers and biological formulas to socializing.

After she scanned outside readings and determined the atmosphere was acceptable, Adam led her to the doorway, pushing the buttons on the pad as if he knew exactly what to do.

The hatch flew open and Eden held her breath. He lowered the stairs and stepped out first, turning and holding her hand as she came down.

She blinked at the landscape, fighting back tears at all they had lost.

Nothing but a barren wasteland. No plants, animals, buildings or people. It was as if Earth had been wiped clean, leaving nothing but a brown landscape.

"It won't be like this for long. I'll take care of it. First, I need replenishing."

They'd landed on a beach, though the sand wasn't white, it was granite black. At least the ocean looked clear and normal. Adam tugged her along and then stopped at a level piece of land near the water. "This is a good spot."

A good spot for what? She was about to ask when Adam closed his eyes. The ground rumbled under her feet, the landscape shimmering like an oasis in the desert. Emerald green grass appeared, along with palm trees and white sand. At least fifty yards of land transformed and filled with sweetly scented flowers, shrubs and trees. Her mouth hung open and she looked at Adam.

"Did you...how?"

"Yes I did and I'll explain later." His gaze turned hot, his eyes a dark, stormy blue as he shifted to face her, caressing her cheek with the back of his hand. "I need you, Eden. I'm weakening already."

Weakening? He looked fine to her. More than fine. His body hummed with life force stronger than anything she'd ever felt. Her body responded with immediate sexual arousal that swelled her breasts, heated her core and shocked the hell out of her.

"You have to help me replenish my power so I can create a new world for us. Your father explained?"

She gulped and nodded, her gaze shifting to his still-erect cock.

"Good. Because I need to fuck you right now or I'll die."

* * * * *

Adam smiled at the wary look on Eden's face. He'd wanted her from the first time he saw her. But Dr. John Mason had refused, saying she wasn't ready yet. So he'd waited, allowing John to experiment on him. Waited two long years while he and John developed their plan. John taught him everything about Earth's science, about war and global weaponry. He taught Adam Earth's language, though Adam was particularly enthralled by the curse words, much to John's chagrin.

Adam had assisted with the blueprints for the space pods, making sure they'd contain all the necessary equipment to remain functional as long as necessary.

John had received all the credit for the breakthrough biostasis discoveries. But none of that meant anything to John. His only interest had been saving his daughter.

Hidden behind the secret wall in the lab, Adam had spent those two years watching Eden. Watching her, wanting her, crazy with the need to feel his cock buried deep inside her energy. He might be Earth's salvation, but she was his.

He'd come to Earth for a specific reason, only he'd arrived too late to save the planet. Instead, John had offered an alternative. Not quite what Adam had in mind, but what was a century or so of sleep in order to fulfill his goal?

One thing he'd made clear to John was that he'd do his part, but he wanted Eden. Considering what John knew would happen to Earth, he couldn't very well turn down Adam's request.

Now she was here and no wall separated them. He wasn't certain how much John had told Eden about him, but there was time for explanation later. Just revitalizing this small section of land had depleted him. He needed her. For the energy she'd provide, yes, but also because he'd waited over a hundred years to touch her. His balls were tied up in a knot from the need to feel her hot pussy squeezing his cock.

No more waiting.

"I...I don't really know what you expect from me," she said, her face turning crimson.

"I'll show you what I need."

He gathered her into his arms and pulled her against him.

Her heat burned through her clothes and flamed his skin. His cock rose heavy and hard between them. He couldn't help rocking against her as it brushed her belly, biting back a curse at the painful pleasure. The urge to strip her of those stupid clothes and sink into her cunt right now was strong. But he knew that as a human she wouldn't be prepared to take him yet.

"Adam, I think—"

He silenced her with his mouth, covering her lips and breathing in her sweet scent. The time for words had ended. Her mouth had been an irresistible temptation for too long. Her lips were tentative as she opened slowly for him, her body rigid, her nervousness palpable.

Okay, she needed to relax. He moved his hands over her back, kneading the pressure points until the tension melted. She sighed and he slid his tongue inside, tasting her warmth and essence. Like sweet nectar from his home planet, she filled his senses with a teasing taste of renewing energy.

Keeping his mouth planted firmly on hers, he reached for the closure of her jumpsuit and tugged it down to her belly, easing his hand inside to touch her silken flesh. He groaned at the buttery soft feel of her, the singeing heat that passed between them. She whimpered into his mouth, breathing her energy into his starving cells.

More than the replenishment, he needed her body. Eden was special. He should tell her what joining with him meant. But he couldn't bring himself to do it, not knowing whether she'd accept the consequences or not.

Later, after he'd had his fill of her, they'd talk. Now he craved more of her skin, needed to feel the soft globes of her breasts filling his hands. He pulled the jumpsuit down her shoulders, leaving her bare from the waist up.

Her breasts were full, with large, round areolas and erect nipples just begging for his fingers to pluck them. A red blush appeared over the creamy skin of her chest and neck. He looked into her eyes. "Why are you embarrassed?"

How could Eden explain that not many men had seen her naked? Her experience with sex was limited, to say the least. To watch Adam, this gorgeous man, stare at her body as if she were the most beautiful woman he'd ever seen was, frankly, a little hard to believe. "Look at me. I'm not exactly attractive."

He frowned. "How can you say that? Your hair is like a sunlit waterfall, your face a golden glow. You have a mouth I'm dying to have wrapped around my cock, and the most beautiful breasts I've ever seen."

Eden shook her head. She'd never felt attractive or alluring. What did he see that she didn't? Could it be Adam's lack of exposure to other women? Considering what she'd read in her father's notes, Adam's contact with other Earth females was practically nonexistent. And who knew what the women on his home planet, or star system or wherever he was from, looked like? Yet the way he stared at her now had emotions rising to the surface that never had before. Stupid, girlie emotions—like feeling desirable.

He reached out and circled her nipples, grasping the tips and rubbing them between his thumb and forefinger. She gasped and shuddered as the sensation shot right between her legs. Her pussy quaked and moistened.

"Do you like that?"

She nodded, then groaned when he grabbed both nipples and plucked, pulled and pinched until she wanted to slide her hand between her legs and rub her clit to orgasm. The way he looked at her, the way he touched her, was unbearable.

"These have to come off. Now." With quick, impatient hands, he knelt before her and yanked the coveralls down to her ankles. He held her hand while she stepped out of them. Now she felt really stupid. Naked except for her boots.

But Adam didn't even look at her feet, or smirk at her too-wide hips and thighs. Instead, his eyes focused on her pussy, currently positioned at the level of his—

"Ohhh, shit!" she whimpered, clutching his hair as he took a long lick of her folds. No man had ever touched her down there with his tongue. No man had ever taken the time to touch her beyond rudimentary foreplay. This was...amazing. Unable to resist, she looked down and watched his tongue roll over her clit, felt the sparks shoot deep in her cunt. Juices poured from her and he licked every drop. She wanted to faint on the spot. She moaned and he pressed his mouth against her clit, sucking the pearl between his teeth, flicking it with his tongue.

She might die right here. So much for seeing Earth again. She was going to explode right on this oasis. Her legs buckled. Adam grasped her hips and without once losing contact with her pussy, laid her onto the grass, spreading her legs and stabbing his tongue inside her.

More. Please, more.

She wasn't sure if she said it out loud, but in her mind she pleaded for this sweet assault to continue. Eden reached for Adam's head, lifting her hips to grind her sex against his mouth, needing him to stay there until she came all over his face.

"What a sweet pussy, Eden," he said, stopping to smile up at her.

Don't stop. Please don't stop now. I'm so close.

His smile turned to a wicked grin. "Now I want to know what you feel like on the inside." He moved his hand between her legs, palm down, and patted her pussy. Once, twice, a little harder each time. The taps vibrated her clit until she was rising to meet his hand. Then he slid his palm down over her slit and drove two fingers into her cunt.

"Ahh, damn," he muttered in a harsh whisper. "So fucking hot."

Her buttocks lifted, nails digging into the soft earth as she twisted to meet his thrusting fingers. Adam pushed her hips down and pinned her there, leaving his fingers embedded in her pussy and once again tortured her clit with his mouth and tongue.

The dual sensation tore her apart. She bucked against his mouth and fingers, surprised to hear wailing sounds pour from her mouth. The lava-hot thrust of his tongue against her clit was more than she could take.

"Please, Adam, please," she cried, her head thrashing from side to side. Insanity had taken over. She no longer cared about anything except Adam's tongue on her fiery clit, his fingers pistoning in and out of her drenched pussy.

She needed to come. Right now.

Chapter Two

Adam felt the tension coiling deep inside Eden's cunt. He knew she was close. With a couple flicks of his tongue and a driving thrust of his fingers, he'd take her there.

But he wanted her come on his cock this first time, wanted his climax to coincide with hers. When he pulled away, her head rocketed up and she shot him a glare so fierce he had to struggle to keep his laughter at bay.

"What are you doing?"

"Relax and lie back. I need to fuck you."

"But I...I haven't..."

She didn't finish the sentence, just laid her head down and looked at the sky. Obviously, Eden had never been one to demand her fulfillment from a man.

That would change soon enough. He'd get her so hot and so ready she'd pummel him with her fists, bite and scratch, anything to claim her release.

Just the way he wanted her.

But not today. Today was the day he'd waited a veritable century for. "You're trying to tell me you haven't come yet."

Her gaze remained fixated on the sky. "Yes."

"I already know that. I'm going to make you come."

"You don't understand."

He read the exasperation in her voice. "Understand what?"

"I can't…I've never…forget it."

He leaned over her and forced her gaze to meet his. "Never what?"

"I can't come that way." Her face reddened.

"What way?"

"By fucking. I can only come by touching my clit."

One corner of his mouth curled in a smile he couldn't hold back. "Maybe before. Not now. Trust me."

"Oh God."

The time for talking about it had ended. Whatever happened in Eden's past with sex was irrelevant. With him she would experience release. They both would.

"Look at me. Keep your eyes focused on mine."

She blinked and chewed on her bottom lip, but kept her gaze on him. He threaded his fingers through hers, raising her arms over her head, and positioned his cock head between the swollen lips of her velvety pussy.

Hot and tight, her pussy sucked the head of his cock between its swollen lips, squeezing as he pushed inside her. Her eyes widened, the greens, blues and browns swirling together in a stormy vortex as he shoved further into her tight sheath. Cream surrounded him, lubricating his way.

Her pussy was taut, pulsing, giving off the life force he so desperately needed. With each clenching spasm, he soaked in her massive stores of sexual energy. Restored, he relaxed and moved against her, twisting his cock in ways that hit her walls just right, knowing instinctively what would pleasure her.

Now it was time to bring her the climax she needed. He focused his energy on extending the small piece of flesh above his cock, wound it around her clit and thrummed the hardened bud. Like a slithering snake, it pulsed along her nerve endings. He may be occupying a human body right now, but there were parts of his original anatomy he could still call into play.

Shock registered in her widened eyes, her lips parting as she fought for words. "What…what is *that*?"

Smiling down at her he said, "Your pleasure, Eden."

"Oh dear God!" She lifted her hips, allowing him to drive deeper. Filling her was ecstasy. Her response gave him strength. He pulled back, drove hard, powering his cock deep. He pummeled her repeatedly, his balls slapping her ass, feeling her muscles tighten as she prepared to let go. Giving pleasure to this woman was the reason for his creation.

Eden gasped for breath, the dual sensation of Adam's cock and whatever that *thing* was that massaged her clit catapulting her into a new dimension of pleasure. Emotions, raw and untamed, bubbled to the surface, giving her a clarity, focusing every sensation between her legs as she felt Adam's strength grow.

He thrust hard, his cock head striking her womb, sending arcing pulses of heat to her clit and pussy.

"Ready to come on my cock now?" he asked.

She loved looking at him, the way his features drew tight and hard, the corded muscles and distended veins in his arms showcasing his incredible power.

"Yes," she whimpered, feeling as if she were suspended in midair, poised at the precipice of some monumental occurrence.

The soft flesh covering her clit vibrated and Adam thrust deep, tensing and holding as his cock head stroked her G-spot. Her climax roared through her body like she was hurtling through space. Time suspended, the rush of pleasure like tiny pinpricks raining over her. Adam reared back and shouted unintelligible words as he jettisoned hot fluid inside her. She watched his face, the intensity of his orgasm creating more erotic pulses around his shaft. The pulsing waves seemed endless, more powerful than anything she could have ever imagined.

Finally the crest subsided and she floated back to reality. Adam withdrew and pulled her against his side, caressing her skin with light strokes.

They spent a few moments in silence. The sound of ocean waves lapping against the shore was the only noise. Eden laid her palm on Adam's expansive chest, feeling the strange thumping of a not-quite-human heartbeat.

She had questions about him and what would happen now. But for some reason the scientist in her retreated and the woman stayed. They had an eternity to figure the rest out. Right now, she wanted only to get to know him better, to discover how he felt.

How she felt.

How *did* she feel? This entire experience had come upon her quickly. Too quickly to even give her mind time to assimilate the information. She just did what her father requested, knowing he wouldn't ask this of her without good reason.

Now that she'd done it, she was filled with questions. First and foremost, how was Adam going to replenish the earth?

Okay, maybe the scientist in her *was* resurfacing.

"Adam?"

"Yeah."

"Now what?"

He smiled at her. Lord, the man had an enigmatic smile, seemingly filled with secrets. "Now we do this again. A lot. I have much strength to amass first."

The *this* he referred to must be sex. Or at least she hoped so.

"Eden, what did your father tell you?"

"His note was detailed in some areas, like the fact I needed to have sex with you because you derive your energy that way. But in other areas it was vague. Only that he placed you in the pod instead of himself because of the assurance you could recreate the Earth."

"That's about right."

"You want to tell me how you plan to do that?"

"It's complicated."

"I'm a scientist. Try me."

"It's a matter of psychic energy and its effect on climate, plant life, water and animals."

She frowned and pursed her lips, trying to fathom a formula for that in her head. "Psychic energy can't create something tangible, especially not living things."

He reached for a lock of her hair, letting it slide through his fingertips. The simple gesture, though not sexual, made her pulse race. Maybe it was the way he looked at her.

"Not the psychic energy you know. But where I come from, we don't build with machinery. We create entire cities with our minds."

She couldn't even imagine creating one's own environment. "Where do you come from?"

"One of the star systems up there," he said, his index finger aiming toward the northeast sky. "When it's dark I'll point it out." He skimmed the swell of her breasts with his fingertips. Eden sucked in a breath, her nipples hardening.

"Why did you come to Earth?" she asked, hoping to keep her mind occupied with scientific thoughts, not sexual ones.

"Two years before the destruction, I arrived to put a halt to the decimation of your planet's resources. I made contact with your father because we determined he would be the most receptive. But I found that war was imminent and global warming and pollution had depleted the Earth of resources. It was too late. The only alternative I could offer was to begin anew, after Earth had recovered."

She pushed away and sat up, staring out at an ocean that looked both familiar and strangely new. "You knew what was going to happen, but you did nothing to stop it?"

Since he couldn't reach her hair or her breasts, he caressed the swell of her hip. She shivered.

"There was nothing I *could* do. It's not our way to interfere once the majority of the population is hell-bent on destruction. The people of Earth were past the point of listening. Suspicion ruled them. They weren't ready."

Her heart ached for the billions who had died, especially the innocent. Children who never had a chance to grow up, couples in love who never had the opportunity to start their lives together. The tears fell and she didn't want to stop them.

"As much as we'd have liked, we couldn't save your planet." Adam sat up and swiped at a tear sliding down her cheek. "You cry for all who were lost, and that's good. Perhaps rebuilding Earth will produce better results this time. Maybe those who were saved will care enough about it, about the generations to come, to learn how to love and respect both nature and each other. And then pass that love and respect down to their children."

He spoke as if he wasn't included in the new Earth. "What about you, Adam? Aren't you part of all this now?"

A shadow passed over his clear blue eyes, but he quickly smiled and it disappeared. "Of course. I am the catalyst for re-creation, for the future of this planet. I am as much a part of it as any of you."

Why did it seem as if he held something back, as if there was more he wanted to say?

"Enough talk. I need you again."

He crouched in front of her and removed her boots, then hauled her up and drew her against him. "There's much I could teach you, if you'll allow."

The seductive way he looked at her told her what he wanted to teach was sexual.

As a scientist, she was ever the student.

"I'm yours, Adam. And very eager to learn."

* * * * *

Eden's trust in him was astounding. She really knew nothing about him other than the information her father left behind, yet she believed what he told her.

Her faith was humbling, her interest in him arousing. He stepped back and looked at her, her rich curves shining golden in the sunlight reflecting off the water. A brilliant mind was enticing enough, but the lush garden of her body sparked his need even higher. There was a reason he fell in love with her when he first saw her in the lab. A reason his desire had never diminished in the two years he had watched her or the hundred years he'd slept, dreaming of her.

Eden Mason was a kind, brilliant woman who didn't have a clue how attractive she was. She had a self-deprecating sense of humor, showed no egotistical characteristics and trusted her father unconditionally.

She also wanted to be loved with a fierce passion she'd never shown to anyone. But he knew. He'd connected with her on a psychic level and had felt every one of her emotions during those years when all he could do was watch. And wait.

He'd wanted her forever, and now she was his.

How would he ever let her go?

"Well?"

He blinked, realizing he hadn't spoken in a while. "Sorry, I was just looking at you. You're beautiful."

Eden rolled her eyes. "Oh please. I'm nothing to look at."

"You underestimate yourself." To prove it, he took her hand and placed it on the center of his chest. "Feel how my heart pounds for you."

The corners of her mouth lifted. "You have a faster normal heartbeat than humans."

"Then feel this instead, and tell me you're not much to look at." He moved her hand over his abdomen and lower, guiding her fingers around his cock. He sucked in a harsh breath at her touch. "Feel what you do to me."

The swirling colors in her eyes deepened, her breathing became erratic. She moved her hand over his engorged flesh, the heat of her body transferring energy to his shaft, expanding the thickness and length. "How do you do that?" she whispered.

"I don't. You're doing it. Your touch determines the level of my arousal."

Arching a brow, she studied his cock as if it were a scientific mystery, her examination so intent that his balls tightened and throbbed. When she dropped to her knees in the sand and took him in both hands, twisting them from side to side as she stroked the length of him, he threw his head back and thanked the stars for assigning him to Earth.

"The textures are so interesting," she said. He wondered if she even realized she was speaking aloud. "Bumpy and ridged, yet smooth and glides easily when I stroke it. The head here is velvety soft." She swirled her thumb over his cock head, releasing silken drops of pre-come. Hell, he was lucky he didn't come right then. The combination of her touch and her avid interest made it difficult to hold back.

"Didn't any of the men you knew before let you play with their cocks?"

She snorted and shook her head. "No. The few sexual encounters I had were mostly in the dark and over way too quickly."

Stupid men. How sad they hadn't realized that much of a woman's pleasure could come from allowing her to touch and taste her partner. He let her explore, not wanting to rush her, forcing the energy to dissipate so she could take as long as she wanted. Eden attacked his cock like any good scientist researching something for the first time. She studied it, touched every angle, experimented with his balls in her hand, from light caresses to gentle squeezing.

But when she leaned forward and used her tongue to swipe the pearly liquid from the tip, he gritted his teeth. Her mouth was a slice of heaven. Or maybe it was hell. Hot, burning his flesh as she swirled her tongue around the throbbing tip, rolling her lips back and forth along his shaft. She took him inch by inch until she could take no more, then drew back, letting her teeth lightly scrape along the ridged surface.

"Fuck, Eden! Are you sure you've never done this before?"

She dragged her gaze from his glistening erection to his face, and shook her head. "No, I haven't done this. But I like it very much."

And he thought he had much to teach her. Eden was very adept at self-education. Though his alien form was similar in many ways to humans, this human body he'd morphed into allowed him to experience senses in ways far superior to his alien body. He still possessed some of the unique qualities of his natural state, so his senses were heightened in this form. The way she tasted, her juicy nectar pouring over his tongue. And the way her body felt under his hands, her muscles rolling, tightening. Oh, and especially the sounds of her whimpers and cries when she came. Now that he really liked.

But this—this was new. The feel of her hot mouth surrounding him, the way her tongue swiped over the tip, the way she swallowed his cock head when he thrust back into her throat. He'd studied the human sexual experience, of course. In books, on the computer that John had provided him, but nothing could have prepared him for how it actually felt, how much of his emotions would be tied into this physical act.

Where he came from, sex was a needed function to sustain life force. Here, it came wrapped up with incredible pleasure and astounding feelings.

Maybe he was the student here. And he had a lot to learn.

He shuddered at the sight of his cock disappearing between Eden's lips. When she reached between his legs to cup his balls, gently squeezing the twin sacs, he tightened and pulled back.

"Oh no. Not yet."

Eden sat back on her heels and looked up at him. "I was enjoying that."

So was he. Too much. "I need to come in your pussy, baby, not your mouth."

Her eyes no longer reflected wide-eyed innocence, but womanly desire. "I'd like to taste you when you come. Let me."

Heat sizzled between his legs at the thought of jettisoning his fluids into her hot mouth. "Soon. Not right now."

Not right now, indeed. Eden might be awed by the situation and her surroundings, including this sexy alien, but she wasn't about to stop what she was doing. Her mouth watered for his beautiful cock, and she was damn well going to finish what she'd started whether he liked it or not.

Instead of submitting to his demand, she lifted up on her knees and grabbed his hips, engulfing his cock and pressing it firmly between her tongue and the roof of her mouth. Expecting a protest from Adam, she was pleasantly surprised and more than a little empowered when he sighed and shuddered, then tangled his hands in her hair, propelling her forward to take more of him. He guided her in the tempo that gave him the most pleasure.

She discovered it varied from slow leisurely sucks to hard and fast. Soon she picked up his signals, the way his fingers tightened in her hair, pulling it to draw her closer, the way his balls tightened when she squeezed them gently and massaged that little area of skin between his scrotum and anus. She might be sexually inexperienced, but she was very well read. For every bit of sex she'd never experienced, she'd studied more than any woman ever should. Now her book knowledge paid off — she was pleasing her man.

Her man. Adam wasn't hers, any more than she was his. Time to cast those ridiculous notions aside and concentrate on coaxing a climax from him. From the way his body shuddered, she knew that eruption wasn't far off. His balls tightened against his body and he began to pump between her lips in earnest.

"Ahh, Eden, you're going to make me explode."

She hoped so! She coiled her tongue around the tip of his cock, flicking it back and forth, then drew his shaft deep, twisting her fingers around the base. With a loud groan he blasted silky fluids into her mouth. She swallowed the sweet juice, milking him with her hands until he muttered a sexy oath and withdrew.

His cock was still hard!

She sat back and looked up at him, licking her lips. His jaw was set tight, his chest heaving with the force of his breaths. The fine sheen of sweat across his brow glistened in the late afternoon sun. Lord, he was magnificent!

And right now, he was hers.

Chapter Three

Adam pulled Eden to her feet and drew her against his chest, capturing her lips in a kiss that curled her toes. His cock nestled between them, still wet from her mouth. Despite the taut desire coiling in his corded muscles, she could tell he fought for control. It was almost as if he feared his own passion. But why?

She raised her arms and entwined them behind his head, loving the silken feel of his hair as she tangled her fingers within the strands. Her heart pounded, her body demanding another release.

He dragged his lips from her mouth and blazed a fiery trail over her neck, testing the tender skin between her neck and shoulder with his teeth. She shuddered and reached between them, winding her fingers around his cock.

"Oh, no," he said, reaching for her wrist and pulling her hand away. "The time for play is over."

He began to move forward, forcing her to step back as he walked his way up the beach. Her toes sank into soft, cool grass, the shade from the fronds of the dense grouping of palm trees cooling her feverish body. Her back brushed against something hard. When Adam stopped, she realized she was backed against the trunk of one of the palm trees. Before she could ask what he was doing, he reached under her thighs and picked her up off the ground.

"Wrap your legs around me," he said.

"I'm too heavy for you to hold me like this," she said, worrying about him using up too much energy.

He stopped and leaned his head back, frowning as he searched her eyes. "Eden, you're no more than a grain of sand in my arms."

Her body melted against him. She was no lightweight, yet he held her with no effort whatsoever. She wrapped her legs around his middle, the position aligning his cock head against her moist slit. Adam reared back and plunged inside her, the motion so fierce and unexpected that her back scraped the trunk of the tree. Lightning struck between her legs, a burgeoning heat that seared her, tightening her pussy around his cock.

So much for restraint. He seemed to have no qualms about banging her back against the tree with the power of his thrusts. Thrusts that hit her deep, his thick shaft teasing her sensitive tissues.

"You're so tight around me, Eden. And wet. Your juice is drowning my cock and balls."

She felt it too, an almost embarrassing flood of arousal that she couldn't contain. But Adam didn't seem to mind at all. The wetter she got, the harder he pounded, that magical extra part of him popping up and surrounding her clit, pulsing, heating it, coaxing it ever closer to an explosive climax.

Sensation took over and her mind shut down. As if she was numb everywhere but her sex, all she felt were the relentless strokes of his shaft, the gentle caresses of that extra flesh around her clit. She tightened and exploded around him, digging her heels into his back to propel him deeper.

"Ah, that's what I wanted," he said, his face tight, his jaw set with determination. Her climax rolled and plummeted, then climbed again as Adam kept up the relentless pace. "Come with me, Eden. Spill that sweet cream over my cock again."

She couldn't. Not again, not so soon. But he held onto her buttocks with just one hand and dipped his fingers alongside her slit, gathering up her juices. Probing between the cheeks of her ass, he found the small hole and caressed her anus. She whimpered at the exquisite sensation, never before realizing her nerve endings there were so alive, so sensitive to touch. When he drove one finger inside her ass she screamed out, tightened and came again. This time, Adam tilted his head back and groaned, jettisoning hot seed deep inside her.

Breathing deeply, he rested his head against her forehead. She gathered him against her, loving the feel of his sweat-soaked body pressed intimately against hers. When he finally set her on the ground, her legs trembled so much she could barely stand. But Adam held onto her and led her deeper into the oasis.

"Hungry?" he asked.

Despite the fact she hadn't eaten in over a hundred years, she wasn't starving. But now that she was completely satiated in other areas, hunger pangs began to rumble in her stomach. "A little."

"What's your favorite fruit?"

"Peaches."

She'd no more said the word than the space just ahead of them shimmered. When the waving ceased, a thick tree appeared, filled with enticing, plump peaches! Eden looked up at Adam. "How do you do that?"

"I told you. Psychic energy. I studied the formulas for all Earth's food groups. I like peaches, too." He pulled one ripe fuzzy fruit from the tree and held it out to her. She leaned in and took a bite, laughing when peach juice spilled down her chin. Before she could swipe it away, Adam leaned in and licked the nectar from her chin, capturing her mouth in a soft, but all too brief, kiss.

She sighed at the unexpected sensual tenderness, realizing how quickly she'd become tied emotionally to Adam. Considering he was a stranger and they stood in this tiny corner of a completely devastated Earth, she had no business thinking of relationships or, God forbid, love. Adam fucked her because he had to, because it was necessary for his survival. And that was it.

Quit thinking about him in any way other than a marvel of science, Eden.

"So, what now?" she asked.

He finished off the peach and stepped toward a small stream to wash his hands and face. When he straightened he said, "We have a journey to make."

"Where to?"

"There's a specific location we need to get to in order for me to do the job I was sent here to do."

"Location? Where?"

"I have the coordinates. It's about a day's walk from here."

She needed to wake the others in the space pod. "I should go back to the ship."

He squeezed her hand. "I need you to be with me when I do this, Eden. Don't worry about the others. They'll be fine in stasis for a while longer."

It irked her that he knew more about her father's plan than she did. Then again, her father hadn't shared any information about Adam with her. "Why didn't my father tell me about you?"

Adam's brows lifted. "For the same reason he wouldn't allow me near you. He wanted you focused on your experiments, and he wanted me focused on learning about Earth and assisting him with creation of the pods. I think he realized immediately that I connected with you psychically, and that I would be a...distraction to your work."

It was so unlike her father not to share everything with her, though. "He knew what was going to happen to Earth, didn't he?"

Adam nodded. "Yes. I told him, because I realized as soon as I arrived on this planet that my help would not be needed until years after the obliteration. You can't save a world that is hell-bent on destroying itself, Eden."

She knew that. Her father had known it, too, and had sacrificed his own life for a new world, a world that somehow Adam was supposed to create. Obviously her father had wanted her focus on the propulsion and maintenance system for the rockets, not on an alien who intrigued her from the first moment she saw him. If she'd met Adam before Earth had been destroyed, she would have wanted to drop everything and study him. Then they'd all be dead.

Knowing her father was right didn't make this any easier. But if her father trusted Adam, then she would, too. "Let's get to the location, then. We have work to do."

* * * * *

They trudged over the soft ground, mile after mile. It felt good to stretch his muscles again after so long in stasis. This human body had such limitations, specifically taking so long to traverse anywhere on foot. But it was important he remain in this form. He had to, in order to fulfill his function here. Besides, Eden seemed to like his human body, and pleasing her was important.

She seemed to have progressed past the point of worrying about being naked. After all, it wasn't like anyone would see her but him. The rest of the ships hadn't landed yet, a fact he and John had made certain of when they'd been sent into space. He needed the time to set things in motion before the others came down. Once that was complete, all the pods could be opened and they could start their new lives.

Somewhere on one of those ships would be a man to care for Eden. Pain lanced his heart at the thought of another man touching her, caressing her soft skin and sinking his cock inside her tight cunt. Duty had never seemed so agonizing before.

"Why a specific spot?" she asked, lacing her fingers through his.

"It has to do with the Earth's pull in a specific location and my ability to draw psychic energy from a position of strength."

"Where exactly are we?"

"From your old Earth charts, a position somewhere in the southern hemisphere. Tropical, yet with mountains close by. You'll need a good start in a warm location."

"Why?"

"Be patient, Eden. I'll explain it all when the time comes."

He kept moving, but realized after a few seconds that she'd slipped her hand away from his. When he stopped, he turned and saw her standing still a few yards back.

God, she was beautiful. The soft flesh of her hips just begged for his touch. Holding onto her and thrusting deep into her hot pussy was as blissful as anything he'd ever experienced. He walked toward her. "What's wrong?"

"I don't like being kept in the dark, Adam. There's no reason for you to withhold information."

He fought back a grin at how feisty she looked right now. Jaw set, hands on her hips, tapping her bare foot against the ground. Fire blazed golden in her eyes. His cock twitched.

She noticed, momentarily distracted enough to glance down at his growing erection, and then back at his face. "Quit getting hard. I'm trying to be angry here."

This time he did laugh. "I'm sorry. I can't help it. When you get pissed off it turns me on."

Her nipples puckered, her skin glowing with a faint blush. "Well, it's difficult for me to focus when you're waving that...thing at me."

When her lips curled upward into a faint smile, he stepped toward her and gathered her in his arms. His mouth covered hers, his tongue sliding inside to taste the lingering peach flavor, mixed with a deep passion that pained him.

He moved his hands over her body as if he could memorize every inch of her skin. The way she smelled, so arousingly female, so musky with desire that her scent called to him in a way he could only describe as...primitive. The tight points of her nipples scraped his chest. He soaked in her cries with his mouth, rocking his shaft against her soft flesh, spilling drops of pre-come along her skin.

This time, he didn't want to savor every moment. Need grew within him and he had to be inside her now. He concentrated and created a soft patch of grass around their feet, wide and long enough to accommodate their bodies.

"Get down on your knees," he said, his voice sounding harsh, but unable to help his overpowering lust.

She complied immediately, casting him a saucy grin before turning around and crouching down on all fours. Adam dropped to his knees, sucking in a shaky breath at the erotic view of her backside. Glistening beads of moisture clung to her pussy lips, beckoning him to slide between the swollen folds. The puckered hole of her anus teased him, the soft globes of her buttocks calling to his hands.

He nestled between her legs, widening them with a nudge of his knee. Lust overcame him in a way he hadn't expected, making him want to possess all of her in any way he could.

"Eden."

"Yes."

"I want to fuck your ass."

Eden stilled, heat washing over her. She closed her eyes and imagined how it would feel to have Adam's thick cock buried in her ass. The visual was so wickedly arousing that her pussy clenched, pouring juices from her cunt.

Adam rocked against her, his cock banging against her clit, his fingers digging into the flesh of her hips. She struggled for breath, aroused beyond the point of speech. His sudden desire for her, his request to fuck her ass…it was all too much. Could someone die from being this turned on?

"Tell me if it's not what you want. But I have to fuck you now. I can't wait."

The excitement in his voice tripled her desire. She wanted, needed his possession of her in every possible way. "Fuck my ass, Adam."

She heard him exhale, and then he was searching between her legs with his cock. She tensed, waiting for him to shove it in her ass, but instead he slid gently into her pussy, burying every glorious inch of his thick shaft inside her. His balls tapped against her clit as he moved slowly in and out, teasing her. Her pussy lips grabbed onto his magnificent rod and refused to let go, sending sparks of intense pleasure to her womb when he withdrew.

"God, you're wet," he whispered, running his palm reverently over her buttocks. When his fingers slipped into the crack of her ass to tease the puckered hole, she gasped, dropping down on her elbows to give him better access. Splinters of fire danced along the sensitive nerve endings as he caressed her, drenching her hole with her own juices.

"Hurry, Adam," she whimpered, desperately needing him to fill her.

With a low growl he probed her tight entrance with the head of his cock. Well-lubricated, he pushed past the barrier with ease, sliding partway into her anus. The shock of pain mixed with heady pleasure stunned her and she tensed.

He stilled, and his patience relaxed her. After a few seconds she grew used to having something huge buried in her ass. She had no idea she could be so sexually stimulated by having something in her anus. Knowing it was Adam's cock was even more enticing.

Adam pulled back and slid home again. With each thrust she gritted her teeth, the sensations exquisitely unbearable. She reached between her legs to massage her throbbing clit, the added stimulation bringing her ever closer to orgasm.

"So tight, such a beautiful ass," he murmured. He grasped her hips and drew her hard against him. She cried out and thrummed her clit faster, timing her strokes to each of his pounding strokes.

How could something hurt and feel so damn good at the same time? White heat intensified between her legs until she teetered on the very edge.

"Now, Adam, hurry!" she cried, already feeling her pussy tighten. When he reared back and buried his cock deep, she splintered, a cry tearing from her lips as she burst into a shattering orgasm.

Adam groaned and dug his fingers into her buttocks, powering his cock hard and fast as he shot a stream of hot come deep in her ass. He shuddered and collapsed onto her back, pressing his lips against her nape. His heart pounded fiercely against her skin, equaling her own racing beats.

He pulled out and drew her to her feet. Eden's eyes widened as she spotted a small lake in front of them. Where had that come from? No doubt another of Adam's instant creations. He led her into the water where they bathed and played, the cool refreshing liquid releasing the heat saturating her body.

She wrapped her legs around him and kissed him, pouring out the passion she could no longer contain.

They were the only two people on Earth, and she felt destiny surround her as the enormity of it hit. Eden was desperately in love with Adam.

Chapter Four

Adam paused, feeling the heat simmer under his feet. Too subtle for a human to notice, but he knew exactly when they'd arrived at the correct location.

"We'll stop here."

They'd walked the rest of the day and into the night. Fortunately the day had turned cloudy, shielding them from the bright sun. He hadn't wanted to expend too much of his energy creating shade trees along the path.

"Why here?"

"It's on the equator, and the exact spot where we must create the new world."

"Okay, I'm a little vague on the 'create the new world' part."

Her abrupt transition from pure woman to scientist amused him. How quickly she could change gears. It was one of the things he loved most about her. Such beauty and astounding intellect wrapped up in a lush, desirable package.

It was going to kill him to leave her.

"Sit here with me and let me explain." He pulled her to the ground and they faced each other. "I need energy, and a lot of it. I'll center the energy within and use my knowledge of your world to re-create it."

Her eyes widened. "Re-create it, how? In what form? A certain era?"

He shook his head. "No era. Earth will be as clean and untouched as when it was new. As far as the 'how', I told you that my abilities involve being able to create things."

"Okay we'll get back to that in a minute. What about technology?"

"Whatever you and the others possess, intellectually, will be preserved. But there will be no computers, no labs, nothing like what you had before."

She exhaled. "Why?"

"Because technology got your world in trouble in the first place. Do you really want what you had before? With cars and factories to pollute, with the ability and devices at hand to create weapons of destruction?"

She didn't answer. "This is your chance to start life over again, to teach your children and the generations to come about right and wrong. To build from the ground up, discarding the mistakes of the past and focusing on a world that is created the way you know it should be. The right way."

"But Adam, the advances we made in medicine, in other areas of science…"

"Will still be here," he explained, placing his finger to her temple. "You have the knowledge, you and the others, to do great things. You know that most cures for disease can be found in simple plant life. You'll have that in abundance. Animals too."

"And we'll have to hunt for our own food."

He nodded. "Yes."

She went silent, and he let her mull it over. After all, he'd just hit her with some devastating news. Though John had been aware of Adam's plan, he vowed not to tell

Eden or anyone else about it. John had agreed that they'd outgrown their own technology, had created massive ecological and human social problems with no clear idea how to fix them. Now they wouldn't have to.

"Did my father know about this?" she finally asked.

"Yes. And he agreed."

Eden sighed. "I suppose we should be thankful to even have this. After all, if it wasn't for you there wouldn't be anything left. Thank you, Adam. I'm sorry if I seemed ungrateful. It's just a lot to comprehend."

"I know. That's why I saved it. I wanted time with you, to get to know you, to love you, before I had to break this news and risk the possibility of you hating me."

Her eyes swirled with myriad colors, filling with moisture as she shook her head. "Oh, no. I could never hate you. I love you, Adam."

His heart both swelled and crumbled with her words.

"What do we do now? Should I stand back?"

"Oh, no. You're an integral part of all this. That's why I needed you with me. I have to make love while I'm gathering energy, Eden. I need your help to make this work."

Eden stilled, realizing why she'd been asked to accompany him. As a scientist she found it difficult to believe that one man could restore Earth's former beauty, especially via psychic energy. Then again, what she'd seen from Adam already proved he could do things no human could do.

"Tell me what I have to do."

He leaned back onto the grass and held his arms out to her. "Ride me, Eden."

Her womb quickened, her sex awakening to his command. Eager for the experience of loving him again, she straddled him, reaching for his already hard cock and stroking its length. Adam's eyes darkened like a storm-laden sky. Drops of silken fluid spilled from the tip of his cock and she wanted to sweep them away with her tongue. But something told her there was a sense of urgency here.

Urgency was good, since she was ready for him. She lifted and positioned his cock head between the pulsing lips of her slit, then slid down over his shaft, feeling him stretching her walls, filling her completely.

"Ahh, Eden, you and I fit together so perfectly." He reached for her hips, lifting her up and down over his cock. Sparks of intensity arced within her as she rocked her pelvis against him.

The ground rumbled and the clouds turned a threatening dark gray. The wind picked up, swirling around them, the brown Earth floor turning over like an invisible shovel had attacked it.

"Whatever you see or feel, don't break contact with me," he said, his voice rapid, urgent and breathless. "I'll protect you."

She believed him and focused her energy on joining with Adam instead of on the chaos surrounding her. His energy was sizzling. She felt it in every cell of her body, like an electric shock to her system. Only this kind of shock was pleasurable instead of painful. So pleasurable her body trembled. She heard the whimpers coming from her throat, but was powerless to stop the chain reaction from his psychic pulses surrounding her.

The sensations were so intense she wanted to break away, fearing she'd lose her sanity. It was as if she was transported out of her body and jolted by lightning. But she held on, leaning forward to entwine her hands with Adam's.

His eyes were closed, his hair flying in the torrents of air swirling like a vortex around them. She could no longer see her surroundings because her vision was distorted by a white tornado of wind circling them.

She could only see Adam, the connection of his hands, his thighs, and his cock pounding into her savagely. A keening wail tore from her lips as she climaxed, flooding his cock with her come. She felt her body lift off the ground and begin to hover, spinning as wildly as the air current around them. Adam squeezed her fingers and forced her attention back to him.

Strangely, she felt no fear. Only a weightless euphoria as she continued to orgasm, gripping his shaft with quick, forceful pulses. Adam tightened against her then yelled, his voice dark, deep, spouting unintelligible words and phrases as he came hard inside her. Her pussy was soaked as he continued to jettison his seed until she collapsed onto his chest and squeezed her eyes shut, no longer able to bear the stimuli around her.

Adam's muscles relaxed and the wind died down. She felt them float back to the ground. But she still held onto him, afraid of what she might see.

When she opened her eyes, her heart slammed against her ribs as she took in the scenery around her. The tiny oasis he'd created for her earlier was nothing compared to the sight that greeted her now.

White sandy beach, turquoise water, palm trees with fronds gently swaying back and forth in the light breeze, bushes with berries, tropical fruit trees….everywhere! As far as she could see.

Looking ahead in the distance she saw steep mountains and hills with emerald green slopes.

Her ears perked up and she looked skyward to see birds flying over, happily chirping. Before her eyes could drink their fill, she heard splashing and turned her gaze to the ocean.

Dolphins and whales frolicked within viewing distance!

Tears filled her eyes and spilled down her cheeks. She looked down at Adam in awe, realizing that he created the awe-inspiring scenery around them. "Oh my God, it's beautiful."

He offered her a half-grin, then shifted and helped her up, slipping his hand in hers and pulling her close. "Anything and everything you need is here."

She sighed, overwhelmed by the pristine beauty of unspoiled Earth. "It's breathtaking."

They would share a lifetime of happiness together. With his knowledge they'd rebuild Earth the way it should be. Her heart swelled to bursting with happiness.

"I have to leave now, Eden."

"What?" Her gaze shot up to his, her soaring heart shattered. "I don't understand."

"I was never meant to remain here. My duty to Earth has ended and I have to return home."

She couldn't believe this. "I assumed you'd be staying."

He caressed her hair, his eyes filled with the sadness she felt in her soul. "I know you did. I'm sorry I didn't tell you sooner, but I couldn't."

This wasn't happening. She was in love with Adam! He couldn't leave her now. "When?"

"Now."

A blinding light appeared overhead and hovered, casting a spotlight over the ocean in front of them.

"No!" It was some kind of dream, not reality. Adam wouldn't leave her. Not now.

But his words penetrated the fantasy she'd created. "When I disappear you'll be transported back to the landing site. You'll wake the others. The rest of the ships will be landing within a day or two, all in different locations throughout the Earth. They will be given a program to view that explains everything I've told you."

Her chest felt as if a boulder sat on it. She couldn't breathe. "Adam, I love you."

His eyes squeezed shut for a second, then opened again. "I love you too, Eden. And there's more I need to tell you."

How much worse could it get? His leaving devastated her. How cruel could fate be, to give her a man she could love only to rip him away? She wouldn't ask. She didn't want to know.

"You're pregnant, Eden. He will be the Earth's leader."

Pregnant? How could he know that? "What? How do you...are you certain?"

His smile broke her heart. "Yes, love. Absolutely certain. He will possess the knowledge of my species, and the talents. And his descendents will rule after him. He will take good care of Earth."

"This isn't fair." The tears wouldn't stop, and she didn't care. She wanted him to see her pain.

"I know it's not fair. But I will love you until I no longer exist, Eden. Distance won't separate my heart from yours."

Something was happening. The light overhead shifted, pouring over him like white rain. He began to grow fainter, almost as if she could see through him. "No, Adam, not yet!"

She reached for him, but her hand sliced through his body as if he were a ghost.

"I love you, Eden. I always will."

He was gone.

She blinked back tears and suddenly found herself at the site of the space pod.

Alone.

Oh, God, how could this have happened so quickly? One minute he was in her arms, the next gone.

Forever, gone.

Eden palmed her lower abdomen.

A baby. Adam's baby. Was it really true?

God, how could she have a baby out here with no medicine, no hospital? What if something went wrong?

But just as she thought it, she knew nothing would go wrong, that somehow Adam had taken care of her and their child.

Misery settled over her like a dark cloak, shutting out the renewal of life around her. She felt like a widow.

She'd just lost the love of her life, the other half of her soul, and she'd never recover.

With a heaving sigh, she dropped to her knees and let her tears wet the newly created sand beneath her.

* * * * *

Three months later

Adam stared at the floating visual, wishing he could reach out and touch Eden. She worked tirelessly alongside the others, fishing, creating clothing and testing plants for medicinal value.

Her slightly rounding belly was clearly outlined against the pale animal hide she wore. He couldn't help but feel the greatest pleasure knowing that was his child inside her.

A human child. A son. But also part of him.

What worried him was the misery on Eden's face.

She never smiled anymore. Other than interacting with the others in necessary work, she didn't socialize. Some of the men made gentle overtures, but she never returned their interest.

She ate well, making sure the child she carried was well-nourished. But Adam knew the Eden he loved didn't exist inside that body any longer.

"Troubled?"

Adam felt Ignon's presence. "Yes."

"Your human?"

His woman. His love. "She's not happy."

"It has been a while since you departed, Adam. Surely she has chosen another mate to care for her by now."

The thought of another man touching her made him feel uncharacteristic anger. Ignon picked up on it, too. But he wouldn't hide his feelings.

"I love her, Ignon. I deserted her when she needed me most."

"It is the way of our species. No more is required of you there."

But part of him had stayed on Earth with Eden. Duty warred with selfish need.

"Interference isn't allowed, Adam."

He could always trust Ignon to read his mind. "I've already interfered. Can't you see that? This didn't work as we thought it would. She's embedded in my heart, and I'm in hers."

"You want to go back."

"I *have* to go back. I belong there. My woman is there. And so is my child."

Ignon sighed. "You are right. We all worry for the babe. It is imperative he survive. The only way to ensure that is to make sure his mother is happy."

Adam turned and regarded the ruler of the stars. "Are you saying I can go back?"

Ignon smiled and nodded. "I feel what's in your heart, Adam, as well as what's in hers. The love you have for each other is pure, and exactly what the struggling planet needs. Go to her. May the stars watch over you."

* * * * *

Eden choked back a sob, forcing back tears she was too damn tired to shed. Her child moved, no doubt feeling the emotions she tried to keep at bay but couldn't.

She missed Adam. The hurt never went away. Instead, it grew until it was nearly unbearable.

She stood at the edge of the water and stared up at the clear night sky, trying to remember which star system contained his planet.

"I can't remember, Adam. Somehow if I could pinpoint which one, I'd feel closer to you."

It had to be pregnancy hormones. This melancholy depression wouldn't go away, no matter how hard she tried. She knew she had to remain upbeat for the baby. She ate well, God knows she got plenty of exercise. They'd worked tirelessly the past few months setting up shelters and learning how to harvest and hunt for food.

When Adam had first mentioned the fact they wouldn't have the technology they'd been accustomed to, she'd been shocked. But now she realized the pleasure they all derived from working the land and creating something from nothing.

That part was exhilarating.

But at night when she crawled into her hut by herself, she curled up and wrapped her arms around her middle, feeling so lonely she was afraid she'd die from it.

Somehow, looking up at the stars helped.

"I love you, Adam."

"I love you too, Eden."

She shook her head, trying to eliminate his voice from her memories. Sometimes he felt so real, so near, she could swear he was with her.

"Eden."

No, that wasn't her imagination. She whirled around, her eyes widening as a...mirage appeared before her. She was losing her mind! "Adam?"

"Yes. I'm really here."

He stood proud and naked before her, his body as magnificent and breathtaking as it had been the first time she'd seen him. She took a tentative step forward, then two, reaching out to see if she could actually...

...touch him! "Oh, God. You're real!"

He gathered her into his arms and covered her lips with his. She felt an explosion of emotion that she couldn't contain and poured out her feelings, her love for him, with her kiss.

When they finally broke apart, she reached for his face. "I can't believe you're really here. How?"

"I can't exist without you. Though it goes against the principles of my species, I was allowed to return."

She didn't dare to hope. "Forever?"

He nodded and grinned. "Yes. Forever. We'll spend the rest of our lives together. I'm human now, so don't expect any of that fancy stuff. Our son will have more powers than me."

She didn't care if he came back as an old man. She loved his soul, the man he was inside. "Part of me died when you left."

"It was your love that allowed me to return."

He held her hands, pressing his lips against hers, filling her with a love that had nothing to do with psychic energy and everything to do with two hearts that had found each other.

"Forever," she said again as if she couldn't quite believe it.

"Forever."

He led her toward the grass, dropping to the ground and shielding her body from any impact by holding her above him. He pulled her against him, sweeping her hair aside and cupping her cheeks with his palms.

"If I don't fuck you right now then *I'll* be the one who's dying," he said, raining kisses over her neck and breasts.

When he took her aching nipple in his mouth and suckled it, she cried out and pulled his hair. "Then fuck me, Adam. I need you inside me."

He looked up at her, his gaze like a steely-eyed warrior. Nudging her legs apart with his knees, he probed her slick entrance and buried his shaft inside her.

Shock hit her as she felt the impending rush of orgasm. She pulsed once, twice, them came, crying out into the night, oblivious as to who might hear her.

"Eden," he murmured, taking her mouth and plunging his tongue inside, mimicking the hard, quick thrusts of his cock as he took her once again over the edge. He came with her, hard spurts of hot come pouring inside her. Adam rolled over and pulled her against him, stroking her sweat-dampened hair as they both looked up at the stars.

She'd gone from misery to elation in such a short period of time it was overwhelming. "You gave up a lot to come back."

"Not really." He pressed a kiss to her temple. "The only power I'm interested in is the power of love I feel from you when you look at me."

Their child kicked, and Adam's eyes widened. He placed his large palm over her abdomen and grinned. "My baby."

"Your son."

"Our future," he said, pressing his lips against hers.

A new Earth and a new beginning. One that would begin and end with love.

About the author

In April 2003, Ellora's Cave foolishly offered me a contract for my first erotic romance and I haven't shut up since. My writing is an addiction for which there is no cure, a disease in which strange characters live in my mind, all clamoring for their own story. I try to let them out one by one, as mixing snarling werewolves with a bondage and discipline master can be very dangerous territory. Then again, unusual plotlines offer relief from the demons plaguing me.

In my world, well-endowed, naked cabana boys do the vacuuming and dishes, little faeries flit about dusting the furniture and doing laundry, Wolfgang Puck fixes my dinner and I spend every night engaged in wild sexual abandon with a hunky alpha. Okay, the hunky alpha part is my real-life husband and he keeps my fantasy life enriched with extensive "research". But Wolfgang won't answer my calls, the faeries are on strike and my readers keep running off with the cabana boys.

Jaci welcomes mail from readers. You can write to her c/o Ellora's Cave Publishing at 1337 Commerce Drive, #13, Stow, Ohio 44236-0787.

Also by Jaci Burton:

THE
ELLORA'S CAVE
LIBRARY

Stay up to date with Ellora's Cave Titles
in Print with our Quarterly Catalog.

COMING TO A BOOKSTORE NEAR YOU!

ELLORA'S CAVE
2005

BEST SELLING AUTHORS TOUR

Lady Jaided

The premier magazine for today's sensual woman

Lady Jaided magazine is devoted to exploring the sexuality and sensuality of women. While there are many similarities between the sexual experiences of men and women, there are just as many if not more differences. Our focus is on the female experience and on giving voice and credence to it. Lady Jaided will include everything from trends, politics, science and history to gossip, humor and celebrity interviews, but our focus will remain on female sexuality and sensuality.

A Sneak Peek at Upcoming Stories

Clan of the Cave Woman
Women's sexuality throughout history.

The Sarandon Syndrome
What's behind the attraction between older women and younger men.

The Last Taboo
Why some women – even feminists – have bondage fantasies

Girls' Eyes for Queer Guys
An in-depth look at the attraction between straight women and gay men

Available Spring 2005

Lady *Jaided* Regular Features

Jaid's Tirade
Jaid Black's erotic romance novels sell throughout the world, and her publishing company Ellora's Cave is one of the largest and most successful e-book publishers in the world. What is less well known about Jaid Black, a.k.a. Tina Engler is her long record as a political activist. Whether she's discussing sex or politics (or both), expect to see her get up on her soapbox and do what she does best: offend the greedy, the holier-than-thous, and the apathetic! Don't miss out on her monthly column.

Devilish Dot's G-Spot
Married to the same man for 20 years, Dorothy Araiza still basks in a sex life to be envied. What Dot loves just as much as achieving the Big O is helping other women realize their full sexual potential. Dot gives talks and advice on everything from which sex toys to buy (or not to buy) to which positions give you the best climax.

On the Road with Lady K
Publisher, author, world traveler and Lady of Barrow, Kathryn Falk shares insider information on the most romantic places in the world.

Kandidly Kay
This Lois Lane cum Dave Barry is a domestic goddess by day and a hard-hitting sexual deviancy reporter by night. Adored for her stunning wit and knack for delivering one-liners, this Rodney Dangerfield of reporting will leave no stone unturned in her search for the bizarre truth.

A Model World
CJ Hollenbach returns to his roots. The blond heartthrob from Ohio has twice been seen in Playgirl magazine and countless other publications. He has appeared on several national TV shows including The Jerry Springer Show (God help him!) and has been interviewed for Entertainment Tonight, CNN and The Today Show. He has been involved in the romance industry for the past 12 years, appearing on dozens of romance novel covers and calendars. CJ's specialty is personal interviews, in which people have a tendency to tell him everything.

Hot Mama Cooks
Sex is her food, and food is her sex. Hot Mama gives aphrodisiac a whole new meaning. Join her every month for her latest sensual adventure -- with bonus recipe!

Empress on the Mount
Brash, outrageous, and undeniably irreverent, this advice columnist from down under will either leave you in stitches or recovering from hang-jaw as you gawk at her answers to reader questions on relationships and life.

Erotic Fiction from Ellora's Cave
The debut issue will feature part one of "Ferocious," a three-part erotic serial written especially for Lady Jaided by the popular Sherri L. King.

Why an electronic book?

We live in the Information Age—an exciting time in the history of human civilization in which technology rules supreme and continues to progress in leaps and bounds every minute of every hour of every day. For a multitude of reasons, more and more avid literary fans are opting to purchase e-books instead of paperbacks. The question to those not yet initiated to the world of electronic reading is simply: *why?*

1. *Price.* An electronic title at Ellora's Cave Publishing runs anywhere from 40-75% less than the cover price of the <u>exact same title</u> in paperback format. Why? Cold mathematics. It is less expensive to publish an e-book than it is to publish a paperback, so the savings are passed along to the consumer.

2. *Space.* Running out of room to house your paperback books? That is one worry you will never have with electronic novels. For a low one-time cost, you can purchase a handheld computer designed specifically for e-reading purposes. Many e-readers are larger than the average handheld, giving you plenty of screen room. Better yet, hundreds of titles can be stored within your new library—a single microchip. (Please note that Ellora's Cave does not endorse any specific brands. You can check our website at www.ellorascave.com for customer recommendations we make available to new consumers.)

3. *Mobility.* Because your new library now consists of only a microchip, your entire cache of books can be taken with you wherever you go.

4. *Personal preferences are accounted for.* Are the words you are currently reading too small? Too large? Too...**ANNOYING**? Paperback books cannot be modified according to personal preferences, but e-books can.

5. *Innovation.* The way you read a book is not the only advancement the Information Age has gifted the literary community with. There is also the factor of what you can read. Ellora's Cave Publishing will be introducing a new line of interactive titles that are available in e-book format only.

6. *Instant gratification.* Is it the middle of the night and all the bookstores are closed? Are you tired of waiting days—sometimes weeks—for online and offline bookstores to ship the novels you bought? Ellora's Cave Publishing sells instantaneous downloads 24 hours a day, 7 days a week, 365 days a year. Our e-book delivery system is 100% automated, meaning your order is filled as soon as you pay for it.

Those are a few of the top reasons why electronic novels are displacing paperbacks for many an avid reader. As always, Ellora's Cave Publishing welcomes your questions and comments. We invite you to email us at service@ellorascave.com or write to us directly at: 1337 Commerce Drive, Suite 13, Stow OH 44224.

Discover for yourself why readers can't get enough of the multiple award-winning publisher Ellora's Cave. Whether you prefer e-books or paperbacks, be sure to visit EC on the web at www.ellorascave.com for an erotic reading experience that will leave you breathless.

WWW.ELLORASCAVE.COM